THE

HEALERS

Also by DK Williams

Burn Baby Burn

Eli's Secrets. Trust No One

THE HEALERS

DK WILLIAMS

The Healers is a work of fiction. All incidents and dialogue, and all characters with the exception of some well-known historical figures, are products of the author's imagination and are not to be construed as real. Where real-life historical figures appear, the situations, incidents, and dialogues concerning those persons are entirely fictional and are not intended to depict actual events or to change the entirely fictional nature of the work. In all other respects, any resemblance to persons living or dead is entirely coincidental.

The content in this book is for fictional and entertainment purposes only and should not be construed or used as medical advice or practice. Always seek the medical advice of your physician or other qualified health care provider with any questions you may have regarding a medical condition or treatment, and never disregard professional medical advice or delay in seeking it because of something you have read in this book.

DEDICATION

I thank my family for supporting my dreams and bringing me joy everyday. To all my friends, Beta readers and sensitivity readers, that read what I write a very big thank you. I also thank God for His many blessings.

Faithful readers, I hope you enjoy this work of historical fiction loosely based on imagining the life experiences of my 5x great grandmother: Sarah Naky Tatsi Canoe Ward, (B 1765) Wife of Nathan Ward and mother to 19 children. Sarah and Nathan Ward, Sr. are buried at Osborne Fort Cemetary, Brush Creek, Grayson County, VA.

Sarah is the daughter of Dragging Canoe, a Cherokee War Chief, and granddaughter of Chief Attakullakulla. She married Ward, a white settler from Osborne Fort, when she was about 14 years old. Attakullakulla was the tribes First Beloved Man. Her cousin, (Nancy Ward) was honored as a "Beloved Woman" for bravery and leadership in battle. Attakullakulla and Dragging Canoe are written about in Capt. Timberlakes writings, noted in the bibliography.

ONE

Current Day

Annie's spirit hovered overhead watching the EMT's desperate struggle to free her body from the mangled Range Rover holding her captive. She then realized she was dead.

An early spring day brought with it heavy morning dew coupled with a fine drizzle, falling like tears making the roads wet and grass slippery. The men's boots created a mud hole around the car causing them to slip on the incline of the steep hillside. The fog was thick, and the air smelled of burning rubber, oil mingled with anti-freeze, gasoline, and fresh blood.

Wisps of steam drifted upward, the vapors rolling and twisting, resembling tormented souls rising to the netherworld. The gaping black body bag lay on the ground prepared to receive the remains housing her spirit but a few moments before.

An EMT fought with the car door while wrestling a giant piece of machinery resembling an alligator's gaping mouth. It opened and closed by slicing the metal like a warm knife through a stick of butter. As he worked in his long canvas coat, sweat drenched his body and his breath became visible with each exhalation as it collided with the chilly air. Wet hair hung down over his eyes, dripping the cold and steady rain down his face.

Annie careened down the highway heading toward work just a few minutes before the crash, steering with her knee while pouring more vodka into a red-plastic cup of orange juice for her morning pick-me-up. Some people used caffeine, but she preferred alcohol. This would be her third drink of the morning, but she told herself an exhausting day awaited her at the hospital, and she needed the calming effects of the tart liquid breakfast. She could handle her liquor, knew her limit, and knew she shouldn't drink and drive. But she felt fine and didn't think a couple of drinks would hurt, after all she wasn'tdrunk. Lately, she progressively needed more alcohol to face her day, followed by one more at lunch from the bottle she kept hidden in her locker, and another couple of swigs before the drive home. Once home, she opened a bottle of wine while cooking dinner, finishing it off before stumbling into bed to repeat the process again the next day.

Today her luck ran out as she sipped her drink, the car hydroplaning in a puddle of water and began skidding down the highway. While clenching the steering wheel and slamming on the brakes, which only made matters worse, the car started spinning. The brakes locked up and the car fishtailed right then left, careening off the roadway. The initial jolt as the tires bit the gravel and then the ditch caused her head to first hit the side window and then ricocheted forward smashing into the windshield knocking her unconscious and coming to an abrupt stop when colliding with a telephone pole. The airbags deployed too late to protect her head, but did save her from the ejection from the vehicle.

When first responders arrived on the scene and checked her body for signs of life, she had no pulse, so they were in no rush to remove her from the metal womb. The EMT workers used the jaws of life to pry open the driver's door and extract her body like delivering a newborn by caesarean. As they pulled her from the wreckage an empty vodka bottle rolled out onto the grass. Placing her into the gaping cadaver pouch covering her with a white sheet—the grim visual signifying a fatality and shielding her from 'rubber neckers' driving by in the morning rush hour. Those are the last memories Annie had at the accident site.

Annie felt a whoosh as her spirit was pulled toward the stars and she found herself standing alone on a vast desert plain. Hot winds blew while lightning flashed around her, but there were no claps of thunder, or any sound. It was eerily quiet. She was afraid but felt no pain. Annie's senses were heightened, exhilarated, and her body had a lightness of being—almost floating.

This must be a dream. Where am I?

She took in her surroundings and saw clouds swirling ominously in the purple sky against the red rock mountains. The colors were brilliant and unlike any she had ever seen. She tried to gain her bearings, but didn't recognize any landmarks. Upon a far hillside she saw a paint stallion and upon its back a woman with long dark hair swirling around her in the wind. Annie cried out reaching with outstretched arms toward her for help.

"Help me, help me, please."

In an instant the horse and rider were by her side. The woman spoke in the kindest voice but in syllables she did not recognize, and yet somehow, Annie understood their meaning. They communicated with each other through their thoughts.

"Where am I? Am I dead?"

"My child, you are in the 'land that knows no time.' Here there is no yesterday and no tomorrow. All souls must pass through this place on their way to the Great Spirit."

"I don't understand what you are saying. Who are you?" Annie asked calmly, afraid that she might scare her away to find herself alone and abandoned in this strange place, if she displayed her true horror.

"You should not be in this place yet, you must return from where you came. I will greet you when it is your time to journey into this land." The woman said, waving her hand and shouting, "Be gone."

A jolt ran through Annie and suddenly she was back in her physical body on the ground under the white sheet, her body racked with pain. The EMT heard her gasps and moaning, and he timidly lifted the corner of the sheet. Peeking underneath Annie's eyes fluttered open as she struggled to suck in the air. She was fighting for each breath and bleeding profusely from her injuries.

The EMT shouted orders to his partner scrambling out of the back of the ambulance.

"Oh my God, she's alive, bring a crash kit. Get a backboard. Looks like she has a severe head injury with chest involvement, and an open fracture of the left tibia. She's bleeding out, apply pressure to that head wound. Let's get some O2 going, hang a bag of fluid, and splint that leg. Call it in Joe, we're losing her. We need to transport now."

The other EMT came over to assist and said, "hey, I know her, she's that lady doc from St. Vincent's hospital—Dr. Hayes. We need to get her out of here fast before she crashes again. The way she's struggling to breathe, I'd guess she has a collapsed lung and probably internal injuries."

The highway patrol officer arrived and gathered her personal belongings from the wreckage to notify next of kin. After snapping pictures of the wreckage, he picked up the empty vodka bottle and placed it into an evidence bag.

As the EMT's were loading her into the ambulance the officer said, "I want a full toxicology panel on her at the ER. From the looks of her I don't think she'll make it to the trauma center alive."

However, she surprised them all. Annie was a fighter, she needed to be to survive her childhood, her mother's negativity, and incessant need to control every aspect of Annie's life growing up. As early as Annie could remember her mother had told her *'Don't.' Don't* run Annie, you'll fall. *Don't* try to play ball Annie, you're not athletic and you'll get hurt. *Don't* be friends with those girls Annie, you're not their type. Even in high school and college she told her don't…*don't* take chemistry, you'll never pass, *don't* try for that college, you'll never get accepted. *Don't* go to medical school, you'll end up with a lot of debt. *Don't* always *don't.* However, Mom wasn't around anymore to tell Annie *don't* drink and drive, you'll have a wreck and ruin your life. She had to learn this lesson the hard way.

Annie usually did some things anyway when told not to, and paid the consequences, like the time she told her *'Don't'* ride your bike down the big hill." Annie wrecked and broke out her four front teeth. She got a lot of *'I told you so's'* after that one, but sometimes things worked out for her. Like Chemistry, she was a natural science nerd, the college of her dreams became a reality, and now she was a physician. Why couldn't her mother have been her cheerleader, happy for her, and encouraging her? Instead, she instilled a lack of self-confidence in her only daughter, something Annie dealt with every day of her life as an adult.

Annie drifted in and out of consciousness for the next several days, living somewhere in the fog between reality and purgatory. When she finally awoke in the ICU, she remembered nothing of the wreck, transport, or her time in the trauma bay. She recognized her husband, Tom, standing beside the bed as the ventilator pushed oxygen into her damaged lungs. She tried to fight the machine breathing for her, and get up from the bed, but a nurse appeared and injected something into her IV. The fog possessed her once again. The next time she awoke in a private room on the surgical floor, off the respirator, and breathing on her own.

Tom was again by her bedside; he had on his scrubs so he must have come from work. He gently stroked her long black hair still matted with blood from the large gash on her scalp. He counted 30 staples closing the head wound.

"Hi there. Hey, look at you and those big brown eyes finally open. It's good to see you awake. How do you feel? Your pupils are equal and reactive, and you recognize me, all positive signs for someone with a traumatic brain injury." Tom said.

Her throat was sore, and she ached deep inside. It hurt even to nod her head or breathe deeply. When she tried to move her legs, something was wrong, one was heavy and immovable. Fighting the pain to crane her neck and look down but doing it anyway, she saw the halo fixation device with pins piercing into the skin on her left leg. The leg was purple and black from the knee to the ankle with remnants of dried blood, and she saw a long gash snaking down her shinbone, with staples holding it together. No wonder she was in pain.

This doesn't look good.

"What happened to me, what's going on?" She asked, surprised at how she sounded, her voice was hoarse and weak, and it hurt to inhale, so she took shallow sips of air.

"There was an automobile accident, you hydroplaned in a puddle of water on Hwy 256. You should see the car—it's totaled. But thankfully, no one else was injured," Tom said.

"My head and chest hurt like hell, oh man my leg. How long have I been here? I need to get up and go to work, I have patients to see." She grabbed the side rails and attempted to pull herself out of the bed. It was excruciatingly painful, lighting bolts shot through her body. Tom gently urged her back down onto the bed, she didn't resist.

"Wait a minute, whoa…..You've been here about a week you've been out of it, but you moved out of the ICU yesterday. You have an open fracture of your leg, and cracked a few ribs, which punctured and collapsed your lung. You've also suffered a head injury, that's why your memory is a little sketchy. But you have a good prognosis. It will take a while along with physical therapy in rehab, but you're out of the woods and you'll be as good as new."

He took her hand in his kissing her fingers and smiling at her, but she could not keep her eyes open, and the fog moved in again.

She awoke to a nurse arousing her to administer pain medication, and to clean the pins on her leg device. She knew she was in for torture, and she was right.

Later, lying in the hospital bed, alone in her room and bored between ten-minute cat naps, she saw her cell phone charging on the nightstand. She tried to reach over the rail to retrieve it to no avail. She refused to call the nurse's station to help her with something so trivial, but she needed to check her texts and voice mail. She had patients in this hospital and needed to see that her colleagues were taking care of them. She couldn't stay awake though and drifted off to sleep again.

Tom was there when she opened her eyes. "Hey there, sleeping beauty, I didn't think you were going to wake up for me today."

"How long have I been here? I feel like I'm in *Groundhog's Day*." Not waiting for an answer she said, "Please hand me my phone. I need to check on my patients and get back to work."

"You've been here almost two weeks, and if you keep improving, you'll be discharged to a rehab facility in a few days according to Dr. Green." He pushed her phone on the nightstand further away from her, "Don't worry about work, the other doctors are covering for you. You just focus on getting better."

"Green, she's the one treating me?" she asked, not expecting an answer.

She knew Dr. Judith Green very well, they were peers, and she knew if Green was on her case, she had been in bad shape, because she headed up the Level 1 trauma center. She was a good doctor, and all the males in the hospital had a crush on her—including Tom.

Annie still couldn't remember the wreck or what day it was. She asked the same questions every day. Tom would visit like clockwork, during his lunch break or after he finished his work in the Radiology Department. He was very patient with her, and each time she asked, he would explain what happened to bring her back into the present day.

She felt lucky to have him. They met in college a year before both graduating from medical school and after dating a year, they married. They enjoyed each other's company and at one time shared lots of common interests. They were the picture-perfect pair; he was six feet tall, blonde hair, blue eyes, handsome, intelligent, and looked perfect standing next to her. Their college dream was to eventually open a medical practice together. But they seldom talked about their dreams and ambitions anymore. Tom hadn't shown interest in owning his own practice since they started working at St. Vincent's over 10 years ago. He was content working for the hospital, and she let her dream languish. She could still hear her mother's voice in her head telling her *'Don't do that,'* and this time she listened. She knew something was 'off' in their marriage, and had been for some time, but it didn't seem important to her anymore. Tom would come home to her each night, and they would go through the same routine. It was how life was between them, like a pair of old shoes. They may not look the best but were comfortable and she didn't want to break in a new pair of shoes. Something more important was consuming both of their lives; she had a career that took center place in her life, just as Tom's did for him. She honored her marriage vows and promised she would never leave Tom.

Since the accident she sensed something different—a nagging feeling that something miraculous happened to her in the wreck. She had flashbacks of visiting an ethereal place where she met a woman, with a kind presence emanating from around her. The woman seemed familiar, as if she knew her from somewhere, she felt like a grandmother. Annie knew that was not possible, because she was adopted and there were no living relatives. Her only family was Tom. But she could not shake the feeling that she knew this woman who appeared to her in the dream. At least she thought it was a dream but wasn't sure and she had many unanswered questions.

Did she have a near death experience, and visit the afterlife? Had she suffered a cardiac event in the wreck, and resuscitated or was the memory just a hallucination?

When Dr. Green came to check on her, she would ask about her injuries in more detail. She got her chance later that afternoon.

"Annie, how're you feeling today?" Dr. Green asked as she opened her chart and began scribbling notes, not waiting for a response.

"As well as can be expected," she said. "I do have a question for you though…..did I die?"

"We have a report from the EMT that you were unresponsive at the crash scene upon their arrival, and they did resuscitate with CPR. You suffered significant trauma to your head and chest and lost a lot of blood. We transfused you in ER." Dr. Green answered bluntly.

That explained a lot to Annie. Her heart stopped beating and coupled with the massive blood loss depleted oxygen to her brain causing confusion, making it difficult to determine dream state from reality, she reasoned.

Later that same day, another visitor—the Illinois State Police came to the hospital room and served papers charging her with DUI. Her blood alcohol tested in the ER at two times the legal limit. She thanked God she had not injured anyone else in the wreck, but she knew she was in big legal trouble. It would appear at first glance that she may have a drinking problem, but she believed she could quit anytime she wanted. The stormy weather had caused the wreck, not the alcohol.

As days went on snippets of the accident started to return to her. Haunting her thoughts by the memory of a woman on a horse, the one in her dream from the day of the wreck. She would never forget her; something unspoken transpired between them and it remained in her soul and buried deep in her damaged brain.

Was there someone at the crash on horseback, or was I imagining it? Who was that woman and what significance did she have to me?

She was released to a rehab facility three weeks after the crash and began working to get back on her feet. Annie progressed with her recovery. While in rehab, a fiberglass cast replaced the halo device on her leg, allowing her to ambulate more easily. She also began hard physical therapy, learning to stand up and sit down, take a shower, walk on crutches, and conquering stairs all by herself.

Tom hired a lawyer to manage her legal issues in court. The judge gave her probation in lieu of jail time and ordered attendance into a rehab program for her alcoholism.

While Annie didn't know when she would have time for rehab, she was grateful to Tom for wrangling the slap on the wrist. She vowed she would never drink and drive again. She heard her mother's voice in her head saying, *'I told you so'…..*

Cherokee Country
Approx. 1765

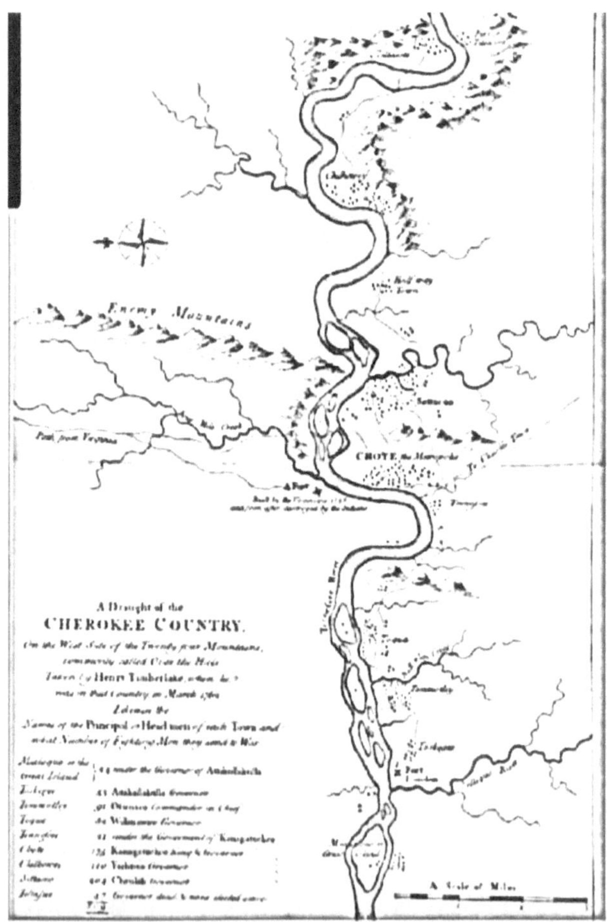

Timberlake, Lieut. Henry, The Memoirs of Lieut. Henry Timberlake, LONDON Printed for the Author, MDCCLXV (1765), Collection University of Pittsburgh Library System, Americana https://www.archive.org/details/memoiroflieuthe00tumb/page/62/mode/1u p?q=dragging+canoe

TWO

1830

New Echota,
Northwest Georgia

Sitting on the rocks at the river with her feet submerged in the water soaking her swollen feet. From the corner of her eye, she caught the movement of a dark shadow darting about in the canopy of the trees. Squinting her eyes to focus, she saw nothing there. This all added to her unease for something that had been stirring in the air of the camp. She couldn't see it, but felt it deep inside, the presence of a dark spirit buffeting her soul looking for a soft spot to bur its way inside. As an empath, the granddaughter and daughter of Cherokee spiritual healers Running Deer sensed the danger surrounding the tribe. She possessed a gift of communing with spirits, visions, and revelations.

A gust of wind caught her silky black hair swirling around her head like a crown. Her hair was long, reaching to her knees, and ornamented with ribbons of assorted colors. Her dress was much like the white European settlers living near their camp, today she wore a dark calico print fashioned loosely and adorned with elk teeth and a wampum belt tied high over her big belly. The elk teeth valued by the Cherokee, as only two are harvested from each kill. Running Deer's dress was highly regarded among the tribe since it displayed 100 or more teeth, proving her husband a great hunter.

Suppressing her fears and concentrating on the coolness of the water, which felt good on her ankles, she thought of the new life growing inside of her. She had 'come to the water' at the river to bathe, think and pray, as she did every morning to cleanse her spirit. She sat watching the crawdads and tadpoles darting in and out of the shallow water rippling toward the bank, while thanking the

Creator for life and the plants and animals to sustain it. The forest was beautiful this time of year, dressed in its spring finest. The weather had warmed after a hard winter, the deciduous trees sprouting greenery, and the early redbuds and dogwoods already in full bloom. The birds had come back to nest singing, announcing their arrival this morning. It was now the cusp of the full Flower Moon, which occurs in May and signifies the coming of spring with the arrival of flowers. After that, the next new moon would be the Planting Moon, when the moon waxed fully signaling readiness for crop planting.

Today in this place, she felt bad spirits, even amidst all the beauty of new life surrounding her. She was anxious about the imminent birth of her first child, she had heard and seen births go wrong. She also worried about the murmurings of the locals against her tribe due to the recent actions of the U.S. Government. At the river, while praying to Earth Mother and the Great Spirit for help, for an easy birth, a healthy baby, the protection of her people, for wisdom, and peace with the white settlers.

Caressing her large stomach overpowering her sleight athletic frame all while rubbing and speaking softly to the treasure kicking and squirming within. She watched the baby's foot move from inside her womb leaving a trail behind on her large belly. She traced her finger along the foot's path connecting to the child held captive within.

"Settle little one, you will soon be free and have more room," she smiled and spoke softly, focusing on the active baby she carried within.

Her time to deliver would be any day, the milk engorging her breast for a few days now. Suddenly she felt tightening starting in her sides, back, and spreading around her belly, and when the pain hit, she could not move. Her birth water gushed and began trickling down her legs. These birth signs came as no surprise and she was ready but scared of what was to come, as it was her first.

Running Deer strolled the shady trail casually from the river counting between contractions, waddling toward her grandmother's lodge. Her mind now on the impending labor and delivery, as she walked, she needed to stop and stand still as each contraction came on, panting while the tightness of her belly subsided, before resuming her trek. It took longer than usual for her to reach Grandmother's lodge.

Grandmother was the medicine 'woa-man' and healer of the 'Paint Clan.' There are seven clans in the Cherokee Nation: the '(Red) Paint,' the 'Wolf,' the 'Blue Clan,' the 'Long Hair' or 'Twister,' the 'Wild Potato,' the 'Deer Clan,' and the 'Bird Clan.' Each clan inherits a specialty and conducts certain functions for the tribe. Running Deer's clan, the (Red) Paint clan – the 'Aniwodi,' was the smallest and most secretive group of healers, sorcerers, and medicine men and medicine 'woa-men.' They are the teachers of life, birth, death, and regeneration and the secret keepers of the hidden things, having second spiritual sight, seeing visions, and creating illusions. The protector of ceremonies, rituals, and tools, they are the only ones that make the special 'red' paint used in ceremonial rituals, warfare, and healing. Prior to battle, they mix and paint the horses and warriors for protection. When healing, they paint the red medicine onto a patient's body after harvesting, mixing, and performing the healing and cleansing ceremonies over them.

In a few hours, Mother and Grandmother would help deliver her first baby. Grandmother midwifed for countless other Cherokee women for over fifty years. She was highly revered, and recently named the 'Beloved Mother' by the clan, a high honor. She readied to meet her first great grandchild days ago. She stocked the birth lodge with fresh water, decoctions, tinctures, tonics, herbs, bear grease, and firewood needed to minister to the laboring mother and to welcome the new soul into the light.

Running Deer sent word to her mate, Black Fox of the wolf clan it was time. He left to join the other men far away from the lodge to await his offspring's arrival. He was handsome and of muscular build. The skin of his upper face—from lower eyelids to scalp was painted red, and arms marked with black tattoos of animals designs permanently pricked into his flesh with gunpowder. The hair of his head clean-shaven except for a patch on the top and backside, which he ornamented with beads, feathers, dyed deer hair, and other baubles. Both of his earlobes had slits and hung down to his shoulders, wound with silver wire and adorned with pendants and rings, which also pierced his nose. He wore a collar of beads cut from clamshells, a hammered copper breast plate, and bracelets on both arms and wrist. His shirt traded from the English, and his moccasins ornamented with colorful beads and painted porcupine-quills. Black Fox was very gentle and loving to Running Deer, but his enemies feared him as a fierce warrior, and he looked the part.

Running Deer entered the birthing lodge she had watched the men build a few months earlier. They began by setting thick posts fixed into the ground creating a circle, measuring around 16 feet in diameter. Between each of these thick posts they set a smaller one. Then the women wattled it together with twigs like weaving a basket and covered the exterior with an exceptionally smooth clay dug from the earth, which they then whitewashed. The roof covered with narrow boards, and a small hole venting the top for the smoke to escape. It was very dark, warm, and sooty inside.

This was her first time entering this new lodge and she began chanting to enter a spiritual state as she walked around inside. Grandmother placed a large mound of leaves near the fire in the center of the room. She would not lie down for the delivery, but stand, or squat over the pile of leaves to catch the baby as it fell to Earth Mother, but that was still many hours away.

Grandmother opened the medicine bundle skin, preparing Running Deer a special tea of wild cherry bark and blue cohosh root, to help speed labor. She then filled the medicine pipe bowl with tobacco and other herbs, and holding it aloft began offering prayer. This sacred vessel had passed down for generations from healers before her. The pipe was over two feet long, with a hollow cane for the stem adorned with copper pulled from these ancestral mountains harboring extraordinarily rich stores of gold, silver, and lead. The ore was melted, poured while a hot liquid upon a flat rock and then pounded when cooled into a cylindrical shape used to adorn the pipe stem. The pipe was also decorated with porcupine quills, painted very colorfully in red and yellow sacred symbols, while the bowl was fashioned from a hollowed out red stone found in the earth. The stones outside honed round, and polished smoothly, when lit it glowed fiery red with each puff. Two blessed eagle feathers hung down from the stem, where they joined to the bowl.

Grandmother lit the pipe, holding it aloft and began offering smoke to the four corners —North, South, East, and West, to represent the ebb and flow of life and to carry her prayers up to the Great Spirit. The clan's fire keeper had earlier prepared a fire in the center of the lodge with large stones encircling it. Once the logs burned down, Grandmother pushed the stones into the embers to absorb and later emit their retained heat. She placed the mullein leaves onto the hot rocks and dripped water onto them to produce medicinal steam, which Running Deer straddled as she labored, to soothe, soften, and prepare the birth canal.

During her pregnancy, Running Deer had been careful, avoiding all foods deemed dangerous to the baby by the elder mothers. They warned her not to eat raccoon, pheasant, or squirrel, and to avoid speckled trout so the baby would not have a birthmark, and black walnuts, which would cause a big nose. Grandmother cautioned her about wearing belts or necklaces, for fear it would cause umbilical strangulation. In the last weeks of pregnancy, her mother and aunts began shouting at the baby to scare it from the womb. Each time they did, it made her jump.

After four hours of hard labor she said, "Grandmother, I'm scared and the pains hurt, I feel like my body is being torn in half. It doesn't seem like the baby is moving down."

"My granddaughter, it is supposed to hurt, nothing great in life will find you without pain and sacrifice. Open your mind to the world around you and become one with the spirits, they will help your pain and help lead your child into this world."

Grandmother offered her another sip of yellow root tea, to help the birthing pains and checked her progress. She handed her the bear grease to rub and stretch her perineum, while placing more mullein leaves on the fire allowing the steam to relax the muscles of the birth canal. As the labor became stronger, she straddled the hot stones allowing the smoke from the fire to soothe her. Grandmother smudged her forehead with sage, then fanned the smoke around her with an eagle feather to ward off evil spirits. She then cleansed the room with the pipe smoke again.

The pain grew more intense as nighttime arrived, when the pain was unbearable, she chewed on a leather strap and grunted with each hard contraction. She would make no sound for fear she would frighten the baby back into the womb. Grandmother rubbed her back with herbs infused in oil, and placed cool cloths on her forehead as the pains drew closer. Mother continued to give Running Deer brews of wild cherry bark tea to sip, which helped calm her fears and anxiety. Running Deer saw dark figures in the room startling her. At first it was only one body; now there were several shadows slinking and dancing around inside the lodge. She didn't mention the intruders to anyone, but Grandmother noticed her focus change and her eyes appear to follow something around the room.

Grandmother heard a raven's cry from outside in the darkness and felt the strong wind blowing against the lodge. Her senses amped and the goose flesh covered her body. She knew something was wrong. The dried bones and owl feathers suspended on leather strips and tied above the doorway to serve as an alarm for intruders started to shiver and shake, yet there was no breeze.

"What is it my child, why do you fret, what do you see?"

"It's nothing Grandmother, but I thought I saw dark figures lurking around the room. I saw the same shadows while I was at the water this morning also," she tried to downplay her paranoia.

"My daughter, this is not something to ignore, the dark figures will come for you when you are weak. The talisman moving above the doorway signifies the evil Raven Mockers are here and seek to destroy you and your unborn child. They prey on those who are sick or dying and steal their heart without leaving any marks on the body. Once they feed on the heart, they add a year of life for each year their victim would have lived, which is why newborn babies and young mothers are prime targets.

They know you carry a special soul, which is pure and feeds their evil spirit. The baby will be powerful, a chosen one, who will do important things for our people. They will pursue the child's soul for generations in this world. They are normally invisible and only those with strong medicine can see them. If the Raven Mocker does not feed within seven days, it will rot and die. You must be aware of the evil one, shielding yourself and the child until it grows strong enough to fight these evil spirits."

Recognizing the danger, Grandmother knew she needed to bring stronger medicine. Placing Evergreen on the fire to repel the evil ones, she took the sage again smudging Running Deer's forehead and fanning the smoke around her head with the eagle feather. Taking an amulet from her medicine bag—a piece of stag horn shaped into a circle with a hole to hang from a leather strap. The circle engraved with figures depicting the four corners of the earth, with arrows pointing left and right around it. The arrows symbolize safety and peace. Grandmother tied this charm around Running Deer's neck as she chanted a prayer, while dabbing the sage on her swollen abdomen to protect the baby. Grandmother puffed the pipe again seven times offering the smoke to the four winds, and instructing Mother to retrieve the sacred crystals, eagle feathers, and other secret talismans from within the medicine bundle. Then placing them in a circle around where Running Deer lay, beginning at her head. Grandmother chanted and prayed, calling on all the powers that night to protect the two lives in her care.

Finally, the baby's head crowned, and the time came for Running Deer to push. She stood over the warm stones bending her knees slightly. Mother stood facing her, holding her hands, while speaking soft words of encouragement and helping balance her so she would not topple forward.

"I must push."

She moved to stand beside the stones, crouching over the deep pile of leaves. With one great push and a hard grunt, she felt the baby's head emerge. Using her hands she guided the head and then the shoulders out, gently gliding the baby onto the leaves and into Earth Mother's embrace. With a cry of relief, she picked up the wet baby, held it by one foot upside down, rubbing its back with her hand until it cried. She used her fingers to clean the mouth of liquid, then placed it into a soft buckskin the father tanned in preparation. Mother watched with pride and tears in her eyes as her daughter dried and softly cooed to the infant.

"It is a girl," Running Deer announced with a broad smile, as she handed the baby to her mother.

Earlier in the day, Grandmother dug a shallow hole in the dirt floor of the lodge, buried hot stones and covered them with soft pelts for the new mother to rest upon after the birth. Running Deer began to cry, as she lay down on the warm pelts, grateful for the healthy baby, as Mother and Grandmother sweetly tended to her body and soul.

Grandmother's midwife's work was not yet finished, as she prepared tea of smooth sumac to help the new mother's milk come in and delivered the afterbirth. Her focus remained on Running Deer, exhausted from the long labor, watching for hemorrhage or any other complications, while Mother tended to the newborn.

Mother opened the skin blanket covering the baby, rubbing her all over with a small amount of bear fat while tying off the umbilical cord and cutting it with a knife. After grandmother delivered the placenta, Mother would bury it in a separate ceremony along with the umbilical cord, returning life back to Earth Mother, as a gift in exchange for the safe birth of her first grandchild.

Mother swaddled the infant tightly and carried her outside into the crisp night air, where the women of childbearing age gathered around the front of the birthing lodge. They were there waiting and chanting all day for the safe arrival of the new soul. Mother placed the baby into the waiting arms of one and then she passed her onto the next, until all the women in the circle held and greeted the tiny baby. The ceremony signified they were all new mothers with this birth, welcoming the child to the Cherokee.

Mother then carried the baby to the corral holding the scout horses. In the center of the dirt arena, amid the horses, the father had prepared a small wooden box lined with straw. Placing the baby into the box, she backed a few steps away, watching as the horses came to investigate the squirming noisy thing in the box. Most of them would sniff and snort and then walk away. All but one, a young paint colt with a blaze on his forehead and four white socks stood steady beside the box. He did not move away, and he continued smelling and snorting at the baby, while pawing the dirt with his front hooves. Mother knew this was a spiritual bond, signifying a connection and link to the supernatural realm. The colt would be given to the child representing strength, courage, and freedom.

Mother returned to the center of a circle formed by the gathering of women with the child. Unwrapping and holding her naked, offering her up toward the full moon. The cool spring night enveloped them, with the moonlight shining upon the baby's face and reflecting from her eyes. The child wailed into the night. Mother whispered a blessing upon her head and thanked the Great Spirit and Earth Mother for the new life.

Mother recited a Cherokee proverb to her new granddaughter for all to hear, "when you were born, you cried, and the world rejoiced. Live your life so that when you die, the world cries and you rejoice."

She swaddled her and returned to the lodge placing her onto Running Deer's breast to nurse. The baby latched on immediately, squirming and making soft suckling sounds. Running Deer had never felt such love for another, and her emotions ran deep—too deep for words. She didn't know the depths of such feelings existed until this moment, and knew she would give her life for this child. She cried silent tears at the beauty of the child suckling at her breast, and for the safe birth.

The new mother and baby would share a laying in period in their lodge home, where they would get to know one another and bond their souls together for eternity. Running Deer would also watch for signs from the spirit world to reveal the name of her child. The elder women of the clan would provide them nourishment and see to their needs during this time. The father came to meet his daughter, but the couple would not lay together until Running Deer went through a cleansing ceremony.

One day soon after birth, and the child's name had not yet been made known to her, Running Deer went to the water to wash herself. When she exited cleansed from the water, she heard doves coo. Peering into the dense brush lining the riverbank, she spotted their nest and saw an unusual white dove perched on a branch. The dove looked straight into her eyes and called out to her spirit, "I am White Dove."

She knew this was a sign the child was to be, White Dove—'Unega Woya.' The child's spirit name, White Dove meant peace and happiness, and one who cries for the people. She thanked

Earth Mother and the Great Spirit for revealing the name of her daughter. The new family celebrated her arrival and on the eighth day, the clan held the naming ceremony. For a season, all was well in their tiny lodge home. White Dove grew tall and true, full of laughter, and much loved. She brought great joy to the Paint Clan.

However, the Cherokee would cry many tears over the mistreatment of their people by the white man in the years following White Dove's birth.

The invasion of the white settlers started with a few and then more and more came followed by the French and the Dutch. These Europeans numbered so many hungering to own all the land and its bounty; not realizing one could not 'own' nature. They would stop at nothing short of genocide, their goal to erase the Cherokee and other tribes from the face of the earth by practicing 'Manifest Destiny.' Their belief that the expansion throughout America was both justified and inevitable, that it was their right. Considering the Native people less than and beneath the white man because they looked, dressed, and acted differently. These invading foreigners practiced killing and paying bounties for Indian scalps. Attacking a people whose only crime was defending their homelands and protecting Earth Mother from the European invaders robbing the gold, silver, and copper held deep within her mountains, raping the land.

The Cherokee Nation had declared itself sovereign in 1827 and Running Deer naively believed once this occurred her people would be free. She once hoped this meant living in peace and respect alongside the white man. Now, just three short years later, they were on the verge of eviction from the forest, rivers, streams, and rich farmland that sustained them since the beginning of time.

Running Deer vowed she would not go peacefully or abandon the bones of her ancestors—her great grandfathers and grandmothers buried here. Her people were the first; they were the "Aniyvwiya," The Chosen People. The Cherokee living in these woodlands since the beginning of time, believed here is where they belonged and would remain forever. However, the white man had other plans for this prime property, breaking treaty after treaty while encroaching upon the Cherokee and their way of life.

THREE

Current Day

Annic was discharged to recuperate at a rehab facility after three weeks in the hospital. She would need extensive therapy on her body to heal while learning to walk on crutches and be able to take care of herself with a broken leg. Due to a bruised brain, she also had trouble with her short-term memory, double vision, and balance issues. Life was more difficult for her now, and she worried would she ever be well enough to practice medicine again. The only bright spot to her day was Tom's visits, he tried to come every day after work. Sometimes she didn't see him for a few days, but she understood his very demanding job. She had stood in his shoes and spent a lot of time away from family due to her work schedule too. She regretted that decision now, because she realized how lonely it was to be by yourself all the time. She promised herself that after this was over that she and Tom would reconnect, and she would be a better more attentive wife. He would come first in her life from now on.

Rehab was not a walk in the park, it was hard work, painful, and mentally grueling. She had to relearn simple things again but progressed rapidly. The halo device was removed from her leg before she left the hospital, and now she was in a cast from the knee down. It was better, but still cumbersome and difficult maneuvering on crutches.

The facility Tom chose was not the best in the area, but affordable with their insurance plan. There were a lot of elderly people recuperating from falls and fractures. Each night she could hear the patients screaming out in confusion and pain, and the smells were not pleasant. She prayed for her healing so she could get out of this place while the headaches and short-term memory lapses persisted. She missed Tom and her own bed, crying herself to sleep most nights.

Tom hired a good lawyer to represent her in court, and since it was a single car accident and no one else injured, the judge granted probation with the stipulation she would enter a rehab program. If she had another accident, the court would not be so lenient the next time, revoking her probation and she would go to jail. She didn't believe she had a drinking problem; it was just a bad set of circumstances that led to the wreck. She was in a hurry, the road wet and drizzling rain causing her car to hydroplane then colliding with the pole. However, the court must blame someone and since she had a little alcohol on her breath, she paid the consequences.

Her roommate in the physical rehab facility was a young woman named Miranda. Miranda was raven haired with dark eyes and bronze skin, she was a free-spirit and embraced all things natural. She was there with a broken leg too, having fallen downstairs and banging herself up badly. She didn't want a cast on her leg, as she was a naturalist and vegan, but the doctors insisted on that treatment. Her lifestyle was eye opening for Annie, they quickly became good friends. Miranda helped fill the empty hours for Annie and she offered Annie advice on her own healing journey and life in general. Miranda encouraged Annie to order several books on herbs and healing and they had conversations all day long about Miranda's practices. By the end of Miranda's stay in rehab, Annie began to see logic in her ethnobotany.

Miranda was her only friend in rehab—really in life, and when she was discharged Annie was lonelier than ever. But Miranda phoned Annie every day to check on her. Annie also read the books studying cover to cover. She implemented a more natural lifestyle and healing along with modern medicine, adding supplements, and homeopathic remedies.

After Annie was released to go home, Tom's schedule was still very erratic, and she never knew when he would pop in at home. Sometimes several days would pass before she would see or hear from him. She started to worry about his health with the long hours spent at the hospital. Being alone gave her plenty of time to work on her body and a new healthy lifestyle. One of the first things she did when she got home was to remove all the plastic ware from her kitchen. She kept only a few pieces of clay pottery, glass bowls and dishes. Everything else went into the trash bin. Then she started filtering out all the condiments and jars with harmful ingredients from the fridge, along with wine bottles chilling and the bottles of vodka in the freezer. After the purge was done, there was not much food left in the house, and she needed to restock the pantry. Before she did, she would stop by the hospital and surprise Tom.

Since replacing the halo device with a fiberglass composite cast it became easier to get around, but she was still a bit apprehensive to drive. This would be her first outing alone, and first-time driving since the accident. Getting into the car was difficult as she maneuvered the crutches into the backseat and hobbled into the driver's seat of Tom's car. She had never driven this vehicle. She started the engine and began slowly backing out of the driveway. The memory of the accident flashed in her mind, and she braked suddenly. Her breathing became rapid as she broke out in a cold sweat with sharp pains in her abdomen. Chest spasms were so severe for a minute like having a heart attack—then she realized it was a panic attack. She put the car in park, closing her eyes and leaning back onto the headrest trying to slow her breathing, deep in and then out. She turned the AC on full blast adjusting the vents directly onto her face. She steadied her breathing focusing on each breath, in and out, while intentionally relaxing her extremities beginning at her feet and working upwards. After a few minutes, she calmed down, and her breathing returned to normal. She gave herself a pep talk.

I can do this. Easy peasy, just go slow.

She stayed well within speed limits and was extra cautious, she could not afford another ticket or accident. Her hands gripped the steering wheel, the hair around her face and neck became wet with sweat. But she did it, she made it to the hospital.

She circled the hospital parking lot looking for Tom's old truck but couldn't find it. Thinking that she had overlooked it, she parked in the closest handicapped spot nearest the door and began extricating herself from the vehicle. It was much easier getting in than getting out. She used both her hands to lift her cast left leg out of the car and onto the pavement, rocking herself from the seat until she was standing upright. Retrieving her crutches from the back seat, she began to clump across the parking lot toward the emergency entrance of the hospital.

It was her first time back in the hospital since the accident. She saw some co-workers, but they acted strangely toward her, ducking their heads, or turning to go the opposite direction when they saw her coming.

They heard about my drinking as the cause of the wreck. I don't know if I can show my face here again.

But she held her head high and continued to find Tom. She hobbled into the Radiology Department where he worked, finally reaching the front desk.

"Hi, I'm Dr. Tom Hayes's wife, can you tell him I'm here? It's a surprise," she told the receptionist.

The woman looked at her with a tilted head, her face flushed, and said, "I'm sorry, but I believe Dr. Hayes is off today. I haven't seen him all day, but the other doctor is here. Would you like to see him instead?"

Annie felt like she had been punched in the gut.

She stammered, "No, I must have made a mistake, never mind. Oh, and don't say anything to Dr. Hayes about this, I don't want him to worry about me."

Limping on her crutches back to the car, her eyes began filling with tears.

What's wrong with me? Was Tom at the house and I didn't see him? I'm losing my mind.

When she pulled into her driveway at home, there was Tom's truck.

Had she missed it when she left earlier, had he been home all the time?

She entered the house trying to be quiet, but he met her at the door.

"There you are. Where did you go?" Tom said.

"Out…I went out. I haven't been out on my own for months and I wanted to see if I could do it, and I did." She lied.

She could not confide in Tom, that she left the house looking for him. She didn't want to worry him; she was worried enough for both. She feared her mind was damaged and she would never recover enough to practice medicine again. She could have sworn that he was not there when she left. Was he? She was afraid she was going mad and there was no one to confide her fears to but Miranda.

Tom did not raise the subject again, but all afternoon he acted distant. She tried to engage him in small talk to no avail. It was apparent he was ticked at her about something, but she pretended not to notice. They were both good at avoiding the difficult discussions they needed to have these days. She clanked pans around in the kitchen trying to make a healthy lunch for them, which was difficult because she never made it to the groceries store. The only thing she had in the fridge was eggs and salad mix. She scrambled the eggs whites and dumped them onto a plate of organic greens, cut up canned beets sprinkled on top, along with shredded goat cheese, and chopped walnuts finished off with a homemade balsamic vinaigrette dressing. Granted it didn't look like a four-star meal, but it was clean, healthy, and tasted good. She thought it checked all the boxes.

"You expect me to eat this garbage?" Tom said scrunching up his nose.

"It's not garbage, it's good for you. It's part of a clean diet."

"Well, you can eat this slop, I'm going out to get me something. I'll be back later." he said, as he grabbed his jacket off the back of the chair and went out the kitchen door slamming it behind him.

She was alone again and felt reprimanded like a child. She tried not to cry but couldn't hold the tears inside. She cried often nowadays, and they came without warning since the car wreck, her emotions were always on the edge of erupting and rolling down her face. She sat down in the kitchen chair and played with her salad. Her appetite had vanished along with her husband.

She always thought when she found a career she wanted, a man she loved and their perfect home she would find happiness. If she was happy, why was she a lonely alcoholic crying in her salad? Something was very wrong, and she didn't know how to fix it.

At 10 p.m., Tom still wasn't home, the house was silent except for the clock ticking on the mantle. It ticked in time with her heart. For some reason, an empty house where no one is coming home is always sadder than when you expect someone to walk in through the door. It was as if she was a widow but there was nobody to claim and bury, and yet she suffered from the same grief and loneliness. She mourned her dead marriage.

She headed to bed alone again, struggling to get up the stairs on her crutches and the extra weight on her leg from the cast threw her off balance. She finally made it safe and sound. Opening the door to their perfect looking bedroom, furnished with matching nightstands, matching lamps and decorator pillows piled high on a custom comforter on the large king-sized bed with matching drapes.

How ironic, this is an example of something that looks perfect on the outside but is dreadfully wrong inside.

It had been weeks since Tom slept in their bed, and well before the wreck since they shared intimacy.

He has not been here one night since I returned from rehab.

She folded the comforter back, throwing all the pillows over onto the other side of the bed. She didn't even bother to put on pajamas but crawled straight into the small hole she opened for herself. She hugged the edge of the bed, almost to the point of falling onto the floor.

This bed is much too big for one person.

She lay there replaying the day's events in her mind.

Where was Tom? What was he so angry about? Am I losing my mind, was he home and I didn't see him? If not, where was he all day?

She dozed off and on until about midnight, finally giving up on the thought of Tom coming home tonight. She realized they needed to have a heart-to-heart and get whatever was bothering him out in the open. Their current situation was as a splinter buried deep, causing infection and festering. The pus eventually pushes out the foreign body, but potentially causing sepsis affecting the whole body—poisoning the heart. She believed it was time to excise it to prevent further damage. It would be painful, especially when she didn't self-medicate with alcohol anymore. However, it needed to happen sooner rather than later.

She felt so alone, as an only child she always longed for a brother, or a sister and it was at times like this she wished she had family to talk to and share her troubles. She discovered her adoption in the sixth grade when given a school assignment to create her family tree. She went to the family bible finding her birth certificate folded up between the pages with the mother and father blocks whited out, and adoption papers. When Annie asked Mother if she was adopted, she became furious with her. Mother claimed she always intended to tell Annie the truth, but never found the right time.

Annie had no complaints with her adoptive parents, they doted on her and she led an idyllic childhood. However, it was another great loss when they both died within five years of each other while she was in medical school. Her dad suffered a massive heart attack at 56 and her mother followed him a few years later from metastatic breast cancer. Not only was she an only child, but she was also now an orphan. She had no other living relatives and was all alone until she met Tom. The loneliness tonight reminded her of that time in her life, Tom was her only family. If he left, what would she do without him?

She rolled over and looked at the clock on the nightstand beside the bed. She had been lying there for hours staring at the ceiling and still sleep evaded her. She craved a drink, thankful she had thrown all the bottles in the trash earlier and knew she needed to get to a meeting, or she would go to a liquor store instead. She picked up her cell phone and began searching for AA meetings near her; this would be her first one, but what better time than when you are jonesing for your drug of choice.

Probably less crowded in the middle of the night anyway.

Thirty minutes later she was in a dark room with ten other poor souls at 5 a.m. They sat on hard metal folding chairs in a circle and went around the room introducing themselves. Admitting to themselves and each other, they were alcoholics.

When they got to her, she said, "Hi I'm Annie"…she stopped before saying she was an alcoholic.

She couldn't finish the sentence, she had to be convinced this was true before she could utter those words. The people in the room didn't seem to even notice or care. They responded in unison, "Hi Annie."

Then one by one, these imperfect strangers began telling their sad tales of how they wrecked their marriages, health, jobs, and lives, by alcohol. How they finally turned to their 'Higher Power' and how many days of sobriety they had—usually brandishing a wooden chip to mark their days, while everyone applauded.

She felt sorry for them, but her situation was different, she just had one little wreck due to a wet road. She didn't hurt anybody but herself. These people were down and out, they were real drunks.

She didn't belong here and was only there because the Judge was a teetotaler, and the terms of her probation meant she had to attend meetings. So, she would go to please the court, not because she thought she needed to.

After the meeting was over while trying to sneak out of the room unnoticed, a friendly looking man approached her. He was middle-aged with a paunch belly stuffed into beige khaki pants giving him a square appearance, and on top of his head sat a green plaid golf cap, which he never removed.

Offering his hand he said, "Hi Annie, my name is Ray. I'm glad you're here tonight, I believe you're new to our little club?"

"Hi" she said coolly while she slung her purse over her neck and gathered her crutches, trying to make a hasty escape.

"Would you have time for a cup of coffee at the deli across the street, just a friendly gesture to make you feel a little more welcome to join the group?"

She paused and thought about it before answering.

What else did she have to do at this time of the night? There's nobody waiting at home for me.

Then she said, "Sure, why not."

Ray was engaging and liked to talk—a lot. He was a sponsor, and of course an alcoholic. He had been coming to this meeting for many years now and knew all the others. He told her his story and how low in life he sank before getting sober 25 years ago. Now retired, but at one time a heavy equipment operator and managed to never work a sober day, and yet no one died. He stashed bottles in the cab of his big machine and would drink all day until quitting time. When the workday was over, he'd stop by the local bar and drink until time to drive home where he would stagger inside and fall into bed, repeating the scene again the next day. His last arrest for DUI blew three times the legal limit. Almost unconscious behind the wheel when he ran off the road, they found him passed out with his head on the steering wheel and his idling car sitting in a ditch. Losing his license, he was fired from his job. His wife stayed with him through all those years and, evidently, she was a Saint on earth. Soon after he was hospitalized with pancreatitis, stage 4 cirrhosis, and almost died. Finally realizing he needed help, or he would die, by either drinking himself to death or because of drunk driving. He still carried the guilt for endangering the lives of others, and the pain he caused his family by his selfishness to drink.

All these years later, he attended weekly meetings, not so much for himself anymore but for those he could help, a part of the 12-Step program he still followed.

"I noticed you didn't admit you are an alcoholic, but that's common for first timers. It's something you must accept to heal from it, just keep coming to meetings. You'll get there. The cravings will lessen, but you should find a sponsor as soon as possible. I'll try to help you find somebody you mesh with."

His words led her to confide in him and share her story of the accident and the court ordered program, yet she didn't think she was so bad.

"Just a lapse in judgement, one time act of stupidity. Won't happen again," she said.

As they said their goodbyes Ray offered, "Take my number before you go, if you need to drink and can't get to a meeting call me. Anytime, it's ok."

She added his number to her contacts list on her phone, but doubted she would ever need to call him. After all, she wasn't really an alcoholic.

Slave Bill of Sale

Know all men by these presents, That I, *Sam Dent* ,
of the county of *New Echota* and state of *Georgia*
have this day, for and in consideration *Five hundred*
dollars to me in hand paid by *John Hightower*   his
wife and children, bargained and sold unto him. a
certain negro *Girl*   named *Molly*   about age
of *Fourteen* Years; which said slave I warrant to be
sound and healthy; and I also warrant the right and
title of said slave, unto heirs, executors, &c. &c. and
that said *Negro girl Molly* is a slave for life.

Witness my hand and seal, this *Sixth* day
of *November* 1833 .

John Hightower   Nov 6. 1833.

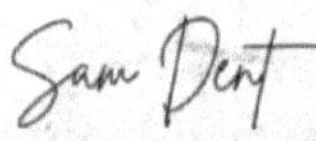

Sam Dent

FOUR

1833

*New Echota,
Northwest Georgia*

The People remembered the night the sky rained down fire before our great walk westward. On that night we shivered and huddled close together as the wind blew from the north, cold and hard against our lodges. We kept fires burning inside our dark and smoky dwellings and made beds upon heated stones buried in the ground then covered with buffalo hides to keep warm. Outside the snowflakes spit down upon us, as the fire keepers kept the fire by the council house, which was in the center of the village, burning high. The first stars began falling at nightfall, we had seen them before and were not afraid. We thought it was the pranksters the Thunder Boys playing tricks on us. But hours later we were awakened by the brightness of the sky, it was not yet dawn and the sky was bright like noonday. The shouts and screams from our People drew the crowds outside to see the sky white with many stars falling from the upper world. The women and children crying and afraid the hot fire would land on them and burn them up. Was the Creator throwing balls of fire from his hearth to destroy us? Hundreds more stars fell from the heavens and the People believed it was the end of their time on earth.

The elders roused the medicine man, asleep in his lodge, outside to interpret what this sign from the upper heavens meant. The medicine man revealed the Creator was angry, so the men danced and gave offerings trying to placate him. Using amulets and eagle feathers from the medicine bag, he called upon his most powerful medicine. He joined the dance around the sacred flame, tossing dried powders into the fire to appease the Lady of the Flame asking her to talk to The Creator on their behalf. The elders joined the dance, chanting all night as the multitude of stars continued to fall from the sky. The People knew this was a bad omen and daybreak revealed another attack by the white man.

As the sun rose the next morning White Dove's mother—Running Deer, stood outside her lodge watching the young children already playing in the dirt close to the fire, including three-year-old White Dove. There were lodges built around in a circle and in the center was the shared council house fire. The fire smoked under a suspended pot cooking venison stew. Two white men rode into the center of the village on fine horses, stopping in front of the council house. The men sat high on horseback looking down onto the women and children of the camp, as if they were beneath them. The riders covered their noses and mouths with handkerchiefs as they shouted, afraid of breathing in the same air and catching some horrid disease from the savages. Running Deer ran to grandmother's lodge and bid her to come quickly to see what the men wanted.

Soon a muttering crowd gathered around the white men, the horses pranced at the sight of the bright feathers the Cherokee men wore in their hair, and the colorful blankets draped around the women. A few cur dogs barked while running around between the horse's legs, further agitating the large animals.

Sitting high upon the white horse, the big man in the center, said, "we have come to take possession of Molly the slave, and her two sons. We know they live here. They are slave property, and we have a bill of sale for it from the trader Mr. Sam Dent to Mr. John Hightower. We are slave catchers here to collect this property and deliver it to Mr. Hightower's plantation in South Georgia."

Grandmother knew the story of Molly—born a slave, who became an adopted Cherokee daughter, Chickawa, and mother to Isaac and Benjamin, sons of a full-blood Cherokee man. This is the story she told Running Deer of how Molly came to the Cherokee.

Sam Dent was a white fur trapper and trader, and at one time, the Cherokee thought he was a man of means. He took a young girl from the Deer Clan as his wife, and they built a lodge on the outskirts of the village. After marriage, Dent isolated her from her clan and worked her like an animal. If Dent was awake, he was usually drunk and abusive to her. He denied her food and mistreated her, but her clan brothers and sisters were unaware of the harsh life she lived while married to Dent. Unfortunately, she became pregnant with his child, and one day in a drunken rage, he beat her to death along with the baby she carried in her womb. When the Deer Clan learned of this, they enacted the Cherokee 'Law of Blood' and meant to take Dent's life to avenge their daughter. This was the Cherokee way. Dent escaped to Georgia for a time, while the Deer Clan continued to pursue him and a few years later, they finally caught up with him.

When they found him, he possessed a young slave girl, known as Molly. In addition to trading guns and furs, he had also started trading slaves. Molly was barely 14 but wise beyond her years.

She had already been sold twice since birth and for a short time worked in the kitchen of a great plantation house until the 'Massa' started leering at her with side eyes from across the room making her feel uncomfortable. He would also visit the kitchen while she worked, rubbing up against her as she peeled the potatoes or fried chicken. One day she spilled gravy staining a tablecloth, the 'Missus' got angry and forced her husband to sell the girl. She was glad the 'Missus' sold her, until she became the property of Sam Dent. Things got worse for her, but he didn't beat her on her face or anywhere that showed, he needed to keep his inventory in good shape. He used her as collateral in poker games, placing her ownership papers as bets, if he lost, they would skip out of town before the winner was able to collect her. They were always on the run, and he was usually drunk and abusive.

When the Cherokee finally found Dent in South Georgia, as custom allowed, the despicable man traded Molly to the Deer Clan scouts under the 'Law of Blood' to replace the life of their sister.

According to this law, they would take her and let him go free in exchange, a life for a life.

They brought Molly back to the Cherokee village in north Georgia at New Echota, at the headwaters of the Oostanaula River, and the same village where White Dove was born. Adopting her as a full-fledged Cherokee, she became one of them in all ways. The color of her skin was irrelevant, as she was now full Cherokee. She finally had a family, was free and happy to be one of them and no longer a slave.

She became accustomed to the Cherokee ways and blossomed in her new life and freedom. The Long Hair Clan, known for taking in adoptees, welcomed Molly renaming her Chickawa. Over the years she grew into a beautiful woman for she was a mere child, when Dent traded her under 'Law of Blood.' She was a hard worker mastering the language and customs of the Cherokee quickly. The other women took her under their wings and taught her what she needed to know to survive and prosper. She became their sister. Soon finding favor and love with a young Cherokee man, and bore him two sons, Benjamin, and Isaac.

When Molly heard the man on the horse profess to claim her, her knees buckled. Her past as a slave finally caught up with her, threatening all their freedom. She was inconsolable, as she tried to understand what the bounty hunter said.

Evidently, the no-good Sam Dent traded Molly to the Cherokee to save his skin, but later lost her papers as a bet in a poker game to Mr. John Hightower. Mr. Hightower wasn't going away like the others who Dent cheated, Hightower wanted his slave property back, hiring slave catchers to track her down and to collect the debt he owed. U.S. law deeming that as Negroes Molly and her offspring were legally considered slaves without papers conveying their freedom. The Cherokee, however, refused to let these men cart their daughter and sons away. According to the Cherokee law, they adopted Molly, and she was now Chicawa of Cherokee blood. Molly was no longer a slave, she was now Cherokee as were her sons, and her people would fight to protect them all.

Amid the barking dogs and bright feathers, the big man's white horse became skittish and started rearing on its back legs. Jerking hard on the reins as the horse reared, he caused it to lose balance, stumble, and fall backwards into the crowd. The rider jumped free, but the horse landed on top of the group of children. Running Deer heard the babies crying and realized what happened.

"My baby," Running Deer screamed while scrambling to find her daughter White Dove.

Several of the children were injured and not moving, White Dove among them. When they freed the unconscious baby from under the horse and pile of children, she was bleeding from her nose, and barely breathing. The full force of the horse landed directly on top of her small body.

"Grandmother, my baby, help me," Running Deer cried out.

Grandmother took charge, ordering the injured children taken into the medicine lodge.

"Stoke the fire, and get water boiling, I will be right there."

She ran to get her medicine bundle to tend to them.

The man whose horse fell on the children remounted and with a disgusted look said, "Forget all this nonsense, we will be back with the law to claim the property."

The Chief came forth from the crowd speaking loudly for all to hear, "Chickawa, is our sister of the Long Hair Clan. She and her sons are of Cherokee blood, and no longer enslaved by the white man to be treated as an animal."

Raising a spear in his hand toward the sky he shouted at them, "You must leave here now—GO!"

The warriors started war hoops and lifting their weapons in the air. Molly cried as she heard the chief defending her rights as a daughter of the clan. She felt reprieved but knew this was not over for her or her boys.

The man on the horse yelled as he rode out of camp, "This is not the last you have seen of us, heathens, we'll be back with the law next time."

However, he would learn the Cherokee Indian Territory was a sovereign state, not bound by the laws of the U.S. government. The fight they would conduct would be in the Cherokee court system, not in U.S. courts nor on the battlefield. Eventually, with the Cherokee Nation Supreme Court resolving the trial of Molly and her sons' ruling she was full Cherokee by adoption, no longer property owned by another, nor were her children. She continued to live as a daughter of the Cherokee Nation and the white man had no claim on her or her sons Benjamin and Isaac, forever ending their days in slavery. They were now free, and officially Cherokee.

The men rode off and the immediate concern of the village turned to the injured children. After examining them, Grandmother found they would fully recover. They had the wind knocked out of them and were simply scared. However, White Dove was not so lucky, as the full weight of the 1,200-pound animal had landed on the small girl.

She suffered a head injury, no bones seemed broken, but it was serious.

Grandmother prepared a poultice for the baby's head and started thinking of the medicines needed to help her. She instructed Running Deer to put cool wet cloths on the girl's forehead and back of her neck. Grandmother knew if her head injury formed a blood clot, she would need help dissolving it. From her pouch, she pulled pieces of bark from the willow tree and placed it in a cup of hot water to steep. After the bark colored the water, she spooned small sips into the child's mouth. The willow bark was a natural blood thinner and pain reliever.

She placed a poultice on the baby's chest, to keep pneumonia from forming in her bruised lungs. Now, all they could do was wait and watch, and call for White Dove's spirit to return to her body. Running Deer chanted so her daughter could hear her from the spirit world reminding her not to travel too far from her body. Hoping to help her find the path back to them.

Running Deer said, "I see the same dark shadows in the room that were here when I birthed White Dove. I am scared they are here to steal her spirit."

Grandmother performed a sage and cedar cleansing ceremony to the room while chanting prayers for the spirits to guide White Dove back into her body. The baby was unconscious for several hours and her breathing shallow.

Grandmother said, "I must go guide her spirit back to us with a spirit walk tonight when the moon is full. I fear she is lost in the nether world. We prepare now."

When the full moon appeared in the night sky, the elder 'woa-men' of the paint clan joined them in the lodge. Grandmother smudged their foreheads and cleansed them all before letting them into the room—preventing evil spirits attached to them from entering. Prior to the spirit walk she performed a purification ceremony to prepare herself for travel into 'the land of no time.'

Grandmother bathed in the sage and cedar vapors and smoked the pipe while offering the sweet, scented smoke to the four directions. She then prepared a secret mixture to drink.

While her spirit was gone from her body, the women in the lodge would chant and pray to the Great One. Grandmother would search for White Dove on the plains in the spirit world. Their chants would help her come back from that place with the soul of White Dove. This would be an extremely dangerous journey for both of them. She hoped the baby girl had not ventured too far to return.

As a drum beat outside in rhythm to the chants emanating from the room, Grandmother drank the potion and prayed to the Great Spirit to send her spirit animal guide to lead her. It took only a few minutes for the bitter liquid to sedate her. Her head nodded forward as the chanting became louder, she drifted into unconsciousness and her spirit was carried away. She awoke standing on a high mountain looking down into a great valley below. The red-tailed hawk cried out, he was her spirit guide soaring overhead, and circling round her in the sky. She had met him many times before. Looking out over the valley, she saw evil dark shadows running back and forth below her, searching for a host. She must find White Dove before they did and carried her away for eternity.

"Greetings red-tail, I need your help. I have lost a little one in the spirit world, it is not her time, and I have come to lead her back. Will you help guide me to her?"

The hawk circled low and let out a piercing cry, Grandmother understood the animal's language in the spirit world. She extended her arms and with her mind, she began to soar beside the hawk. Soon they flew into the valley near the land and there stood a great paint stallion, upon his back was the girl. The horse ran fast and wild, and White Dove was laughing and prodding him to go faster, with her hair blowing behind her in the breeze like the horse's dark mane.

Grandmother called out to her, "White Dove, it is Grandmother; I have come to take you home my child."

She guided the horse by her thoughts to come alongside Grandmother.

"I got lost Grandmother; I found my spirit guide and he saved me from the darkness. But I don't know how to return to the land of the living."

"It is all good now, I am here to lead you back, take my hand, and we will return to your mother, for it is not yet time for you to leave us little one. You will journey here again one day I promise, and you may visit again in the future, as your gift grows stronger. Always remember your spirit guide is the great paint stallion on whose back you sit. He will be watching and waiting for you to come again," Grandmother said. "Now let us leave here, the longer we linger the harder it will be for us to return home, and we risk being lost in the darkness."

White Dove reached for Grandmother and as their fingertips touched, there was a great flash of light. She then heard chants of her mother and the others and awoke in the lodge with Grandmother standing over her with her hand on her forehead.

White Dove's health took many months to return to normal, she had trouble walking and talking at first, but eventually made a full recovery. She never forgot her first spirit walk and the paint stallion. She did not talk of these things, as they were sacred to her and Grandmother. However, when they looked deep into each other's eyes, they remembered the Great Spirit Walk they shared which would connect them for eternity.

Escort orders from
Capt. Benjamin T. Watkins,
June 9, 1838

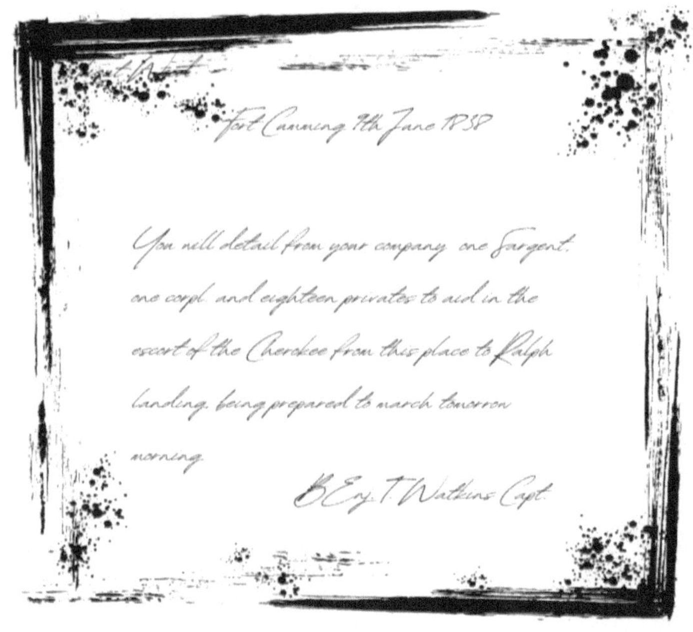

FIVE

Summer 1838

White Dove was eight years old in the summer of 1838 and still too young to understand all the political turmoil surrounding her people. However, she was old enough to sense something was not right in their village. The adults around her carried worried looks on their faces, and she observed them during the day standing and talking with their arms waving and shouting at one another, using words foreign to her. Peace had left their camp, and as an empath, she could feel the disruption to their routine way of life.

One evening as they sat around the shared campfire eating venison stew she asked, "Mother, what is wrong with our people in the village? They seem upset and I can feel something is not right, it makes me ache deep inside. I can hear the disagreements and shouting between them, and it troubles me."

Mother marveled at her daughter's insight into other's feelings at such an early age. She knew this gift was part of her blessing as a healer. However, it could also be a curse, for she would hurt when others hurt, and her people were now hurting badly.

"My daughter, I tried to keep this from you for you are yet young. However, you deserve to know, the white man is forcing us to leave our homes and the land of our fathers. I fear that time is near."

Mother did not elaborate on the politics of the day or that President Andrew Jackson signed into law the Indian Removal Act. Even the name was offensive, written as if they were to be 'removed' like vermin. This Act authorized granting the lands west of the Mississippi in exchange for Indian lands within existing state borders. The government would take their land and relocate them further west. The white men intended to take the rich and fertile land with cleared acreage near water that produced bountiful crops, as their own and push the original People out to parts unknown, in the unsettled dry and dusty west.

Mother's voice was soft and slow, almost a whisper, like a secret that would become true if another heard her, "The white man found a rock called gold in our homeland mountains of New Echota and is greedy for this shiny stone. He will do anything to get it, even harm Earth Mother. He digs into the underworld, disrupting nature, destroying all plants and trees, even if the animals have no place left to hide. He robs what she has hidden deep within her. Now, they want to take our homes from us and steal our land. The settlers have already invaded our hunting grounds, and the wild deer and turkey are not plentiful like they once were." She paused for a moment, to wipe her tears.

"A group of Cherokee men went against Chief John Ross making a treaty with the government, to trade our land for new territory in the west. Our People mourn for the sacred burial places of our ancestors, the hunting grounds that we love and the earth where we have sown corn and replenished with our offerings. This will all be lost to us and our children. We must leave behind—by force, all that we know and where we have lived since the beginning of time. Our departure draws near and is why you hear shouting and feel the fear of our People; we do not want to go. We must plan for a long journey, and it will be a difficult trip, many miles across the great river. Always remember White Dove, your people are brave and strong, and we will once again live free." As if all her hope was gone, Mother cried.

"Where is this new land Mother?"

"It is in the west, into the land where the sun sleeps," she said.

"But isn't west where the spirits go when they die, are we going to die Mother?"

"We must cross the mighty river where we will once again live free. We will live as our ancestors have for centuries, among our people with our ways, far away from the white man. We shall go when the leaves change colors and fall from the trees," Mother said. "Go to your bed now and do not worry about these things. The Great Spirit and Earth Mother will guide our way."

In the weeks that followed, Mother went about her daily chores, worrying as she prepared for her family's journey west into the land of death. She wore a stoic face for her family, but it was difficult for her, as she had never travelled past the river in her whole life. To prepare White Dove had new moccasins sewn for her. Mother gathered panic grass and cut the stems to pad the insides and lined them with deer fur to cushion her feet from the tree roots, rocks, snow, and ice encountered on the trail as they walked hundreds of miles. She wove each of them new blankets, and father tanned long hair buffalo hides for coverings to wrap around them against the cold winds. However, the People were scared and angry over losing their homes and no one felt ready for the unknown.

Early one fall morning before the dew dried off the brown grass, and the steam rose from the water, a great commotion erupted in the camp. There were many men wearing blue coats and riding on big horses charging into their midst. The People watched as wagons loaded with provisions rolled past their camp toward the river.

A bearded man with shiny buttons sitting upon a black horse, holding a sword in the air and a gun stuffed into the waistband of his pants, yelled out, "alright savages, it's time for you to move out."

He then rode to every lodge in the village and kicked at the sidewalls to raise those slumbering inside. As the men came outside to see what was happening, he started poking them with his weapon as he screamed orders to vacate the village. Those that refused were roped and dragged by the soldiers.

Mother watched from her door with White Dove hiding in the folds of her skirt. Then helping her dress hurriedly she whispered, "You must get your bundle, your thick moccasins, your warm blankets, and your buffalo hide coat quickly my child. Run to Grandmother's, avoiding the men on horses, tell her the time has come for us to go."

Mother gathered the gunny sacks of food tied with grass-string she had stowed for the eviction, along with a pot, and a frying pan. In the sacks she had placed prepared dried venison jerky, a few potatoes, apples, skins of water, and anything they could carry that would give them sustenance on the trail. Little did she know their stockpile would be gone and they would hunger before they took one-step on their long journey.

By the time Grandmother made her way to their lodge that morning, the men on horseback had doubled in number as more continued to arrive. The more that came, the meaner they became. They marched the people toward the great river, yelling and hitting anyone that lingered too long or looked behind them. At the riverbank, they had erected a large stockade. The area encircled about two acres and inside there was no shelter, no trees—nothing. It looked like a holding pen for animals with tall wooden walls and only one gate, one-way in and one-way out. The wooden fence held them huddled inside its walls like a herd of cattle. They were confined there many days before the march west, the rain began to fall turning the ground into six inches of mud, and they sank deep up to their ankles in their makeshift prison. White Dove would never forget the sounds of the women moaning, the babies crying, and the men shouting, pleading for help as those around them grew weaker and sicker. They were powerless, they had no weapons, and there were many soldiers guarding them. As bad as this was, it would get much worse before the move westward was finished.

The soldiers locked The People into the stockade to wait, while collecting supplies and hiring contractors needed to make the trip westward. They also looted The People's lodges, and white men moved into them, claiming them as their own before the previous owners were even gone. Days turned into weeks, and weeks turned into months, before they began the forced march. Winter came early and temperatures plummeted, there was nowhere to escape from the cold, and they sat huddled closely together on the hard frozen ground most of the time. The weather worsened, and the first snow came, as they waited. While held as prisoners, dysentery and disease took up residence in the stockade with them, and still they waited. The place began to smell of death. Many of the youngest children died of whooping cough, and still they waited. The old died from the cold and the gripe, and still they waited. Grandmother tried to heal as many as she could, but her healing supplies ran out and she helplessly watched her people die. The white men would not give them medicines or let her forage in the woods to replenish her bundle of healing herbs as more dark spirits and death arrived. Yet they waited for their exile.

After months of living as captives in the squalor of the holding pen, the time finally came to travel westward. The timing meant they would be walking through the rough terrain in the dead of winter, through the bitter weather without much food, no shelter and many without shoes or winter clothing. The army did hire contractors to feed them for a while, but their supplies were inadequate and spoiled with bugs and maggots. The contractors took the army's money and gathered the cheapest supplies they could provide, keeping the profit and the decent food for themselves.

Not only was the trip physically brutal, but spiritually brutal as well. The U.S. government removed over 100,000 people from the eastern United States and 25 million acres of Native land handed over to the white settlements. Forcing The People to march in groups of 1,000 some went on overland trails, and some went on keelboats down the river. The Cherokee called the river the 'long man' his head rested in the mountains, and his feet in the sea with ties to the underworld. Fearful of traveling by boat—but that didn't matter to the soldiers. They forced them onboard the rickety vessels. The boats groaned with overloading. Travel was dangerous and many capsized, drowning the passengers. Those that followed the land routes didn't fare much better as they force marched alongside the supply wagons, pulled by teams of horses.

One soldier they called Nathan, stole White Dove's paint horse, 'Inena'—which means 'let's go,' the one given to her at birth and bound with her spirit. Inena labored under the weight of the big man with his fat belly bulging and straining the buttons on his dirty shirt. The horse's nostrils flared as he tried to buck him off his back, he worked up a lather each time the big man sat on his back. He carried a long leather whip, made from the braided strips of a buffalo hide. When Inena bucked under his heavy weight, he would lash on its neck with the strap. He would also use this strap to whip those walking too slowly. Grandmother received a lashing more than once, and when she saw him riding up from behind, would place her hands on White Dove's shoulders holding her close and protecting her from his orneriness. There was no one to protect Inena from his abuse.

He stank of sweat and whiskey and never bathed in the water. He was especially nasty and cruel to The People and used any opportunity to abuse them, and for some reason he took a great dislike to Father. Any time he could unfurl curse words or get close enough to hit or kick him, he would. He usually had a big wad of tobacco stuffed in his jaw with the spittle leaking out from the corners of his mouth. Staining his gray beard down both sides and resembling a macabre dark frown. While sucking on this plug of tobacco, when he would get near Father, he would spit the juice onto his head. Followed by a heinous laugh, and then yelling out a war-hoop. Each day White Dove learned to hate the white man a little more.

White Dove and her family would walk the overland trail to the new land and at the end of their fifth day of marching White Dove stopped and turned, looking back toward the towering mountains far behind them in the distance. Where there once had been their homes, fertile farmlands, and abundant hunting grounds. The illusion of smoke billowed out of the top of the evergreen trees, while a light rain fell to earth. Grandmother said the Great Sky was shedding tears for them. This was their 'Trail of Tears' and they cried with the Great Sky. They cried not for possessions, but for the bones of their ancestors, the hunting grounds, and sacred burial places—leaving behind a part of their souls. White Dove could hear the wailing moans and cries of the travelers as they force marched westward. She would forever live with this memory and the sadness she would always carry in her heart, proof as to how cruel the white man could be to her people.

Many elders and infants died on the trek; they could not keep up the grueling pace. The snow, cold, and starvation sickened them. Graves of the young and old dotted the paths they travelled on and over 4,000 souls perished on the trails. The Cherokee lost many of their past and their future on this exile.

As much as Mother and her family had done to be ready, nothing could have prepared them for what they now faced. The Cherokee marched many miles a day until their feet broke open and bled or toes turned black from frostbite. They marched while their stomachs growled from hunger, and they watched their neighbors drop along the way. They mourned for their people and their freedom as their way of life was no more.

A few months into their journey on the rocky trail, White Dove could walk no more. She was so tired and hungry, and her feet were busted open, sore, and bleeding. She lay down on the grass beside the path and fell into a deep sleep while others continued their march past her. Mother and Father didn't notice she was no longer with them. However, Isaac following behind saw her laying on the ground while everyone else walked on by her tiny curled-up body. He picked her up and carried her on his back for many hours until the group stopped for the night's camp. He would continue to look out for her on the long journey, watching over her as a protector and friend, a behavior he would continue for the rest of his life.

Peril was everywhere on the trail, everyday held danger. A team of horses pulling a supply wagon spooked and ran over those walking in front of them, killing several and injuring many others. But the soldiers didn't stop, they made them march onward. The surviving family members carried those hurt, after quickly burying the dead in shallow graves beside the trail. After this happened, Mother instructed White Dove to walk alongside the path not on it in case the horses broke free again. However, the grass was as tall as her head and the rocks made it difficult to keep her footing, so she soon forgot about the horses behind her and went back to walking the center of the trail. Isaac made sure he followed her from behind, so he could push her out of the way if need be.

They also forded raging rivers where many drowned. As they crossed, Father sat White Dove on his shoulders to keep her out of the frigid water as much as possible. He tied a rope around Mother, Grandmother, and his waist, while linking arms three wide with him in the middle, they waded into the currents with White Dove on his back. The rocks were slick and the water icy, numbing their feet and legs, making walking treacherous. Father held Mother and Grandmother by their arms steadying them when they stumbled and almost fell. They made it safely to the other side, but others that tried to walk alone were swept away by the current never to be seen again. Their group from Echota arrived in the unfamiliar and unforgiving territory of Oklahoma at the end of March 1839.

Little White Dove and her family survived the grueling trip, walking over 800 miles. Molly's oldest son—Isaac, who was 12 years old, was always near

White Dove during the trek looking out for her, helping, and prodding her to keep going. Molly's youngest son Benjamin, 10 years old, followed Isaac's example taking care of their mother and watching out for White Dove.

Under the terms of the new treaty, the U.S. Government granted land in Oklahoma territory to be Indian Territory and called the Cherokee Nation. For relinquishing their land in the east, they were also promised $5 million dollars. In return, they lost ~90 million acres of fertile developed land to the white settler expansion. The money promised to them was never paid.

They were weak, weary, and had broken spirits, but they would rebuild and learn the new ways of this very unforgiving land. From where they came everything was different. In the east the land was so fertile one barely scratched the surface and planted a seed for it to take root and grow. However, in this place it was arid and hard rocky dirt which would not nourish or reward their labors. They would observe the animals to see what plants were useful and learn how to hunt and farm on the open prairie instead of deep lush woods. In time they would return to a semblance of their old life. In the new place, Grandmother began searching for plants, trees and herbs needed to heal the sick. Some plants were similar, and the animals would teach her about the others.

The recovery of The Cherokee would take many years, but they would persevere and learn to live in these new lands. However, they would never trust the white man, who did not keep his word. Once again, treaties were broken and their lands stolen from them.

SIX

1848

Cherokee Nation
Indian Territory

By the time White Dove turned ten years old she could identify many local plants and their uses for healing. At 18, she had apprenticed with Grandmother for many years, and she was an expert. Walking on the forest floor early in the morning, speaking with Earth Mother, and giving thanks for her bountiful gifts while collecting medicinal plants. The pine trees would whisper to her, while she gathered medicines in the shade of their branches. As she approached a tree, she could physically discern its health and needs. Touching the bark, she felt the sap pulsating through their trunks.

The most treasured item in her medicine bundle was the ginseng root—or 'sang,' because it was hard to find and an important ingredient for special healings. Even the settlers at the trading post were greedy for the dried roots, plundering the woods digging it, or trading flour and other goods with some Natives, making it a scarce commodity. Grandmother taught White Dove to harvest the gnarly roots once the berries ripened in August, making it easier to find. After digging it from the ground, she would replant the red berries to replenish the growth for future years. Once home she washed the dirt from the roots, placing it in the sun to dry. A large root would shrivel and shrink up to a small size, so it took a lot to make a little medicine. After several weeks of drying, she would place the roots in a hollowed-out rock, grinding it with an oblong stone into a fine powder to use in her concoctions. Sometimes recipes called for brewing it as a tea from tiny slivers of the root and the patient drinking it, depending upon their sickness.

Now White Dove was not only harvesting plants and roots, but also decoctions, blending concoctions, making poultices, and practicing 'hands-on' medicine with tribe members. She learned the connection between plants, animals, and the spiritual world. Grandmother taught her the Cherokee way, to skip the first three plants harvesting the fourth, and to replenish what she took. Always offering a prayer to thank the Earth Mother for allowing these medicines used to heal the 'two-legged's'—what they called man. As a healer, she must also seek the Great Spirit's guidance before healing anyone. She would ask permission first and follow the Spirit's leading in the healing process.

White Dove learned the legends of her People, passed down from their ancestors. The legend said that once long ago, the plants, the animals, the stones, the fliers, the crawlers, and the finned ones all lived in harmony with the four winds. They could talk amongst themselves, and they knew that the 'two-legged's' could not live without their help. The animals allowed man to use their fur and their meat for food, the plants for healing, and finned ones for food. However, man must follow the sacred way, to take only what he would use and use all that he takes. The two-legged's were greedy and selfish.

They stopped giving thanks and didn't replenish the forest. The animals cursed man and inflicted diseases for his ungrateful heart. However, the plants were sorry for the man and said that for every illness animal gave to man, we will give a cure. This was the legend the Cherokee lived by passed down by word of mouth for centuries. It was the 'old way.'

They found in the new Indian Territory of the west, that the plants were different from the Georgian forests and valleys. However, with Grandmother's guidance, and by observing the animals, it didn't take long to recognize their uses, replenish supplies, and continue with their healing work. White Dove received a spiritual education at Grandmother's side as well. She learned the strong mind-body connection and the need for the spirit's involvement in the healing process. She blossomed in her role as pupil working and learning alongside Grandmother.

As White Dove grew into womanhood Chickawa's son, Isaac, was always hovering near her. He spoke with a stutter and had wiry hair—not smooth like the other Cherokee men, so he wore a long braid down the center of his head to tame it. He was very dark skinned with dimples in his cheeks that were deep when he smiled. His eyes were wolf gray like his mother's leaving no doubt she was the result of breeding to a white man and born into slavery.

When Isaac eyes met with White Dove's, it was as if he could see into her very soul. She usually had to look away, she couldn't stand his penetrating stare. However, White Dove never saw him as different from any of the other sons of the tribe. He was handsome in her eyes, possessing a sweet soul and his stutter disappeared when he spoke with her. He was noticeably quiet with others, as he tried to hide his speech difference.

She was in her 18th year in the days of the Cold Moon when the preparations were made for the coming spring. The hearth fires are extinguished by the priest of certain clans marking the ending of one cycle and new fires started representing the beginning of the new cycle. It was in preparation for this ceremony that their friendship turned into something deeper. Isaac had looked at her with adoring eyes since their youth. One day she noticed him and touched his arm as he carried wood to the fire pit in the center of the village. Her heart skipped a beat.

What was the feeling she experienced when he came near to her?

The annual Crane Dance celebrated in early spring gave the opportunity for one to make their romantic feelings for another known. They built a huge bonfire at the dancing grounds, and the young maidens wearing their finest dresses created especially for the occasion danced to drumbeats in front of the young bucks. The single men would sit around with their backs to the fire while the maidens circled them.

White Dove had been watching Isaac around the camp for many weeks before the dance. Strong feelings pulled her toward him, and she knew he looked at her in a certain way. She watched him play stickball with the other young men. Stickball played between two teams was an extremely aggressive game and consisted of anywhere from nine to twenty-two players on a team. Each person had a stick at least three feet long, made from hickory with a pocket on one end used to catch and toss a ball, resembling Lacrosse. The ball was about three inches in diameter and made of sinew and leather. The first team to get the ball from one end of the field to the other, through the goal post, would get a point. The first team to reach 12 points won. The players wore no protective gear, they didn't even wear shirts. It was a rough game; the Cherokee call it 'little brother of war.' Many times, the sticks whacked an opponent to keep them away from the ball. When Isaac noticed her watching him, his chest would puff out more and he would play the game harder, trying to impress her.

She and Mother worked for many months on her dress for the Crane Dance. Her father harvested two deer to get the hides for her dress. Mother cleaned and tanned the hides working them until soft, and then bleaching them snow white using lye and sunshine. The dress had long sleeves with fringe hanging down from cuff to underarm. A

V-shape front held the beadwork medallion on the center front. She fashioned a wide belt covered with cobalt glass beads to cinch her waist. Long six-inch fringes fell from the bottom hem to the top of her moccasins. Her stitches were small and tight, and the dress fit her well, showing off her strong form. She, Mother, and Grandmother worked late into the night creating patterns of red, blue, yellow, and purple beadwork onto the white dress and belt while sitting around the fire in their lodge home. The outfit was stunning on her, the white of the hides accentuated her long dark glossy hair and bronze skin tone.

Father stitched her new moccasin boots, from the white hides too. They were tall mid-calf, with rabbit fur trimming the top, and beads all around the toe area in the same design as on the dress. She was a beauty, with a sweetness in her soul. It was as if pure sunshine emanated from her face when she smiled.

The first day of the Crane Dance, the young men watch the women wanting to court, as they dance around the night fire. When one catches his eye, the man approaches his mother, who would then speak with the mother of the maiden. In the Cherokee tribe, the clan membership remains with the woman's lineage—so upon marriage, the man joins the wife's clan. If they divorce, he will leave taking only his clothes. Members of the same clan were considered siblings, therefore forbidding marriages between members of the same clans. All marriage proposals needed approval by each clan's grandmothers. As a matrilineal society, the women were the decision makers and tended to the gardens and children. The women owned all property, and the children belonged to the mother, handing down field rights from mother to daughter. If the mothers approved, the young man could visit the maiden later that night.

He would go to her lodge and light a candle. If she wanted him, she would blow out his candle, and he is then a part of her clan. If not, he must woo her more by playing a courting flute outside her lodge, until she wants to come outside and see him.

The first evening she walked to the bonfire dressed in her white regalia. Isaac was there in a front row seat, anticipating this night also. White Dove began to dance to the drumbeat with the other maidens. As she neared Isaac, she leaned in toward him and smiled her radiant smile. His heart fluttered, and his breathing became rapid. He had eyes for no other, she danced only for him, and he hoped she would be his love for eternity. During a break from the dancing, he went to her, taking her by the hand. They walked away from the fire to sit on a fallen tree nearby where they could talk privately. He must know that she wanted him, as much as he wanted her.

"White Dove, you are so beautiful in all ways, I see your very soul when I look deep into your eyes. I have loved you since we walked the Trail of our Fathers, and I carried you on my back and looked after you. For some reason you have always been in my heart, I believe the Creator gave you to be my soulmate. Before I light my candle for you, I need to know if you feel the same about me. I am not full Cherokee blood; I have slave blood mingled through my veins. I don't look like the others, and our children will not be pure."

"Isaac, you are Cherokee in my eyes and in the eyes of the Nation which adopted you as their own. I see nothing but a brave warrior when I look at you. I too have loved you for many moons, and I would be honored to have you as my other one."

Isaac stood pulling her to his chest and cupping her chin in his hand. He kissed her deep and full of longing for her. She melted into his arms, and her heart and body ached with love for him. When she pulled back and stared deep into his gray eyes, a vision came upon her.

The great paint stallion stood on the mountaintop. It reared on its hind legs, while the dark storm clouds whirled, and lightning flashed. She followed the stallion's gaze and there below on the tundra she saw a solid black lone buck deer with great horns. The lightning flashed striking the deer and it fell over, dead. Gasping, she pulled Isaac nearer to her. She knew she had just envisioned his death, while still in his prime, strong, and agile. She never shared this vision with Isaac but hid it deep in her heart. She knew their life together would be short and she intended to show him her deep love each day they shared.

That night Isaac spoke with his mother Chickawa about his love for White Dove, and White Dove spoke with her mother. The mothers agreed with the joining of clans. After the end of the Crane Dance, Isaac went to White Dove's lodge with his unlit candle. She anticipated his arrival and had placed the best skins near the warming fire in the center of the floor. She had gathered wild strawberries for them to share, which symbolize the heart. The fire cast a soft warm glow in the cabin, and she threw dried herbs into the flame for a sweet smell.

Isaac made his presence known and she called him to come inside. She was sitting on the skins beside the warming fire. The light of the flames bounced off her dark silky hair and reflected in her eyes. She noticed his hands shaking, as she placed hers over his and together, they held the candle in the fire igniting the wick.

"My love, White Dove, will you share this life with me? You are all I think about day and night. I love your ways, your kindness, and your heart. I will cherish you, your mother, grandmother, and our children for all times. I will join the paint clan as their son." He looked pleadingly at her, scared, as he held the burning candle toward her, awaiting her response.

She smiled at his shyness, and he knew the answer was yes before he heard her words. Blowing out the flame, she lay back on the fur skins pulling him onto her. Her arms encircled his waist as she pulled his shirt over his head revealing a solid muscular chest and abdomen. Startled he sat back up, as he didn't know where or how to begin to undress her or what to do. This was his first time with a woman. She took his hand in hers and untied her belt. She then pulled the dress over her head and shed it quickly. Her body was firm and beautiful, the color of sweet honey. He had never seen a naked woman before and tried not to stare at her breasts. He let his eyes move downward to her mound of dark hair between her long legs. His body shook with anticipation and nervousness.

He nodded as if to ask is this ok as he reached out and touched her breast. She groaned and took his other hand and placed it on the other breast and they lay down facing each other. They stared into each other's eyes as their hands explored foreign territory. He was gentle with his rough hands marveling at the softness of her skin. He thought his heart would burst and could hardly keep from crying out with emotion. She gave soft grunts and moans to signal he was not hurting her as he suckled and bit at her and hid his face in her hair and neck, nuzzling her. Her expression changed as she guided his hand to her secret place. His touch ignited the passion in her body. She then found his manhood—shocking him at first, as he had never been touched there by another. He became so excited that he had to stop her for a minute to compose himself before he could continue. She pulled him into her warmth and the feeling was so exciting to him that he could barely contain himself.

What came next was natural but so spiritual, so unexpected. Her body shook with his as the two became one, and when they released from each other, they both knew one would never be the same again. Their lovemaking continued for two-days, and their mother's left food and drink outside the lodge to sustain them, while they bonded for eternity.

SEVEN

1851

White Dove and Isaac began their new life together, each day sweeter than the day before, and their love deepened. Her healing skills became stronger and visions clearer. She developed stronger empath abilities and would feel and interpret the energy of the people around her, just as she had learned to feel the energy of the trees. She learned protection rituals for herself so that the bad or sick spirits would not overtake her. In time, she became an even more powerful healer than Grandmother. The people from neighboring villages started coming for miles to seek her help. She began to carry a healing stick and would snip a locket of hair when someone received a cure then attaching it to the healing stick. She used her stick to gather plants and to push away snakes in the forest, or to dig holes to replant seeds from her harvest. The stick also reminded her of the blessings she had passed on to others and it strengthened her.

However, not everyone was accepting of her power, the tribal medicine man was very jealous. He practiced 'witch' rituals, as well as healing, and dark magic, and he saw her as a threat. Grandmother warned her to be wary of him and to always pray for protection and to cleanse the evil spirits, which he could summon to vex her. He was very powerful and someone to fear. However, she became increasingly learned in the ways of the spirit world, the healing ways, and grew in grace and beauty. She was beloved by her people.

White Dove's visions continued to come, sometimes welcomed and sometimes not. She could not predict the frequency or intensity. Some visions were of simple things occurring in the camp, other times visions were of the governance of the Cherokee Nation. She was functioning as an open receiver, which was always powered on. She had not yet learned to control this skill, nor how to turn off unwelcome transmissions. Grandmother assured her that she would someday. Once this happened, she would be able to spirit walk and to move in and out of spirit worlds with ease. Her ability would allow travel to and from dimensions without time constraints, as spirits are eternal.

One day in early summer, White Dove went to the water to perform the cleansing of her spirit and body. The new moon cleansing ritual entailed disrobing and entering the water, facing the East. She began by offering thanks to the Great Spirit, splashing water upon her head seven times, and then dunking herself under the water seven times. After washing her body clean, she emerged from the stream. She dried, dressed, and rubbed her exposed skin with lavender scented oils. That's when she saw the dark silhouettes dashing through the trees. She tried to discern if they were physical or spiritual. As she watched the shadows circling her hidden in the woods, she then realized she was under attack by demonic spirits. She pulled amulets and crystals from her pouch, and started chanting for protection of the Great Spirit, while sprinkling salt on the ground around her feet firmly planted in the center. The shadows dimmed and slithered into the brush as the sunlight shone on her head and face. From that day forward, she began to see the shadows lurking around her more often and wasn't quite sure why or what to do about them.

A few weeks later after this encounter in the woods, she awoke very nauseously, and no amount of tonic would take away the sick feeling. She thought she had eaten bad food, but Isaac wasn't sick at all. She worried the medicine man had cursed her with a bad spirit. She tried every medicine she could think of, and nothing helped. She couldn't stand the constant sickness, which progressed to vomiting and inability to eat. The smell of cooking food made her wretch. Maybe evil spirits had invaded her body. She was very scared. So, she went to Grandmother for help, she would know what to do.

"Grandmother, I need your healing. I think I have been poisoned with bad food or evil spirits that have entered my body, for I am so sick," she described her symptoms with a worried look on her face.

Grandmother looked into her eyes, and smiled, "My child, when was the last time you had your womanly flow?"

"What? I had not thought of that, do you think it could be?"

"Yes, my dear, you are with child. I believe we will see her when the deep winter comes," Grandmother grabbed her around the shoulders hugging her tightly.

"I can hardly wait to see you as a mother."

White Dove was so emotional, her eyes teared up, and she said, "I hope I can be half the mother and grandmother I am blessed to have in my life. But why did you call the baby a 'her,' do you see?"

"I am hoping it is a girl, to carry on the line, but it doesn't matter. This baby is already so loved. I am happy for you and Isaac," grandmother said.

White Dove left the lodge with happiness in her heart and couldn't wait to share the news with Isaac. When he returned home from hunting with the other men, as she told him he seemed distant and not as happy as she expected.

"My love, why do you not rejoice at the new life we have created?" she asked.

"Dovie, I love you and our child, but I am worried about how our child will be treated. I have slave blood running through my veins and the Cherokee Nation treats us differently. Principal Chief John Ross signed laws that Negro's cannot own property, trade with anyone, and learning to read or write is considered a crime. There are 22 schools on the territory, and not one Negro can attend. It is illegal for marriages between our people. As one of mixed blood, I cannot vote or hold any office in the government. My kind is treated as less than a man; I am only able to be with you because my mother Molly was adopted into the Cherokee. My heart hurts for my people held as slaves to the Cherokee on many farms, there are over 4,000 slaves on this land, and that could have been my fate as well."

"Isaac, look at me," as she guided his face with her hands to look into his sad eyes. "You are enough for anyone. You are a man. You are Cherokee and my husband. I do not care if your skin were the color of the raven, I would still love you and our child. We must work to change these things; people are not property for ownership by another. One day all men will be free like the birds of the air. This I promise you."

They embraced and celebrated their love and new life tenderly that night in the lodge. White Dove did not rest easy though for she had a vision in the night. The vision was of their child, she labored to deliver her, and yet the child would not come. She did see the baby was a girl, just as she hoped. There was a rope tied around one leg suspending her in the air, part of her in one world and part in another. She was very troubled when she awoke but she told no one about her vision.

The months passed as her belly grew, the baby was never still, and when Isaac drew near, it seemed to leap inside her. Grandmother's strength was leaving her bones, she was beginning to stoop and lean more on her healing stick as she walked. She would soon be 80 moons upon this earth, and White Dove already mourned her leaving them. She wanted her to meet their daughter and help teach her the healing ways. Soon the deep winter was upon them and her time came to give birth.

Just as countless other women, including her mother, she went to the medicine lodge when the labor started, summoning Grandmother and Mother to midwife. She had helped deliver many babies herself, so she knew what to expect and what should be happening. Things did not seem right with this birth. She began labor pains on the morning of the first day of the week, and her birth waters broke by sundown. She had walked the forest paths until the afternoon to coax the baby out, to no avail. The pain became stronger and at dusk Grandmother gave her tea to help strengthen the labor. The pain grew stronger and then she felt something hot and sticky on her legs. She looked and saw pools of dark red blood, and she cried out.

"There is something not right, I am bleeding, please Grandmother, help me."

"Lay down on the skins and let me check the baby."

She put her ear to White Dove's belly and heard the heartbeat. She saw the baby's movement and then felt inside her.

"I feel a foot, the child is turned upside down, and she is confused on which way to go. Do not be afraid, we can straighten her path," Grandmother said.

She began to chant, asking the Spirit for the knowledge needed to save them. Pulling a yellow powder from the medicine bundle, she blew this onto White Dove's belly. While rubbing her abdomen with salve, she began massaging her from one side gently tugging and pushing to turn the baby into the correct position. Grandmother did not want to frighten White Dove, but this was bad. She had lost mothers and babies from this in the past. She pressed dried yarrow root into her birth canal to clot the blood and stop the flow.

"Grandmother, the dark spirits are here, I see them dancing around the room. I can hear them hissing, and they draw near to me, taunting me."

Mother quickly lit the sage and began cleansing the room, the chanting grew louder, and Grandmother started shaking rattles to scare the dark shadows away. White Dove lost consciousness. Grandmother prayed and used all the medicine she had in her, asking the Great Spirit to spare the lives of White Dove and the baby. She bargained for Him to take her instead. She was old, used-up, and she had lived a long and happy life. She was ready to move on to the spirit world.

The night turned to the second day, and White Dove grew cold and did not have the strength to push the baby from her body. She lost consciousness, but Grandmother would not give up on them. She thought of the Medicine Man and realized he must have a hand in this. Inviting the elder women into the lodge, she needed their prayers and chants to buffet the attack on the weak ones. She turned her prayers from healing to warding off the evil spirits and pulling out the most powerful secrets in her possession. She had never taught these ways to anyone, she never spoke of these powers, and they would die with her. She invoked them against the Medicine Man's curse. She then prepared to go into the spirit world and rescue her loved ones. She tied a thread to her wrist and the other end to her medicine stick. She gave the stick to Mother and told her not to put it down for any reason. She quickly drank down the bitter potion kept ready for such things and nodded off to the chants of the women in the lodge.

She awoke in the other world and immediately began looking for the great paint stallion not waiting for the red-tailed hawk to greet her. For she knew she would find White Dove there with her spirit guide.

The land was shaking, thunder clapping, and lightning flashing about her. She rode on the back of a white stallion searching over the land, looking for White Dove. There far away on a great bluff, she saw her. She was on the paint horse, with a rope tied around something dangling over the edge of the cliff. Grandmother raced to her side.

"White Dove, I am here."

"Grandmother, I knew you'd come if I could but hold on for a while longer. Please help me, something catches the child and pulls her away from me, I have one leg with a thin rope, but I fear it will not hold much longer, and she will be lost to the spirit world," White Dove cried as the winds howled around her.

Grandmother began shouting prayers to the Great Spirit asking for the soul of the child and her granddaughter in exchange for hers as she loosened the red string from around her wrist and tied it onto White Dove's. A great gust of wind blew toward them, and loud thunder sounded, it was all they could do to stand on the ledge of the bluff without it blowing them over. White Dove's horse reared up on its hind legs. Grandmother lay down and while reaching far over the cliff, she grasped the baby with its left ankle. She pulled with all she had in her, and the child broke free and White Dove caught her in her arms.

Grandmother then yelled, "Great stallion return them now. Go!"

White Dove awoke in the lodge, so tired. The baby lay on her breast and Mother was tending to her. She saw a red thread tied around her wrist and binding her to the medicine stick, she wasn't sure how or when that happened. She smiled toward Grandmother wanting to show her the baby girl. Grandmother sat with her head bowed and her hair hanging down each side of her face hiding her eyes. Her arms were limp at her sides, with her palms opened upward. Then White Dove realized Grandmother's spirit had left her. She was gone, she had not returned from the spirit world where she now walks for eternity. White Dove heard someone wailing, and then realized the sound was coming from her.

Mother gave her a tonic to calm her and help her milk to come in. It also helped her sleep soundly for a few hours. When she awoke, Isaac was sitting beside her. She could tell the great warrior had been crying and looked worried but excited about the birth of his daughter. She loosened the deer skin covering away from the baby to examine her and count fingers and toes. There on her left ankle was a large, red birthmark encircling her tiny leg. This mark was in the shape of Grandmothers hand, and it would remain for her lifetime.

It would take many months for White Dove to heal, but she would recover, and this daughter would continue the family legacy of healing.

EIGHT

Current Day

Annie and Miranda continued to talk frequently after her release from the rehab center, and their friendship deepened. Annie didn't tell her about Tom's attitude toward her, or his escaping to work most of the time. She kept making excuses for Tom's behavior, hoping it would change.

Miranda helped Annie gain more knowledge about her holistic healing journey. Annie found a book defining medicinal plants that Native Americans had used in the past. The book was a goldmine of information, which helped her understand the plants used in ancient days to heal before modern day pharmaceuticals came along.

Many of these she would try, but the problem she faced was finding the natural ingredients to make them. Annie didn't have access to woods and fields where these ingredients grow naturally, but she would try and make do with local health food stores.

Due to the traumatic brain injury from the wreck, she suffered tremendous headaches. The pills the doctors prescribed were habit forming and made her feel drugged and hazy. Researching natural healing she learned the common hop plant, *Humulus Lupulus*, would alleviate pain and help her to sleep. She dried the hop buds purchased from a local brew house in the oven and then ground it into a fine powder. She then filled clear empty gel capsules found on the internet and swallowed two with water. Sure enough, it made her drowsy and when she awoke from her nap, she didn't have a headache anymore. She called this the 'remedy.'

Maybe there was something to this after all.

She also studied the book for more natural remedies she could try to concoct. She could hardly wait to share her success with Miranda.

Tom was still absent most of the time, but Annie no longer made excuses for him. She knew he was avoiding her for some reason. But what could that be? Was he disappointed in her because of her drinking and the car wreck that ensued? Their marriage was in deep trouble, and she knew it, but she didn't have a clue how to fix it.

A few days later and for no reason she decided it was time to finally get to the bottom of things. When Tom came home again, she would confront him as to why he was absent from their home so much. As it happened, today was the day he would show up.

He waltzed into the room like nothing was wrong, throwing her off guard with his nonchalant attitude, when he had not been home for ten days, no phone calls, no nothing.

I could have been dead and buried, and he would not have known about it.

She fumed at the thought but kept a calm exterior.

"Tom, I think it's time we had a talk. Things can't go on like this for me."

"Like what? What are you talking about now?" Tom snarled.

"Well for one, you never come home anymore, nor do you call, or even answer my calls or texts. Doesn't that seem a bit strange to you? Where have you been staying?"

"Where do you think? I'm trying to earn a living since you are not working. We still have bills to pay and there's the added medical and legal cost since the wreck. I'm struggling to keep us above water." He spoke loudly and harshly.

"You're staying at the hospital for ten days in a row? Why don't you call home and check in every now and then?" she asked.

"I just haven't had time. It won't be long, and all this will be behind us, and it will be like old times." he said, softening his tone.

Walking over to her he wrapped her in his arms holding her tight. It felt so good, and she believed him, she trusted him. However, her gut was telling her something was dreadfully wrong.

He spent the night at home, but never came upstairs off the couch. She didn't push it; she made another excuse for him once again. It was his first day off in a long time, and she knew he had to be bone tired.

The next morning when she got up at 7:30 a.m., he was already gone. No kiss goodbye, no see you later, just a wadded-up blanket on the sofa. She felt abandoned again.

She went through her daily routine, a quick shower with a plastic bag taped on her bad leg, while doing a stork dance. Balancing on one leg trying to wash all the important parts without falling. Then struggling as she dressed while on crutches. She had a doctor's appointment today and hoped to be rid of the cast by the afternoon. After the doctor freed her from the contraption she could get back to her old life and job. Tom never asked if she needed help with anything, or if she wanted him to go with her to appointments. She didn't need him to, but she wanted him to come—or at least ask. Her appointment was at 1 p.m., after the visit she would go to the hospital and see when she might be able to return to work.

She was 30 minutes early for her appointment and wanted the leg cast off today. The first thing they did was x-ray the bone and then she waited in a small room for the doctor to come in and tell her how it looked.

The orthopedist pushed into the room and sat at the PC, opening the latest X-ray. After staring at it for a few minutes, he said, "I don't know what you have been doing, but your x-ray is remarkable. I've never seen so much bone growth in a fracture of this type. Especially for a woman of your age, and in this length of time."

"So does that mean this torture device can come off today?" she asked.

"Absolutely, now you will have some restrictions and must continue your physical therapy to gain full use of your leg. But if you continue with your healing like you have that should be accomplished in a few more weeks. Hang on, I'll get the PA, and we'll cut that cast off your leg right now."

Thirty minutes later she was gingerly walking to her car on a pair of crutches with a white, hairy, shriveled leg with a nasty scar snaking down her shin. But she didn't care, she was walking on two legs again.

Now, on to the hospital to get my job back, maybe I'll drop in and surprise Tom while I'm there.

She moved more easily than before with the heavy cast on her leg, making it to Human Resources before their afternoon break. The Administrative Assistant at the desk seemed very uneasy, stumbling over her words. She said Annie would have to talk to the HR Director. She was not able to discuss the situation with her, and they would schedule an appointment specifically for the discussion, as the Director had another meeting scheduled for today. Annie agreed to call and make an appointment for later in the week.

Hmmmm, strange—must have something to do with the accident.

Afterward Annie dropped by the Radiology Department to see Tom. He was there this time, and they had a brief chitchat, but he was terribly busy, and she didn't want to keep him from his patients. Finished with her errands for the day, she limped to the car and drove home.

The mail was waiting in the box when she arrived. There was a very official looking letter from the hospital HR Department.

I was just there, why didn't they tell me about this letter?

She opened the envelope and read:

Dear Dr. Hayes:

We regret to inform you that your services have been discontinued. Your privileges have been revoked from practicing medicine at St. Vincent's Hospital effective immediately......

That's as far as she read before dropping all the mail and sinking to the floor. They fired her.

Just like that, her career was over.

What a fool I am, no wonder the HR Admin was stumbling about and didn't know what to say to me. She probably thought I had already received this letter and knew this news. What will I do now? Did Tom already know too?

She picked up the phone and called Tom's cell. He did answer this time.

"Did you know when I came there today that I had been fired?"

"Yes," he said.

"That's all you have to say to me. You couldn't have warned me, or said something? I feel like a fool."

"Just calm down, we can discuss this when I get home," Tom said.

"Oh, you plan to come home sometime soon I'm sorry, that was a cheap shot, but I am very hurt. Tom you never talk to me about anything anymore, things must change. I am going to hang up now and try to get myself together." She hung up without saying goodbye.

Boy, do I want a drink right now; I need to find an AA meeting fast.

She went to the one where she first met Ray. He wasn't there, but it helped calm her down and quash the craving for alcohol. She was still angry with Tom.

When she got home, she called Miranda and filled her in on the latest happenings. She had never had a close girlfriend before, and she liked having someone she could talk to about her problems. Especially since she didn't have Tom around anymore. Miranda was a good listener, and it helped Annie to get things off her chest. She spoke in a strange cadence; unlike anyone Annie had ever heard before. Miranda never offered advice and Annie liked that about her. Annie gave her the good news about her leg, and how impressed the doctor was with her healing. She gave Miranda's holistic approach all the credit for that.

"No, don't give me the credit, it is a gift from our ancestors and nature to those who listen and practice the old ways. I hope you continue to learn more about this, there is more available to you than just physical healing. You can receive spiritual healing as well. You must learn what has broken you to make you turn to the drink?" She said.

Annie had never considered there was more to her alcoholism, maybe there was a genetic predisposition. As an adoptee, she didn't know what illnesses were lurking in her family tree.

"Miranda, I had never thought much about this before, but I think I need to find out where I came from. Who am I? This has a lot to do with my drinking issues and who knows what else may be around the corner for me, from a genetic standpoint. I'm going to work on that, and why not, I have all this free time now evidently." She tried to chuckle, but it caught in her throat, and she choked back tears.

She knew she was a good doctor and believed that alcohol never interfered with her medical practice, but that didn't matter to the hospital. Her career was over at St. Vincent's, and she was grieving that part of her life ending. She just hoped the medical board didn't try to pull her license too.

"Annie, there's not much you can do about that now is there? Just remember, time heals all things, and your future is already written as is your past. You must now learn what it means to just be and embrace the changes. Don't fight with life; it only makes your time here on earth more difficult," Miranda said.

"How did you get so smart?" Annie smiled as she spoke, it reflected in her voice. "I dunno, must be something I ate…." Miranda laughed.

She always felt better after talking with Miranda, she was there just when she needed her most and she had a soft sweetness about her. Annie had never met anyone like her before and she would make a point to retain this friendship for many years to come.

After hanging up the phone, she needed to prepare for Tom's arrival, if he bothered to come home tonight. She bet he would since they had words today over her job loss. She had made a royal mess of their lives with her drinking and the accident. He wanted to know her plans, it was evident they needed her income to maintain their status quo. She didn't know why though, they never went on expensive trips, they didn't drive new cars, and their house was very middle class. One would think two doctors' incomes would afford them a more lavish lifestyle. She had always let Tom take care of all the money, it was easier, and she could focus on practicing medicine. But now she had doubts about that decision, she didn't know anything about their finances. That was about to change.

She went into Tom's home office and found their checkbook, there was no balance, only a registry of hastily written check amounts. She logged into the computer Tom used for paying bills. She found the bank website and logged in; he had saved the password on the desktop which made it easy for her. She pulled up the accounts and found a checking and a savings account. She was shocked when she saw the savings account balance was $10,000 and the checking account balance was only $500. She gasped and all her air went out, until today she earned over $200 thousand dollars per year and knew Tom made at least the same. But where was their money? What had Tom done? They were broke and now she was without any income. Tom had some serious explaining to do when, or if he came home.

He didn't come home that night, so the next day she would play detective and see where Tom was spending all his time away. It certainly wasn't with her. She knew he usually got off work at 4 p.m. so she went to the hospital parking lot and found his old truck. She parked her car in the back lot where she could see his vehicle, but she was hidden from his direct view. Unless he knew where to look for her, he would never see her car. Then she waited patiently.

She didn't have long to wait, at 4:05 p.m. he exited the emergency room door heading for his truck. She started up her engine ready to tail him. He threw his satchel into the passenger side of the beat up old S10 pickup and hopped in like he was eager to get out of there. She waited until he exited the parking lot and reached the traffic light before she began to follow, hoping it would lead him back to their house. It didn't. She kept a couple of car lengths back, without detection.

*This was sorta fun, I could always go into the private eye business since I no longer have a job….*she laughed at herself.

Where are you going Tom?

She was unfamiliar with this part of town. After a few minutes he turned into a parking lot, but she couldn't make out the business until she got closer. This was the tricky part, trying to get close enough to see what he does without him noticing her. She watched him get out of the truck and almost skip to the automatic doors. The building had a large neon sign that read Crown City Casino and Gaming center. Things suddenly became a little clearer to her.

Tom had gambled all their money away.

She stayed in the parking lot to see how long he was inside the building. At 10 p.m. she was hungry and needed to go to the bathroom, he still had not come out the door. While she was contemplating peeing in the bushes or going home, she saw movement. He exited the front door, and he wasn't as jovial as when he entered. She figured he had lost more of their money. But she was still going to follow him home, to see if that's where he would go.

As she turned out of the parking lot, she said a silent prayer.

Tom, please go home.

She stayed a few car lengths behind, and the darkness helping conceal her identity. She was afraid of losing sight of his truck, but didn't want to get too close to be detected. He turned down the side streets and none of them went in the direction of home. Finally, he pulled into a stranger's drive, parked his car, and went into the house as if he lived there. No knocking, no key, just waltzing in through the door. Maybe he did live there because he certainly wasn't spending time with her. She jotted the address down on a paper napkin she found in the car door pocket and shoved it into her purse. Tomorrow her assignment would be to find out who lived here and why Tom had unlimited access as if he lived there. Of course, when she got home, she waited for Tom's call. But that call never came.

She went to bed crying again, over what she knew was the end of her marriage.

Sequoyah's Cherokee Syllabary
ca. 1820.

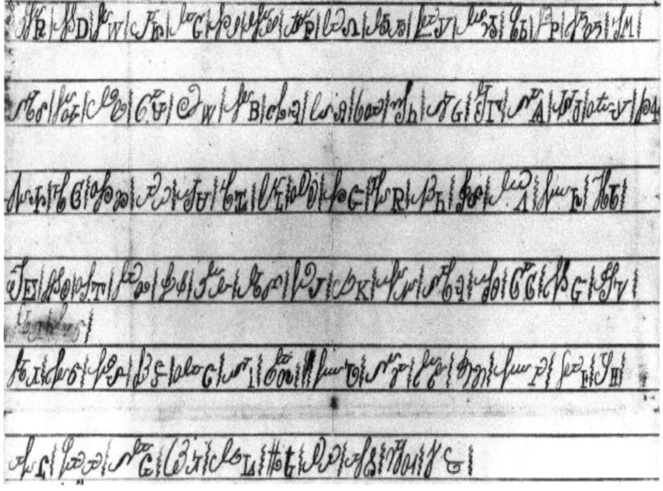

Canva, "Original Cherokee Syllabary.jpg,"
PUBLIC DOMAIN

NINE

1860

Indian Territory
West of the Mississippi

I t was muggy and miserable in the summer of 1860. Dovie celebrated her 30th year, and their daughter was turning nine years old. She carried an English name, Nan, to try to fit into the white man's world. Her skin color was darker than Dovie's, closer to Isaac's deep tone. Her hair was not straight, but kinky, and fuzzy like her fathers, and she fashioned it in tight braids trying to tame it. Nan had a bright smile, and other kids gravitated to be near her, she brought much joy into her parents' lives.

She was of mixed blood, but the Presbyterian missionaries allowed her to attend the grade school on the territory. Excelling in all subjects, she was reading and writing before she started first grade. However much she loved school, her true love was healing and caring for the sick. Since her birth, the elders had told her the stories of her great grandmother the healer. So of course, Nan wanted to learn the healing ways of her people like Mother and Grandmother. Nan had natural talent evident from an incredibly early age, she was also an empath like her mother and carried within her a spirit of love for all living things.

The white man firmly planted the idea of slavery in the minds of most Cherokee, and changing their mindset was not easy. But over the years, Nan's parents, Isaac, and Dovie secretly worked hard to help the slaves in the Cherokee Nation. Together they set up a makeshift school, hidden deep in the woods, to teach the slave children to read, write, and cipher. Dovie also taught the children the Cherokee syllabary Sequoyah invented, which allowed them to read and write the Cherokee language as well. By the time they graduated from the secret slave school, they were more educated than most of the white settlers living around them.

Isaac built the one-room schoolhouse in the woods near the river, furnishing it with long benches and tables. He also found a place downstream in the shallow riverbed with slate rock and there he gathered and chiseled tablets for use with chalk, same as the missionaries used in their schools. Most of the missionaries were secret abolitionists and they helped provide chalk, books, and anything else they could slip to her without raising suspicion.

Dovie told the elders the building was a medical lodge for the slave children, where she would tend to and treat their ailments. It went undetected and prospered. School was in session in the winter months when the children did not have to work in the gardens and the fields of their owners. The first year she had three children on a good day, by the third year she had over 50 students squeezing into the one-room schoolhouse.

The older ones helped her teach the younger ones. By 1860, their school provided literacy to hundreds of people.

Around that time, Isaac also began helping slaves escaping from Arkansas, Louisiana, or east from Tennessee and Georgia. He was a 'shepherd,' someone that encouraged slaves to escape and escorted them on their way west to freedom. Once they reached The Cherokee Nation, they were no longer in the United States. Oklahoma was a territory, not yet recognized as a state, and the law from the surrounding states had no authority to make arrests or to capture fugitives in the sovereign nations of the Five Tribes located there. Bounty hunters searching for runaways were unwelcome there also. The Creek and Seminole Nations welcomed runaways; they would settle on their land or pass onto other 'Underground Railroad' secret locations into free Kansas. In the summer months when there was no school and the children were working in the fields, the school served as an overnight stop for the runaways. Many of the abolitionist missionaries in the territory also helped

Isaac provide food, clothing, and transportation to the next stop on the railway to freedom.

One summer day as Isaac was away leading a group to freedom, Dovie hiked through the woods toward the schoolhouse to do some cleaning before classes resumed in the fall. It was just like any other sultry summer day. However, for some reason, her mind was preoccupied, all she could do was think of Isaac. He had been gone for two days. She missed his warmth at night and worried about his safety. Usually, he would be gone for up to a week or more 'forwarding' runaway slaves from station to station. On this trip, he told her he would be leading a group coming up from Louisiana. She tried her best to persuade him to skip this journey and to lay low for a while. She had a bad feeling for the days leading up to his departure and there was growing talk of war erupting between the North and the South.

Also, the danger heightened as the slave owners, tired of losing their property, began hiring bounty hunters to find runaways. The woods were crawling with armed hunters who would do whatever it took to collect the reward money. Isaac would not listen to Dovie's pleas to stay home for awhile, as people's lives were depending upon him being where he was supposed to be at the appointed time. He could not let them down.

As she walked along the path to the school, she heard the hoots of a large owl overhead in the pine trees. Panic overtook Dovie as the owl was an omen of death, especially seeing and hearing it in the daylight hours. Her legs shook and she sucked in deep breaths as she ran toward the schoolhouse for safety.

Her eye caught something ahead in the distance, a shape moving in the tree limbs. At first, she thought the medicine man cast evil spirits on her again and she was seeing their shadows ready to leap upon her when she got close enough. However, that couldn't be as the medicine man quit vexing her lately with her power and popularity among the people having grown stronger.

"Maybe it was a stranger who came to arrest her for teaching the children?"

Slowing her pace, moving off the trail, and hiding behind a massive oak tree trunk, while peeking toward the floating object up ahead in the branches she stood still and did not take her eyes from it. Her hands shook as she hugged the tree to try and steady herself for a long while. The shape did not move toward her or away from its spot, it was anchored to something, and swayed back and forth in the breeze. She stared at the shape, trying to determine what it could be. Her vision focused as she realized it was something hanging from the tree limbs. Through the dense brush—staying off the main path to remain unseen by the floating object, she began inching her way closer and closer to the schoolhouse.

Then she smelled it, recognizing immediately the foul odor of death hitting her nostrils.

Her heart jumped into her throat. She began to run toward the object, not worrying about her safety anymore. As she got closer, she first recognized the beadwork pattern on the moccasins. The same moccasins she fashioned from the big buck's hide Isaac tanned a few months prior, and she had adorned with the familiar bead pattern.

Her mind questioning, *"how were they in these woods—the moccasins she made for her beloved to wear on his journey?"*

Then, she looked up and recognized Isaac's body hanging from the tree. A rope bit deeply into his neck, while dried blood ran down his shirt in stripes. His black and swollen hands tied behind his back, and legs bound by ropes at the ankle while his body twisting and swinging back and forth in the gentle summer breeze. As she drew closer, she saw the disfigurement of his face, beaten and purple with eyes bulging from their sockets. His tongue swollen and protruding, the flies thick, buzzing and blowing on exposed flesh and crawling in and out of his nose and mouth. She grabbed his legs, lifting him upward to loosen the noose around his neck, but he was too heavy. She dry-heaved when she felt the cold stiffness of his hard body.

"Oh, what do I do…." She cried out to the air, no one heard.

She ran to the school dragging a bench outside underneath Isaac's swinging body, climbing up to cut him down with her knife. She worked hard, sawing at the thick twisted hemp rope tossed over the tree limb, trying to hurry as if some life might remain in him—but, it was too late. His corpse fell with a hard thud to the ground, and she apologized to him, as if he could still hear her and feel pain. It was apparent from the decomposition that he had been hanging for a couple of days. His corpse was gray and stiff, maggots already hatched and working at the flesh of his eyeballs. She worked the knife under the rope around his neck and cut loose the ropes binding his hands and feet to free him.

"My beloved, who would do this to you….I am so sorry I was not with you. I am here now, and I will take care of you. We must warm you."

She flicked the maggots off his face and swatted away the flies, flinging herself across his dead body wailing as her broken heart struggled to beat on without her beloved. She cried out Isaac's name repeatedly, in deep guttural moans with each breath she expelled. She wrapped her arms around him begging him to come back to her. She pleaded for him to live, while wanting to die with him. She lay there upon his chest with her hands and hair covering his face, to keep the flies away until darkness came. Against her will the sun rose again the next morning. She heard footsteps walking toward her crunching in the leaves on the path. Then arms reaching—pulling and tugging her upward. She began to fight with them.

Was it the murderers returning now to hang me too?

She heard Mother's voice. "Ssshhh child, it is us, Mother and Father. We are here for you and Nan waits for you back at the lodge. We will have the priest come for Isaac. Come child, quickly let us leave this place of death. The stench of evil is strong here and it draws dark spirits. We must go."

They half-walked half-carried their distraught daughter to her mother's lodge, and she was inconsolable. Mother brewed tea that would calm her and made her drink it, however it had little effect. She was distraught and wailing with pain, wanting to be with Isaac.

Later that day the priest carried Isaac's body back to the home he shared with Dovie. She insisted that only she would wash and prepare him for burial. She had stopped wailing, but she cried as she boiled willow root and water to make the purifying wash.

Isaac's body lay in the lodge, upon the very table where they shared their meals. She began by closing his bulging eyes and gently washing his face and hair, with the warm water and first with the lye soap. She would then rinse and anoint him with the purifying willow root. She removed his moccasins, shirt, and pants. Proceeding to gently, wash down his body, while touching and etching into memory for eternity each scar and mark on him. She traced her fingertips into the deep gash around his neck to try and soften the edges. His neck lolled to one side, as she touched his face with the cloth, broken by the snap of the rope. She hoped this meant he experienced a quick death with little pain and suffering.

Mother collected his *'dead clothes'* from his mother's lodge. A burial outfit his mother had made for him when he became a man and stored away until needed, as is the Cherokee way. Dovie dressed him, it was difficult as his body was stiff and would not bend. She tried her best to hide the deep red gash around his neck with a necklace fashioned from carved shells, gold, elk teeth, and beads. She tied the cloth turban around his head and fastened the feathers onto it signifying honor, power, strength, wisdom, and freedom. These sacred feathers were gifts from the elders recognizing him as a Cherokee warrior when he became a man.

He was handsome even with the grotesque death mask upon his face because of the hanging. Once she finished washing and dressing his body, she lay down on the table beside him, with her arm across his chest, grieving with deep racking moans. She struggled to breathe; it felt like someone cut her heart out and yet she lived. This was her last night beside her beloved on this earth. She stayed beside him until dawn. Mother came before the priest arrived at daybreak for the burial.

The priest came alone, allowing no one else to touch or see the dead. He carried Isaac, wrapped in a blanket, to the mound where the ancient ones that went before had been interred. Dovie followed behind him crying out Isaacs name in a long deep sorrowful cry. There was a shallow pit dug into the mound, surrounded by a great many rocks stacked nearby. The priest lowered Isaac into the ground on top of his ancestors' bones and said a prayer to the Great One to accept his spirit into the sky.

He then sprinkled scented waters over Isaac and cleansed his body with smoke, while chanting a prayer. After this final cleansing of the body at the burial mound, a reuniting with his spirit occurred.

Dovie gave the priest Isaac's gun, knife, some food, water, and jewelry for him to bury with her beloved for the journey to the spirit world. As he placed them into the grave with Isaac's body, she realized everything she had of his was now gone except Nan.

The priest then placed big rocks upon the body covering it three stones or more deep. The village would continue to use this mound for burials until the priest died and was the last body buried there, and then start a new mound at a new location.

By touching and being near the dead body, everyone and everything in the house became unclean and required cleansing by the priest. The priest returned to their lodge alone to perform the ceremony. He smashed all the furnishings and threw them along with all the food and Isaac's personal belongings into the hearth fire to burn. Afterward, he took the ashes that remained and buried them deep in the woods. He then rekindled a new fire, put on a pot of cleansing water boiled with secret herbs to make a tea brew used for purification. The family members drank and washed in the tea, as he sprinkled the inside of the house with the concoction. He then smoked the house with a cedar bough. After the priest finished with the house, he took all his purification items away and secretly hid them in a hollow tree where they were never to be disturbed. Then he gathered the family and took them to the water, while he prayed, they immersed themselves, facing east and west going under seven times in each direction. As they rose from the water the final time, they loosened their clothing and let it float away with the currents downstream. Now considered fully cleansed they dressed in new clothing and returned to their homes. White Dove went to her mother's lodge, she couldn't stand the thought of being in their home without Isaac. She didn't eat or sleep for four days, mother cared for Nan trying to console the young girl who mourned her father as well.

On the fifth and sixth day of mourning, the family arose at daybreak, cleansed themselves in the water again, and then went to Isaac's burial site. As is custom, there the local women of the village and some neighboring women joined in to wail and cry for Isaac.

Dovie returned to her own home on the seventh day with Nan. She found upon the doorstep a white feather. A reminder that her beloved was near, watching, and protecting her from the afterlife, she picked it up and tied it to her hair. When she got inside, she took her knife used to free Isaac's body from the ropes, cut her hair and placed the braid on Isaacs grave as a sign of mourning. She returned to their home, entering a long and deep grieving period. She would not comb her hair, change her clothes, or bathe for ten months. She sat in the corner of her lodge, mourning her beloved, and eating just enough to survive, while wanting and waiting to die and join him.

The warriors talked about the murder of their brother and tried to find those responsible with no success. After many months, they finally learned a group of white bounty hunters had slipped onto the land of The Nation and recaptured the runaways Isaac was leading to freedom. They murdered him as a message to scare anyone else trying to help runaway slaves, a strong signal that anyone caught interfering would suffer the same fate.

The tactic worked; the underground railroad link broke with Isaac's death. Most everyone on this link was frightened into silence and ignoring the plight of those living as property—not human beings. White Hawk was not afraid to die, and her courage did not diminish, but her grief was too strong for her to function. She could barely live, but she did.

After a while Isaac's murder was forgotten by everyone except Dovie, his mother Chickawa, brother Ben and daughter Nan—the people that loved him most. It remained fresh in their minds, and they would continue to mourn Isaac for their lifetime.

TEN

Current Day

After a restless night Annie finally threw off the covers and padded to the kitchen to brew coffee. Things did not look better in the light of day, and her eyes were puffy from crying herself to sleep.

Annie impatiently watched the coffee pot brew and craved vodka. Thankfully, there was none in the house. She had cleaned out the hidden stashes strategically placed around the house, thrown it all into the trash bin carted away yesterday, or she might have suffered a relapse.

Moments later she stood at the kitchen window with her steaming cup, looking out onto the massive back yard. The trees and hedge hid the view from their closest neighbors. She knew she stood to lose all this, but right now she didn't care. She cared about losing Tom, perhaps it was too late—she may have already lost him. She watched the squirrels' acrobatics while trying their best to raid the birdfeeders. She was not sure how long she stood there lost in her thoughts, but her cup of coffee needed reheating in the microwave.

Time was dragging on today for her, she felt adrift and alone in the empty house. She knew she needed to decide, what did she want out of this situation. Did she still want Tom and all his problems? He had an addiction to gambling just like she did with alcohol. But she rationalized, he hadn't abandoned her when she hit bottom, so should she stand beside him as well? Together she believed they could overcome and build back the life they once had. Wasn't it a marriage worth saving?

Suddenly, she thought of her jewelry box and wondered, if Tom had spent all their savings, what else had he done? She went to the closet and opened the jewelry tray where she kept her engagement ring and the pendant her mother left her. They were both gone. He had pawned the two things most dear to her. She cried again with a gut-wrenching sob. Both items held deep sentimental value and were irreplaceable to her.

"Why would he do this to me—to us?" She whispered between sobs.

She knew the answer, he was an addict and that's what they do, anything to get their fix. Gambling was his drug of choice. She knew then she must confront him tonight and try to get him in therapy, if their marriage had any chance of surviving.

She had some things to take care of today to try and salvage what little was left of their life. She called the hospital payroll department and had her paycheck e-deposit stopped. She would pick up her last check in person, which would at least give her a little stipend in case she needed it. She also went to the bank and opened a new checking account without Tom's name on it. She transferred half of their savings into it. She felt better afterwards but also sad that it had come to this.

Next, she visited pawn shops to try and find her engagement ring and her mother's pendant. She thought this might be hopeless because she didn't know when he had pawned the jewelry. Maybe he even sold it to someone outright? But she had to at least try and find it. At each shop as she talked to the clerk, she would start to cry, unable to get the words to come out to explain what she was hoping to find. The clerks were very understanding; evidently, this happens all the time to them. After the third shop, she realized she'd never find the jewelry—it was gone. There were a couple more shops, she would check out, but hope was gone too.

At the last pawn shop in town she felt her energy sag, her headache returned, and her leg ached deeply. She had overdone it today and needed to get home and take a nap. She had been running on adrenaline, which finally ran out on her. When she got home, she took the headache remedy and lay down drifting off to sleep.

She awoke with a start thinking she had overslept for work. Then remembered she didn't have a job. It was dark in the house and the bedside clock said 7:30 p.m. She wondered if Tom had come home tonight.

Downstairs she found him sitting in the living room mindlessly flipping the remote through the stations. He didn't even acknowledge her presence when she walked into the room.

She started the conversation, "Tom, I'm glad your home, we need to talk."

Sitting down on the sofa facing him with her hands she picked at the nub of the couch cushion fabric, a nervous tic.

God, I need a drink right now.

But she didn't act on her thoughts, not yet anyway. She stayed and faced the fear she felt.

"I know Tom. I know it all," she said.

"What do you think you know, Mrs. Know it all." He said with a smirk on his face.

"I know about the gambling. I know about our finances. I even know about her." Annie was calm. She didn't want to come across as hysterical, but that's what she felt, inside she was screaming. She had to push it down and be calm.

Tom's face fell. "How did you find out?"

"Doesn't matter does it? It's true and it's out in the open now. The question you should ask is what are we gonna do about it?"

"Thank God you know. I have been trying to work up the nerve to tell you, but I just couldn't— not while you were recovering. But now you know we can each get on with our lives," he said.

"So, does this mean you want a divorce?"

Her heart broke when she said the words. As bad as things were, she still had love for Tom. He was all the family she had.

"Well, don't you? I have been awful to you. I stole and gambled away our money; I have been cheating with another woman. You should boot me out the door."

"Yes, I should. But I still love you, I loved our life together. I just can't turn it off like a switch. I am hurt beyond compare, but I would take my old

Tom back and try to rebuild our marriage in a heartbeat," she said.

"Annie don't make this any harder than it is. We are through, I don't love you anymore, I'm in love with someone else, and we need to go our separate ways. Face it, our marriage was crap. We both lived for our jobs and didn't have a real marriage."

She couldn't hold back the one tear that rolled out of her eye and down her cheek. He saw it but didn't comment. She didn't wipe it away either, she wanted him to remember this day and her brokenness when he walked out on her.

"I'm gonna grab a few of my things and get out of here. I plan to move the rest of my stuff next week. You find a lawyer and start the divorce papers; I'll sign anything and give you whatever you want. Let's make this easy for each other. Ok?"

"Sure Tom, I'll make it easy for you."

Then he was gone, and the house was silent except for the sound of the time-bomb ticking mantle clock. Tom had bought it at a flea market when they first moved in together, she always hated that clock. The style was 1950's and it didn't fit into their clean minimalist décor, and she hated the incessant ticking. She went to the mantle, took the clock in both hands, and slammed it out the back door onto the driveway busting it into several smaller pieces. It was now silent.

Good riddance. Damn, that felt good, what else did Tom leave here that I can't stand?

She went through the entire house, purging all the things Tom had left behind that she hated. She had a large pile accumulating on the driveway and topped it off with his clothes. He could pick it up next week, these things were no longer living rent free in her house or her head. It was cathartic. She had cried her last tear for him. She needed to work on herself now and quit trying to fix Tom and their marriage. It was over and done, and she needed to move on.

She called Miranda and filled her in on the happenings of the last couple of days.

"I'm sorry for you, and I'm here for you." That is all she could say about the entire sordid mess of Annie's life.

"We need to work on you, forget about Tom. There is something or someone better that deserves you out there in the universe, you just need to align your stars to find them," Miranda said.

"Don't tell me you have a love potion for that, do you?"

"Actually, my ancestors do have a love brew, but I don't think you are ready for that yet." Miranda chuckled. Annie laughed too; this was the first time she had laughed in a long while. She already felt better.

"I'm going to hang up and find an AA meeting. I have a craving for a drink. So, I'll call you tomorrow and we can discuss my future. Oh, and Miranda, I really want you to know how much your friendship means to me. Thank you for being there for me, you're all I have now."

"No problem sister, we are in this together."

A short while later she was listening to a room full of strangers say, "Hi, I'm *so-and-so* and I'm an alcoholic."

She hadn't said those words yet. She had trouble believing she was an alcoholic; sure, she drank, but an alcoholic? She didn't drink that much, but deep down she wondered if it might be true. Her life didn't sound so vastly different from everyone else in that room. Their stories were different, and yet the same. Most had lost their homes, families, and jobs, or more. The more she listened to them speak, the more she realized they were all drunks, and would always be drunks, but just not drunken at this moment. She needed to keep those moments of sobriety at the forefront of her life, and string them together to make a long lifetime of sober living. Without that, she didn't stand a chance. She would drink herself into oblivion while no one hung around to watch her die from alcohol.

Her drug of choice was vodka, but it could have easily been some narcotic, or gambling.....any type of desire never satiated. There's plenty of things out there to lay claim to some poor sots' soul: some might even be workaholics like her, that one is hard to come to terms with. Because you deliver goodness along with the damage you do, it's a hard one to fess up and recover from. However, it will destroy lives and kill you as sure as alcohol or drugs. It just may take a little longer and you'll have money to numb you as you work yourself into the ground. There isn't a 'workaholics anonymous' to help you through your addiction, too bad for you.

The meeting did the trick, she swallowed a gallon of black coffee instead of vodka, came home and took a hot soak in the tub before bed. She hated going into an empty house, but after Tom's tryst she had lots of experience lately in dealing with being alone. Nothing much had changed for her, except the secret was out and in the open. She did wonder who the other woman might be. That is a private eye sleuthing adventure better left for another day. Who is the home wrecking mystery woman that destroyed their marriage? Whoever you are, good luck to you loving a narcissistic, thieving, gambler.

She felt lucky getting out of the marriage before Tom lost the house and got them in too deep to recover. She'd have to check the mortgage tomorrow and make sure he had not borrowed against the equity in the house. She wished she hadn't thought of that. She would lie awake most of the night worrying about things he may have done that she had not yet discovered.

Finally sleep came to her. The dream started the same as it always did, she was standing on a desert plain. Staring at the red rock hills that looked like sculptures placed by an invisible hand. The wind swirled around her, kicking sand into her eyes and mouth. She was crying and feeling lost and alone. When she spotted a Native woman on a paint stallion. The horse runs to her and then she suddenly wakes up. She wakes up at the same time every time.

What is with this dream? Why do I keep having it night after night? I must talk to Miranda about this; maybe she has some insight for me.

After waking up at 4:30 a.m. she gave up on the idea of sleeping and got up for coffee. She'd watch the sun come up over the trees in the back yard and listen for the birds to awaken and begin to chirp their songs for her. This was her favorite time of the day. However, after the dream, she would always have a nagging feeling inside of her; there is something this woman in the dream is trying to tell me. But what could it be?

She needed to find an AA meeting this morning. She'd go back to the one by the deli where Ray had taken her for coffee, and hopefully he'd be there. She liked talking to him, he made it seem that things were going to be ok for her. She didn't even bother to shower, just threw on yesterday's clothes and went out the door to a room full of strangers that she couldn't wait to hear say. … "Hi, I'm *so-and-so* and I'm an alcoholic."

ELEVEN

1861

Indian Territory
West of the Mississippi

White Dove sat in the corner of her lodge mourning the death of her beloved during the remainder of the sweltering summer, the fall, and into the deep winter. Mother took over the care of Nan,while White Dove tried her best to die from grief. She did not succeed. Meanwhile, the tension between the North and the South grew stronger, and the drums of a great civil war beat louder throughout the nation.

In November of the year of Isaac's murder, the United States elected Abraham Lincoln as president. By the following February of 1861, the

Confederate States of America formed as the first seven states seceded from the Union, elected their own President—Jefferson Davis, and drafted a Confederate states constitution. The Civil War was now imminent. Lincoln's inauguration was in March, and by April, the United States was at war with itself.

The word came in early May to the Cherokee Nation from a band of settlers heading west, running away from the front line at the Georgia and Tennessee border near Chickamauga. They told of the first shots fired at Fort Sumter in Charleston, South Carolina on April 12th. After that strike, three more states joined the confederacy, and then full-blown war broke out. Men and boys raced to join in the war effort and many battles found brother fighting against brother. The new young republic had no clue to the destruction and devastation resulting from a civil war between the states. This war would bleed the blood of all its people and the Cherokee knew they must take a position. However, like most of America, they split apart in their support as well.

Surprisingly to White Dove, the Indian Territory joined the fight with the Confederacy, led by wealthy plantation holder and slave owner Stand Watie. He was one of the original leaders that signed over the ancestral territory to the U.S. government at Echota before the trail of tears. He claimed the collaboration with the South was to get funds and full recognition as a sovereign, independent state for the Cherokee Nation. However, Principal Chief John Ross and his supporters stood with the Union in the beginning of the war. Before long, the Cherokee Nation split in two just as the rest of America had. The Union sympathizers formed the Indian Home Guard, resulting in the Cherokee people fighting against each other in a white man's war.

White Dove felt devastated and betrayed by her leaders. She struggled with what to do to help those like Nan, caught in the middle, and her people. She went to the water to pray, which is where she always felt closest to the ancient spirits, as she sought their guidance.

What would Isaac do?

She already knew the answer to that question. He would fight to free his people regardless of what Stand Watie preached, so she got up and went to work to help the North. She was not sure where this would lead, but she needed to follow her call. However, it would mean leaving everything she held dear to her, her daughter, and her mother. In the end, she realized she could not go, and inside she was torn by her decision. But it was not just White Dove that lost someone; her baby lost her father, and she could not lose her mother too. White Dove was torn.

After she left the river, she went to her mother to end her mourning and get her daughter back. She sat in the floor near the stone fireplace, while mother combed her hair for the first time since Isaac's death. Mother cut mats and clumps of hair to the scalp as she worked the comb through. After brushing what she had left of her hair, White Dove walked alone to the water to bathe. While in the water, a great red-tailed hawk circled around and landed in the tree above where she washed. The bird's piercing call rang out to her. It spoke to her, and she clearly heard the hawk speaking to her spirit with its piercing cries. The Cherokee believed the hawk shares the ability to move between the seen and unseen realms, joining both worlds together. They are the protectors and visionaries of the air and enable an awakening in you to your purpose. She felt this, a new responsibility and now understood her soul's destiny. She went into the river as "White Dove," and emerged from the water as "White Hawk." The name given to her at birth, White Dove, stood for a bringer of peace and purity of love; these things stolen from her when they killed her Isaac. As she emerged from the river, she was White Dove no more.

She dressed in clean clothes, letting the dirty ones float downstream and out of her sight along with her grief. She realized she was now responsible for Nan's future. She was not the same broken woman that washed in this stream after Isaac's burial ten months before.

She now had a fire burning inside her and would no longer hide her efforts in the secrecy of the woods. What good had that done? They found

Isaac and killed him anyway. She would no longer cower and hide, and she would not lay down and die from grief. She must fight for freedom and the rights of the people whose same blood flowed from her and Isaac into their sweet Nan. She vowed to take a visible stand against slavery, no longer a coward, no matter what happens. She would stand strong for Isaac, Nan, and her people.

She hoped for clarity and a sign that she was making the right choice so that evening she would ask the spirit to join her and commune as one in a spirit walk. This would be her first time without grandmother as a guide. It would be extremely dangerous, but she believed she was ready.

She prayed and fasted for the remainder of the day. At evening when the moon was full, she sat around the large bonfire in the center of the village and prepared for her journey. Mother sat beside her, along with many of the elder women who had been friends and midwives with Grandmother, but they could not help her should she get into trouble in the nether world. They did not have the power Grandmother possessed when she had rescued her in the past. White Hawk held the healing stick across her lap; she tied the red string to her wrist. Preparing the pipe with herbs and tobacco, she offered a prayer to the Great Spirit, as she lit the pipe. After blowing the first smoke offering, to the four winds of the North, South, East, and West she passed it to Mother, and it then made its way around the circle of women. She took a sage bundle, lit it, and began smudging herself and cleansing the area of evil spirits with the sacred smoke. She heard the flute player from nearby yet hidden from the light of the fire, the eerie sound echoing around the campsite. The song reminded her of the lone wolf calling to its mate in the cool of the night. Finally, when she had made all the offerings, and knew her heart was right, she drank the special brew to begin her journey. She was not afraid.

Her eyes reopened in the spirit world standing on the vast windswept tundra. There she met her spirit animal, the great paint stallion. He raced to her, and she was suddenly on his back.

He reared then ran across the land; she opened her arms wide as to accept all the spirits had to offer her. The wind swirled around her blowing her hair wildly, while a hawk's cry pierced the sky.

Suddenly she saw her grandmother beside her.

"Welcome my child, I have been waiting for you, not sure when you will arrive. But I knew you would make the journey alone, like we had together in the past."

"Grandmother, I have missed you and needed you. So much has happened since you left us. Have you seen my beloved, Isaac, here in the spirit world? You know of his passing over?"

"Yes, my child, he is here with us. Open your mind to see his new spirit body."

She closed her eyes and willed her mind to receive, and suddenly as she reopened them a large black stag with a massive rack of antlers appeared before her. She cried out, reaching for him.

"My beloved Isaac, it is I, Dovie. I am now known as White Hawk; do you see me?"

The stag ran toward her and morphed into Isaac, as he got nearer, he stopped short. He held out his hands, willing her to come to him so they could touch palm to palm. The thunder cracked and lightning flashed, and the feeling was deep and intense, unlike what she had known before. His spirit was so pure it overwhelmed her senses, she had to release herself from him, for she could not tolerate the power he emitted and remain mortal.

"White Hawk, my heart is rejoicing at your arrival. I have watched you mourn for me, and it saddens me. This spirit body I have now is far better than the earthly body that held my soul prisoner. I now soar with the eagles and commune with the Great Spirit for all eternity do not weep for me."

"My beloved Isaac, I have missed your touch and your nearness, I want to be with you," she said.

"I have been with you since the moment you found me in the woods that terrible day. I have not left you, nor will I ever—our spirits joined as one, and our love is timeless, our spirits are eternal. However, you must mourn no more, there is much for you to accomplish for our people. You were born with a gift for greatness, accept what the Great Spirit has put in your heart. Open your eyes and look around, you will see great things are in store for you. You will find love again, not like ours but one that will see you through until we reunite in the spirit world for eternity."

Then he was gone in an instant. Her breath quickened and her heart pounded, but it did not ache as before. Grandmother approached her as quickly as Isaac vanished.

She said, "Look to the East on the hill, the woman you see standing there, she is yet to be. She will need you to understand her mission and guide her through her walk on Earth. Go to her and begin your work by helping her."

White Hawk looked where grandmother pointed. There she saw a young woman with long dark curly hair and bronze skin standing with her head in her hands and crying. Where her tears fell, flowers immediately grew and bloomed. Drawn toward her, White Hawk found herself standing beside her.

She spoke Cherokee and yet the young woman could understand her meaning. White Hawk knew it was not time for the young woman to be in this chasm between life and death for she had things yet to accomplish in the land of the living.

"What is your name child?"

"My name is Annie. I do not know where I am, I'm afraid and lost. Can you help me find my way?"

White Hawk placed her palm upon Annie's head and felt the connection to her soul.

"You are troubled young one. But accept this blessing and healing for what vexes you. I pray for protection over you. The strength for you to stand upright and discover your ancestors who preceded you, to give you pride, and guide you on your journey. The path you are destined to travel on Earth will not be an easy one, but I am always with you as is the Great Spirit and those of your blood. You must look for us in your heart and there you will find happiness and purpose for being. Now, return from where you came." White Hawk said pushing her away instructing her to leave the spirit world.

White Hawk knew Annie's time was not yet right for her to cross over to the Great Spirit. However, she knew they would meet again someday in the spirit world. Their blood joined them across the eons of time and space.

When Annie vanished, Grandmother appeared beside White Hawk once again.

"Grandmother, what is my earthly purpose, how do I find the path that I am destined to walk? I am torn between staying with my child and avenging the death of my beloved."

"Use your gifts and skills for the ones that need your help the most. It will become clearer to you when you are free of the hatred and grief that poisons your mind. You must let your desire for revenge go. You are destined to become a great healer, and hatred holds your heart captive, you cannot channel your healing gift from the Great One when filled with hate and revenge.

You are destined to become a beloved '*woaman*' for the tribe and do wondrous things, which will live on in stories for generations to come. You will have a long life, walking upon the land of your people. You will see the results in your lifetime one soul at a time, and in the future spirit world you will reap the rewards of your work for our people. Stay true to your heart and love all living things, take care of Earth Mother, and give thanks to the Great Spirit. Now go, return to Nan and Mother, they eagerly wait and worry after you."

She awoke from her walk to find the fire had burned down and all that remained were hot coals amid the ashes. Mother was still sitting silently beside her, the other women long ago retired to their lodges for the night. She could always count on her mother to stand beside her and not grow weary. The others could not keep their eyes open to watch for her return. The last thing she remembered in the spirit world was Grandmother kissing her forehead with love and sending her back to the land of the living.

She would not reveal her words and time she walked upon the sacred land of no time; it was for her only. However, her heart was lighter, and she smiled again for the first time since Isaac's death. She now needed to get to work, to find her path and learn how to become a great healer and a Beloved Woman of the Cherokee.

Harriet Tubman, PUBLIC DOMAIN

TWELVE

1861-1863

Indian Territory
West of the Mississippi

hite Hawk felt the after effects of the spirit walk for several days. She remembered Isaac's last touch, which would sustain her until they could be together again. His desire to help his people renewed her mind, she recalled the faces of slaves of the south passing through led by Isaac to a new life and freedom. She felt ashamed that she had languished in her sorrow and let his work be in vain. Each morning as she went to water and greeted the sun for the new day, she would ask for a sign of how she was to continue Isaac's legacy.

One morning as she approached the water there was a large stag with a great rack of antlers drinking. When she drew near, it raised its head and acknowledged her presence, then walked slowly to the pathway the People used to come to water. This was unlike any deer she had ever seen, they usually jump and run quickly away. This one stood firm, its gaze locking eyes with hers. She took this as her sign to walk the path that Isaac trod. She believed she had found her answer.

She read newspapers from the traders about the civil war fighting in the East. She went to tell Mother about the sign and her plans.

"Mother, I must travel to the east and work to help free Isaac's people. I will be gone for a time and ask you to look after Nan. She has lost so much already, but I know that you will keep me in her mind while I am gone for a little while. Will you do this for me?"

"My daughter, you are a special healer and a spiritual leader, you must follow your calling.

Of course, Nan always has a home with me. I will take care of her like I did you."

Mother embraced her while choking back tears. She hugged her daughter, maybe for one of the last times she would see or hold her in this lifetime.

Preparing for her trek toward war White Hawk knew as a woman that she could not make the journey alone. It would be too dangerous. However, she could go disguised as a man.

Taking the hunting knife last used to cut Isaac free from the tree, she combed and braided her shoulder length hair. Sawing it off with the knife she then placed the braid at Isaac's burial site, symbolic of laying down her grief.

From one of father's tanned deer-hides she cut and stitched a pair of pants. Using cotton cloth from an old flour sack died red by using the bloodroot plant, she sewed a loose-fitting shirt with long sleeves to hide her spindly arms. For healing while on the road, she prepared a medicine kit with herbs and packed a special potion to stop her womanly flow if she drank it. To further conceal her identity, she tied a tight band of material around her bosom binding her breasts flat. She then wrapped a piece of leather that once served as a bridle strap loosely around her waist for a belt and hung her knife sheath. The next day, at the trading post she bartered prime fur pelts for a pair of leather boots replacing her moccasins. Donning a floppy felt hat to hide her feminine facial features, she smeared her face with dirt and ash to look like days old whiskers.

Her transformation complete, and she went to test her new identity on Mother.

As she approached the lodge, the old cur dog began barking, alarming those inside of a stranger who was nearby. Unafraid she kept walking toward the door, as the dog bristled the fur on its back, growling and showing his teeth. She knocked on the doorframe. Her mother peaked out and shouted, "What do you want here?"

White Hawk removed her hat and sheepishly smiled, "Mother it is I, White Hawk."

Mother opened the door, grabbed her by the shoulders, dragging her inside and said, "My daughter, I did not know you, what is this?"

"I can't travel as a woman to the war, but I can as a man. What do you think? Will this work to disguise me?"

"Yes, even I did not recognize you."

"I came to see you and Nan before I go. I do not want to leave either of you, but it must be, at least for a season," White Hawk said.

After a short visit, White Hawk next went to Chickawa's lodge to tell her and Benjamin about her journey. They did not recognize her shocking transformation either. They were also worried about her traveling alone and did their best to change her mind about going.

Ben was not like his older brother Isaac; he was softer and had kindness in his eyes. His face had the same shape and similar nose, but he had a stockier build. Ben was not an adventurous spirit like Isaac, and he was against her leaving to go alone.

Trying to persuade her not to go Benjamin enticed her to stay with gossip about Isaac.

"I know who killed Isaac, the rumors have been heavy around the camp. Why don't you continue Isaac's work here? Together we can find and punish those that stole his life."

Ben relayed the story circulating in the camp. Renegade followers of the medicine man supporting the Confederacy, and some slave owners followed Isaac the night he died. Murdering him to send a signal to warn others not to interfere or they would suffer a similar fate. They were angry about Isaac's work on the Underground Railroad helping to free run-aways. White Hawk was not surprised the medicine man was involved. He hated her for a longtime and would stop at nothing to rid her from the camp. He was always putting spells and bad medicine on her.

However, there was no changing White Hawk's desire to go east and help fight in the great war against slavery. Isaac died for the cause, and she was willing to lay down her life too, if necessary.

Benjamin knew it was far too dangerous for her to travel alone and ultimately decided to gowith White Hawk. By doing so, Ben was placing his life in jeopardy and didn't believe either of them would live to return home. He was willing to go because he could not bear the thought of her going alone.

Together they would leave on the next full Flower Moon, when the first plants of the season erupt from the soil and the time of new births occur. The glow of the moonlight would light their path in the dark of night when it was safer for them to travel. They would sleep in the daytime and travel by night. It would take six weeks at a fast pace to reach New York.

Her mission was to find a conductor named 'Moses' whom Isaac had told her stories about. This one named 'Moses' led many to freedom and northern newspapers wrote about the daring escapes. But no one knew this person's real identity and White Hawk didn't know how she would ever find them, but she had to try. White Hawk's destination was Mother AME Zion Church in Auburn, New York. There she believed she might find 'Moses.'

White Hawk spent her few remaining nights at Mother's lodge loving on Nan. The memories at her cabin were too painful for her to stay there, as she saw Isaac's presence everywhere. She explained to Nan about the terrible war between the states in the east and how the fight for freedom from the white man who sought to own other people—like her father and herself. For Isaac's slave blood ran in Nan's veins and she was doing this for her and those like her, for their future. White Hawk promised she would return to her with the help of the Great Spirit.

This journey would be especially dangerous for Benjamin, as a mixed blood for he had no papers to prove he was a Cherokee Freedman. If bounty hunters caught them, he would be taken and sold into slavery or worse. Most owners tied the captured runaways to the whipping post and lashed them almost to death, made to wear heavy neckchains and hand cuffs. Some even suffered severing of their Achilles tendons or limbs so they could not run away again. The master's sometimes even killed the repeat runaways in the most brutal and violent of ways, serving as an example to dissuade those still on the plantation. Slavery was an ugly and brutal business.

White Dove and Ben departed for the coast on a Friday night. They feared the medicine man or Isaac's murderers would post a bounty in the newspaper for Benjamin's capture outside of the territory. This early departure meant the news would not be broadcast until Monday's edition, giving them a three-day head start, and they would be out of the local area. She would follow the route that Isaac drew to connect with the Underground Railroad to the east. He prepared this map for her to share with other conductors passing through the territory while he was away on his missions. She and Ben would make a slight change, instead of turning north into the freedom of Canada, when they reached New York City, they would head the opposite direction south toward Auburn.

Along the route they kept a lookout for quilts hung in windows, on fences or painted on barns which signified safe haven for runaways. The various patterns were a form of communication with the railroad travelers. The names and locations of abolitionist sympathizers made known to conductors so escapees could find refuge on the trails. Different signs signified the type of help available, some meant food, some clothing, or lodging. It was an elaborate secret code used on the road to freedom for escaping slaves. They would make use of these stops to replenish supplies and rest for a few hours or sometimes hide for days to avoid capture by bounty hunters in the area.

In the beginning White Hawk and Ben raced through the woods under the cover of darkness. A full moon shone to help them to navigate the rough terrain. The North Star guided their way at night, and the sun's rising in the east and setting in the west led them by day. When they couldn't find an abolitionist's house, they would sleep in ditches or hollowed out rotten logs at midday to avoid catchers. They carried dried biscuits, jerky, and fried hush puppies to eat on their trek. The 'hush puppies'—fried meal balls and thrown down to distract hound-dogs that might be following their trail, thus deriving the name. The food silencing the bays of the hounds. They carried deer urine harvested by the hunting parties and stored it in the deer bladder. Sprinkling it around their camps and tracks to kill their scent, so the tracking dogs wouldn't be able to pick up and follow.

After weeks of running, they found themselves approaching New York. However, their ordeal was not over, now they must find this person called 'Moses.'

It was easier than envisioned; they went first to the church Isaac had spoken of introducing themselves to the Pastor. He remembered Isaac from a group he led through his church to freedom in the past. After listening to their story about Isaac's murder, he told them he knew this 'Moses' they spoke of and agreed to arrange a meeting. They hid in the basement of the church while waiting for the meeting.

Several days later, one evening when the lights were low in the church, they sat in the back pew enjoying an hour outside the stuffy cellar while finishing a few bites of stale bread and dried jerky. The double entry doors from the street creaked open. The pair feared they were caught and realized they had nowhere to hide, when they noticed it was a petite dark-skinned woman with the Pastor. She had a meek countenance and dressed in a billowy cotton skirt and blouse, with a cloth tied around her head. She bore a scar snaking down one side of her forehead beginning at her hairline and ending at her cheekbone. Her head and neck tilted to one side, cocked as if she was trying to hear a whisper.

White Hawk was confused.

Who was this person, why did he bring her here? Maybe she needs escorted to freedom, and he wants us to take her with us?

The Pastor said, "I want to introduce you to someone…..my friends, this be 'Moses'."

"My free name is Harriet, some call me Minty, and others call me Moses." The woman spoke as she offered her small—yet strong calloused hand to White Hawk.

This introduction changed lives that night. Harriet Tubman, also known as Araminta 'Minty' Ross, would help White Hawk and Ben travel to South Carolina and gain work as spies in a washhouse and Confederate hospital. They carried counterfeit free papers made for Minty Ross and White Hawk—identified as Billy Bird with ownership papers of one Negro male known as Benjamin. With these documents, they would travel down to South Carolina during the war. Gathering information to aid the northern troops and secret it out to the Union encampment only a few miles away. They would also travel deeper into slave territory with 'Moses' to lead people to freedom in the North and up into Canada. Their lives were in constant danger.

In the spring of 1862 Ulysses S. Grant's Union army fought and won at Shiloh in southwestern Tennessee, one of the costliest and bloodiest battles of the entire war resulting in nearly 24,000 casualties. By fall, the Union had fought and won the Battle of Fort Henry and taken Fort Donelson on the Tennessee/Kentucky border opening the Cumberland River to the North for supplies.

One night in the sweltering summer of 1863 in the South Carolina Low country Harriet took them on the Combahee River Raid where she piloted the lead boat on the marshes and river, which she knew so well. There were 150 African American Union soldiers in six boats that night, commanded by Colonel James Montgomery. The lead boat guided by Harriet with Ben and White Hawk in another one beside her. Harriet's eyes and knowledge of the river helped them avoid the Confederate mines, tree stumps, and sandbars that would sink vessels and result in them all rotting in Confederate prisons or worse, hung as traitors and spies.

The word had spread throughout the area for slave families to be at the riverbank that night to find freedom. The people waiting on the banks got scared, as they found themselves caught in the crossfire between angry plantation owners behind them and Union soldiers ready to rescue them in the water. They started to turn and run back to their plantations, which could mean certain death; Harriett began singing in her deep soulful voice.

*"Swing low, sweet chariot, coming for to carry me home. Swing low, sweet chariot coming for to carry me home. I looked over Jordan and what did I see, coming for to carry me home. A band of angels coming after me, coming for to carry me home."**

The crowd calmed down, began singing along with her, wading into the water, and clambering aboard the boats. Over 700 enslaved people gained their freedom with 'Moses' that night, still few would know it was a young woman called Harriet along with her friends White Hawk and Ben that would help carry them home to freedom.

In 1863, the Union marched on with the South falling in Gettysburg, Pennsylvania, and Vicksburg, Mississippi, taking over Port Hudson and giving the North complete control over the Mississippi River forcing the Confederates out of the North. By June, the Chattanooga Campaign in Tennessee commenced as the South attacked the North at Chickamauga Creek. Finally, Grant

---

* Swing Low Sweet Chariot, Words: Public Domain

pushed the South out, taking control of the Confederate rail center.

After many months working with Harriet, White Hawk and Ben returned home to the Cherokee Nation to rest and to see their families. However, the war between the states raged on, battles fought, and soldiers continued to die. They had seen first-hand the atrocities of war, and it changed them. They had seen enough fighting and watching young boys from both sides die to last their lifetime. This was a white man's battle, and they wanted no part in the fighting, but they were still committed to fight against people owning other people and helping lead runaways to freedom. They assured Harriet after a brief visit home; they would return to help her fight for freedom for their people with renewed strength.

THIRTEEN

1863

Indian Territory
West of the Mississippi

White Hawk and Ben's return home from the war and back to the territory coincided with the Green Corn dance held in late July—August. This annual dance celebrates the first corn crop harvest, the white traders called it 'busk.' The ceremony represents new beginnings, and the people sacrifice the first green corn to ensure the rest of the crop will be abundant for the village. It is a celebration of thanksgiving to The Breath Maker for the first fruits of the harvest and a New Year festival.

For several days prior to the busk drink ceremony, the medicine man each morning goes to the top of the council house in the center of the village and makes a howling, yelling and harrowing sound to frighten away evil spirits. The seven-day ceremony begins on the first day with a great fire in the center of the dancing stomp grounds. The fire summons the "Lady of the Fire," which represents the Earth Mother. She resides with the Great Father and the Child God in the spirit world. The ceremonies consist of dancing, a feast on last year's crop, fasting by the men, and a social stomp dance.

Day two of the ceremony was the busiest time for White Hawk and her family. In addition to taking part in the ladies' dance, their clan is responsible for gathering and preparing the special ingredients to concoct the "White Drink" used in the purification ceremony. The white man called this the 'Black Drink,' or 'Carolina Tea,' it is dark and frothy when shaken before drinking.

The jug holding the drink was handmade by using the red clay near the river. Holding roughly 20 gallons and set on the fire as several gourds of river water poured into the pot to steep the ingredients. When the water reaches boiling, Mother opens her deerskin pouch containing various roots, herbs, and fine salt. A portion of the salt thrown onto the 'head-man's seat, and the rest into the clay pot. She then takes the wing of a swan, and waves it over the pot while offering a prayer to the Creator while in a trance-like state. Next, she breaks sprigs from a bush of laurel and sassafras and places them into the pot with the Dahoon Holly berries along with 14 different secret ingredients. After the brew is ready many of the men drink so much it causes them to throw-up, which they believe is cleansing physically and morally preparing them for the new year. The ceremony and dancing continue for up to eight days.

White Hawk felt the connection to Earth Mother so strongly during this weeklong ceremony.Especially today when she visited the corn field with her basket to harvest some tender ears. Her hands glided along the lush green leaves giving thanks to Selu, as she walked the lumpy ground up and down the rows selecting the perfect ones. She looked for those with the silk turning brown, filled out and round with many kernels. The crop was bountiful, and the corn stalks were tall and waving over her head.

Suddenly, in front of her the medicine man jumped into the row and began shouting menacing words at her. He wore a booger mask, carved out of red clay, and painted with plant dyes, representing evil spirits and their enemies. He was a frightening sight, as he drew closer raising his war stick over his head as if to strike her down. She dropped the basket, turned, and ran back to her lodge, shaking with fear. Mother returned to the field to retrieve the basket and the corn, and he was gone. She comforted White Dove and gave her a talisman to wear to ward off the evil spirits and thoughts that plagued her. She felt better with the talisman around her neck and began to rub it between her fingers and thumb when she got nervous or afraid.

Mother also took her to the priest and asked him to call upon Great Thunder and his sons, the two Thunder Boys. Asking for their blessing upon her daughter vexed by the medicine man. These beings live in the land west above the sky vault.

The priest prepared a pipe of the four sacred medicines— tobacco, sage, cedar, and sweet grass and blew the smoke onto White Dove. He then took two deer antlers and waved them in front of her, and while chanting, banged them together with clashing sounds numerous times to ward off evil spirits.

Later at the ceremony, as she danced around the fire, she could feel the vibrations of the drums and chanting rising from her feet to her core. The Cherokee way is to love and respect all things, the earth, fire, land, wind, and people. All her senses heightened as the drum beat to the rhythm. She danced with a happy heart and prayed that Selu the Corn Goddess, who planted her heart, and the corn sprouted from it, so the People would not go hungry, would bless them in the upcoming year.

As she danced, she prayed to the Great Father Spirit that war would end, and freedom would come to all people. She also prayed for the freedmen to find safety in the Cherokee Nation and for peace. A few months before in January, President Lincoln signed the emancipation proclamation, freeing all slaves. Shortly afterward, the Cherokee Nation also adopted a second emancipation act that freed any person or persons held in slavery and declared them forever free. They became 'Freedmen.' However, the Cherokee Nation did not automatically grant citizenship to them.

Ben watched White Hawk dancing in the light of the campfire on the humid summer night closing her eyes and tilting her chin upward toward the sky. This is what he imagined she would look like as he made love to her, which he fantasized of often. She was beautiful to gaze upon. Her face glistened with beads of perspiration as she moved. Her hair stuck to her neck, which had partially grown back into a curly shag. Her clothes hugged her figure with her breast jiggling as she moved in the circle around the fire, her silhouette lit by the full moon. He had fallen in love with his brother's woman, and he prayed she would grow to love him in return.

He imagined them together in one another's arms sharing their love. He wanted to hold her close and profess his love to her in soft whispers. He fell more deeply in love with her each second, yearning for her, but could not tell her or anyone about these feelings. She was still his brother's mate, until she decided it was no more, and her grieving period ended. There was no set time, it was up to her when the grief period would cease, and she would take another for a partner. She mourned for Isaac and spoke of him constantly to Ben. Ben knew he could only love her from afar, no one must know his true feelings, until she was ready to love again, and there was no guarantee she would choose him to love in return.

After dancing while sitting on a log around the fire, in the dim lighting, she glanced over toward Ben. For a moment she thought it was Isaac she looked upon. She didn't realize how much the two brothers were alike until now. They sat in the same posture —leaning slightly to the right. Their hair was the same wiry texture, and

Ben's profile in the campfire strongly resembled Isaac.

She knew Ben cared deeply for her and she wondered if there could be anything more between them. How her heart ached for Isaac, but lately it raced when she was near Ben, she couldn't control it. She felt something in the pit of her stomach when Ben was around her, and she found reasons to try to find herself closer to him.

After her breath slowed from the exertion of the first dance, White Hawk joined the other women circling to the rhythm around the fire again. It became time for the men to enter the circle, and Ben timed it so that when he did, he would be dancing next to White Hawk. She felt a strange welling up in her chest and her heart pounded. She had not felt that sensation stir since Isaac's last touch before his death. She tried to push it back down, but she flushed even more. She hoped he could not see the color in her face and turned away from the light of the fire. She had butterflies in her stomach, her breath quickened, she had goose flesh, and the hair stood up on the nape of her neck. She hoped Ben didn't notice, and she tried to focus on her dance movements not her physical reaction to his nearness.

When the dancing had finished for the evening, Ben walked White Hawk back to her mother's lodge. It was awkward for both, as if they just became aware of each other physically. She was aloof on the outside but trembling and shaking on the inside. Ben wanted to take her in his arms and profess his love to her, but he knew he couldn't…..not yet. She had to make the first move.

Mother was smoking the pipe and offering thanks to the four winds as White Hawk entered the lodge. There was a smoky herbal flavor in the thick air. There were no windows in the round lodge, only a fireplace vent at the top of the structure. So, the smoke hung deep and thick in the hot night air, as the thunder sounded bringing with it the sweet cleansing smell of summer rain.

"Sit with me my child and give an offering on this special day. The Thunder Spirits have heard our plea and bless us with rain this night, and Selu has blessed us with a bountiful corn crop," she said.

White Hawk sat across from her, and took the pipe in her hands, lifting it to the four directions and thanking the Great Spirit before she puffed the smoke to each of the four points. She inhaled deeply and tried to decipher what herbs were in the pipe, she couldn't name them. Mother still harbored some secrets from her.

"My child you seem troubled, and you look flushed. Do you have peace in your heart, are you sick? What bothers you on this special day?"

"No, Mother, I'm not sick. I am heartbroken from all the sadness in my life and the hurt I have seen. I need to move on from the grief I carry for Isaac. But I don't know how to find this place of peace, or how to lay this burden down. Can you help me, is there an herb or concoction you have for my distress?"

Mother reached into the medicinal pouch on her waist and took a pinch of a finely ground yellow powder, placed it on her palm, and quickly blew it into White Hawk's face. Causing her to sharply inhale automatically and cough. Before she could even get any words to come out, she started feeling woozy.

She started to speak, "Mother….," then she was unconscious. The spirit entered her and took control of her mind.

When she awoke, she was standing on the chimney rock with the arid plains before her. This was the same spot where she saw Isaac morph from the black stag. Her heart leapt as she hoped she might see him again. She recognized the great white hawk circling overhead and heard its piercing cry. Her spirit guide the paint stallion appeared on the cliff near her and reared upward, then began racing toward her. She was on his back before she knew what was happening. Her arms outstretched with palms open, and she was one with the universe. She knew all before and all to come as pure love and filled with light. She then saw the black stag in the distance, as it drew closer it became the semblance of Isaac, and she was off the horse standing face-to-face with him. Enveloping him were bright white points of light bouncing off his human form, almost blinding her. They placed their palms together and once again knew each other's minds with no words spoken between them.

He said, "I am a spirit that resides with the Great One, and am no longer one with you, my love. My spirit lives in the land unbound by time or place, or physical body. There is a great chasm between us, and you can't join with me yet. You must not mourn for me anymore. Live and love in the physical world where you reside until you travel here to be with me and the Great One for eternity. I will be here waiting to greet you when your time comes. Now return to the land of our people, teach them of the ancient ways, and become the beloved woman and great healer that you are destined to be."

Their lips briefly touched and then he was gone in an instant.

When she awoke in the lodge later with Mother, she felt strangely comforted. Her heart didn't ache deep inside like it had since Isaac died. She sensed a renewed hope that good things would come to their people, and the war would soon be over with peace in the land. She had joy in her heart and soul. She could hardly wait to tell Ben about seeing Isaac in her vision.

"Mother, I must go find Ben, I have something to tell him."

Mother chuckled softly, "Of course, my child, I understand."

She didn't have to go far to find Ben. He was still sitting on the log around the fire in the center of the stomp grounds staring into the remnants of ashes and dying coals deep in thought. He looked like he had lost his best friend, appearing very dejected.

"Ben, there you are. You will never guess what just happened to me," she said.

She didn't wait for him to answer. "Mother just sent me into a vision to see Isaac. I saw him before me, I touched him. He told me to end my mourning for him and to live my life in the present. For the first time since he died, I have peace in my heart. The pain is gone."

She continued, "Guess who the first person I wanted to tell this news to?" She paused, "It was you."

She then continued rapidly before she lost her courage, "I have a special feeling in my heart for you. Do you think you could ever love me like Isaac did?"

"No," he said, and she felt foolish. Her face showed her surprise, and she was embarrassed that she had shared her heart with him.

The he continued by taking her hand in his, "I would love you better than he did, if that is possible."

She fell into his arms, and he kissed her for the first time, he was timid at first then his tongue explored her mouth and found hers. Kissing her was better than he ever imagined. She returned his kisses while his hands explored her body. They made love that night and joined their souls together for the rest of their life on this earth, from that time forward all they had were eyes and hearts for each other. Ben would join her clan and live together, but first she must get approval from the elder clan mothers. The mothers were thrilled at their joining, and they became a family again for Nan.

As for the war, White Hawk and Ben had promised Harriet they would return to help her, and they would keep their word. However, they would not return until after the Snow Moon had passed, the 'Snow Man' brings the snow and cold to cover the high places while the earth rests. Once the winter, ice, and snowstorms had passed, they would bind their souls together as one in a joining ceremony. This would happen when the thaw came in the early spring brought by the Windy Moon. Once the new fires were lit in the hearths by the fire-keeper, the trees sprouted buds, and the birds returned to nest, they would leave for the east to find Harriet.

When they departed, they would not say goodbye to their family, as that is not the Cherokee way. They would say until we see you again—never goodbye. Since her latest vision of Isaac, she now fully understood that custom, after death she would see them all again, just as she had seen Isaac in the spirit world. She knew he was waiting for her there, but she still had work to do in the physical world. While she waited to join him, she found love again this side of eternity in Ben's arms and together they would work for the good of their people: the Cherokee and those still suffering the bonds of slavery in the South.

FOURTEEN

Current Day

After the AA meeting, Annie felt a little better, but was still upset and teary eyed. Her shock and sadness were growing into anger toward the man she once believed to be the love of her life. She felt abandoned, as if he had thrown her away.

Who was the homewrecker he cheated with?

She fished the napkin with Tom's mistress address from her purse. She sat down at the computer, typing it into the search bar but it returned no results.

How can I find out who lives at this address, think Annie think.

Then it dawned on her, the property tax rolls. She pulled up the county tax records website, plugging the address into the search bar, holding her breath as she hit enter. She was unprepared for the name that popped up as the owner of the property, Dr. Judith Green.

Are you freaking kidding?

The same doctor that patched her up in the emergency room and tended to her in the ICU was the other woman in their marriage. The doctor she had shared lunch with many times at the hospital cafeteria. Her peer was sleeping with her husband. She felt sick as nausea swept over her. Her hands shook.

When did this betrayal begin? Had this affair been going on before the wreck or was the accident the catalyst for bringing them together?

Her mind reeled with unanswerable questions. She sat there stunned, her mind swirling with unwelcome thoughts of the two of them together. She began crying again.

What would she do with this newfound information? Should she confront the other woman or let it go. Tom had made his choice. Should she let him go or fight for her marriage?

The only decision she could bring herself to make was to call her AA sponsor Ray and ask him to meet her. She needed a friend, someone to talk to and out of binge drinking. The bottle was beaconing her and she wanted a drink—no, she needed a drink, lots of them.

She and Ray met at the usual coffee shop to talk. She unloaded all the baggage that was her life onto him, and he listened with a sympathetic ear but didn't offer any solutions. She knew he had been down this path with others before her. He didn't have a savior complex, and firmly established boundaries. He was there to listen, but these were her problems to solve, not his.

As they sat in the booth of the dimly lit space with red-checkered plastic tablecloths and tired servers, Ray asked, "Annie, why do you drink? Because it tastes good, is not the right answer. It can't be because your husband left you, you were a drunk before you discovered his infidelity."

"I'm not sure, haven't really thought of the reason, been too busy hiding my drinking while trying to keep all the balls in the air, just juggling life."

"Have you ever thought about therapy, finding someone that can help you get to the bottom of this? Answer the question as to why you need to drink?" Ray said.

"Not really, I'm the doctor, the one that treats and cures others."

"You could find out why, you should consider it. I did and it was the best thing I've ever done for myself in my life. It saved me, it could save you too. I think you're worth saving." Ray said as he reached over the table and patted her hands.

She pulled away and wrapped both hands around the coffee cup looking into the dark liquid as if it would reveal something to her in a vision. His words were balm to her wounded soul. He never took his eyes off her, but she didn't want to look back, until the silence became awkward between them.

"I'll consider taking your advice, but I make no promises," she said.

In her mind she heard her mother say, *'don't do that, you're fine. It will label you an alcoholic with mental problems and destroy your career.'*

"Do you feel any better than when you called me this morning? Think you can hang on to your sobriety for one more day?"

Not waiting for an answer he continued, "You know the walk we take is just getting by for one day at a time. I'm still a drunk just taking it day-by-day."

"Surprisingly, I do feel better. I'm still heartbroken over my marriage, but I think I can do this for one more day. I need to get home now. I must find a good divorce lawyer and look for a shrink," she said.

"I don't want to unload on you all at once, and I know you're still new to this, but you also need to start working the 12-Steps if you want to get better.

The first step is to admit you are powerless over this—admit you are an alcoholic, which I've noticed you haven't done yet in meetings." Ray said.

"Yes, I know, but I'm not sure I am one. Maybe I just had a lapse in good judgement. You know what I mean?"

"Annie don't try to con me. I've been around drunks for far too long to buy that. Just get with the program, that's all I'm saying. It works, and it'll work for you if you work it."

He stood up taking the check to pay the tab, as she collected her things.

"This is on me; you pay next time." He hugged her sideways and said, "Take care of yourself Annie, don't blow your chance to save your life."

She thought about Ray's words all the way home, and pulling into the driveway, she noticed Tom's junk was gone. He must have stopped by, collected what he wanted, and trashed the rest. That job was done, and she felt some relief along with deep sadness. Another layer peeled away, leaving her raw and more exposed. She went into the empty house and tried to follow Ray's advice.

While googling therapist, she found one that looked promising, Dr. Carol Beech. Dr. Beech had all the necessary credentials, her office was relatively nearby, and she had a nice face in her on-line profile. She looked like she was in her mid-forties, with short curly graying hair and kind eyes. Annie made an appointment for the next day.

Finding a divorce attorney took a little more time; there were too many results to choose from when she entered the search parameters 'near me.'

She finally gave up and called Miranda, "I'm stuck, and I need the name of a lawyer for this divorce."

Miranda assured her it was a straightforward process; just pick one from the internet. Annie called the first one that came up on the search bar and set a meeting for the end of the week. She would need a few days to pull all their financial documents together for the initial consultation, but he assured her an uncontested divorce, no children, and an equitable settlement with both parties in agreement would have her divorce finalized in 60 days.

She hung up the phone from the lawyer and began crying again. After all their years as a couple and the shared dreams of growing old together, life as she knew it would be over in as little as 60 days. Her heart ached, but she didn't drink and that was good.

The next day filled with dread as she walked into Dr. Beech's office, unsure she should be here and damn sure she was not going to like it. She sat down in the waiting room listening to calming flute music playing on the speakers strategically hidden around the room. She was just about to turn and run when the inner door opened and a young female patient walked out, obviously upset. The woman dabbed her red-ringed eyes with a tissue and swiped her nose. The older woman behind her, Annie recognized from the website as Dr. Beech, placed her hands on the girl's shoulders and turned her around embracing her with a bear hug.

Before releasing her, she said, "Hear me, it's not your fault. You did great today, just work on what we talked about, and I'll see you at the same time in two weeks. If you need me beforehand, just call my answering service and they can get a hold of me. OK?"

The woman shook her head yes, turned and left with her head down, clearly broken.

"Hi, you must be Annie, I'm Carol Beech. You can call me Carol." She said in a warm voice as she extended her hand and smiled. She did have kind eyes just like her picture and pretty teeth.

"Yes, I'm Annie." She placed her hand in Carol's, it was inviting, and she led her inside.

The room was small, just a chair and end table on one side of the room facing the only window in the space. The table held a small lamp and a diffuser blowing a scent into the air. A two-person loveseat sat on the other side of the room facing the lone chair only a few feet away. A speaker played the same flute music in this room as well, the volume was low but soothing. The diffuser misted a sweet-smelling natural fragrance into the room.

She could make out the smell of cinnamon, but the other fragrance was unknown to her. It was pleasant and calming. The lighting was dim and closed mini blinds shielded the windows from the world outside. It felt peaceful and it enveloped her like a womb.

Annie was not sure which seat to take, she decided on the loveseat due to proximity of the box of tissues sitting on the floor next to it. She plucked one from the box before she started to speak. She also didn't know where to begin her story, or how much she should reveal in the first session—maybe the only session. Depending on how things went today.

Carol opened the conversation; she had a way about her that made Annie feel she was the priority in that room, and it was a safe place to be. Her deepest and darkest secrets could come out in the light of day in this room, would go no further and without placing blame, Carol assured her.

"What brings you here today?" Carol asked.

"Well, my life is in the toilet right now. My friend Miranda, we met in PT rehab, suggested it might be beneficial to talk to someone for help, so here I am." She answered purposely incomplete, holding back more details.

"Ok, what do you want to talk about? Tell me as much or as little as you want to today—what we discuss in this room is confidential. But before we started, where were you in rehab? I'd like to get a copy of those records for my files, because of the traumatic brain injury diagnosis you noted on your intake form." Carol said.

"Sure, I'll leave all that with the front desk on my way out."

Carol sat very still, patiently waiting for Annie to speak first, afraid she might scare a timid bird into flying away if she moved. She was comfortable with the silence and waited for Annie to speak.

"People think I may be an alcoholic. I've been abstaining for eight weeks, six of which I spent in the hospital and rehab facility, the result of a car wreck due to dangerous weather. I admit it, I did test over the limit and the time in rehab probably shouldn't count as sober. The only good thing is in rehab I met my only friend Miranda.

When I got home, I found out my husband gambled away all our savings and is having an affair with a colleague of mine. He's asked for a divorce. Oh, and I lost my job due to the DUI and the wreck."

She paused then said, "Are you sure you want to deal with this mess? I wouldn't blame you if the answer were no."

"I've seen worse, I'm up to it if you are and it sounds like we have a lot to unravel. First, are you in an AA group or under a doctor's care and taking medication to help you stay sober?" Carol asked matter-of-factly.

"Yes AA, that's what ultimately led me to you. My sponsor, Ray, asked me why I drank, and I didn't have a satisfactory answer for him. I thought maybe you could help me figure that out if there is one."

"Ok, absolutely we can find out together. But I do have one rule, you must remain sober as long as I am your therapist. I need you to affirm that you will before we continue." Carol said.

"I will do my best you have my word." Annie said.

"I guess I'll take that as a yes. All right then, why don't we start? Annie, you already have all the answers inside of you. We just need to coax them out into the bright light of day where they are not so scary anymore and you can deal with them as sober adults. So why don't you start at the beginning and tell me about your childhood? Where you are from, and tell me about your family," she said.

"I wish I knew."

Annie focused on the tissue in her hands and began shredding it into small pieces as she spoke. Annie told Carol the revelation of finding adoption paperwork hidden in the family bible when she was a child. Her right hand released the tissue to start picking at the fabric's nub on the loveseat.

She explained that no one sat her down one day and told her how special she was and why they chose her. Instead, her mother was furious when she stumbled upon the records and asked about it, flatly refusing to talk with her. Her father would not go against her mother and tell her anything. Nevertheless, she was without answers and today still didn't know who she really was and felt her whole life was a lie.

Her parents had no siblings so there were no other relatives to help her piece together the puzzle of her life. It was a deep family secret that she bore alone, she felt like a fraud from the day she learned this news.

Lost, alone and afraid, she still felt that way. The only person that ever chose her was Tom and she thought he'd always be there for her. That's why his cheating and abandonment cut her to the core. It was more than just a marriage between them, he was her only family. Someone she thought loved her unconditionally. His leaving reinforced the belief that she was expendable, just as her birth mother threw her away. It was almost more than she could bear, her mouth was dry, and she craved alcohol to wet it. She paused her story and sobbed.

"Annie, hear me, you are worthy of love. Tom left you long ago you just didn't notice because you were numbing it with your drinking. About your adoption, from my experience most birth mothers struggle with giving up their child but do it because they love the child so much. She was willing to suffer the loss of her flesh and blood so you could have a better life than what she thought she could give you. Who knows your birth mother's story, but I can guarantee you she believed she was doing the best thing for you—not throwing you away. Have you ever thought of trying to find her and get the facts straight from her?"

"I used to dream of finding her all the time when I was younger, but Mother was so against it."

She heard the voice in her head, *'Don't do it Annie, don't. Opening a can of worms.'*

"So, I just dropped it and pushed the feelings deep down inside. Still, I sometimes imagine her, and wonder if I look like her? Sometimes in dreams she comes to visit, she is tall and thin with straight black hair, olive skin, and brown eyes. My adoptive mother was a blue-eyed blonde; we were nothing alike, in looks or temperament."

Annie looked up with blurry vision as her eyes filled with tears and Carol making notes on her yellow pad.

"Well, there's no one stopping you from searching now. Is there? You don't need anyone's permission but your own. You're not a little girl anymore, you are an adult, you don't need Mother's approval," Carol said.

"I guess I could, do you think it would help with my drinking?"

"Everyone should know their story, I believe you need to find closure on this part of your past. You may not like everything you find, but knowing is better than not knowing. Just like exposing the truth in the cold light of day is better than buried secrets, which tend to grow in the dark. I think it may help you with your feelings of abandonment and self-worth."

The phone alarm dinged to signify their time was up, and Carol closed her yellow pad.

"Well, that's about all the time we have for today. Shall we pick this up again in a week and dig a little deeper?" Carol asked.

Annie left the office lighter than when she arrived and with more insight as to why Tom's betrayal hurt her so. Before Carol's visit, she believed that he left her, not their dysfunctional marriage. She now realized the marriage had been on life support for months, maybe even years. They lived separate lives and only came together out of habit before the accident. She should not have been surprised that he strayed. She really couldn't blame him, maybe they should have split up long ago.

She would come back to see Carol again. Maybe Ray was right about therapy, and all the other bits of wisdom he shared.

The next day she attended an AA meeting, and it was her turn to speak to the group. As she nervously approached the podium, she was rubbing the 30-day chip in her pocket between her finger and thumb. This was her first time sharing her story with them. Ray was in the audience, and she caught a wink from him as she cleared her throat to begin.

Looking around the room at all the faces tuned into hers was quite intimidating, so it was nice to see his kind face. Her mouth dry, she licked her lips wishing she had a bottle of water, or vodka.

Summoning her courage she said. "Hi, I'm Annie, and I….um, I'm an alcoholic," speaking louder than she meant to do.

Everyone responded in unison, "Hi Annie."

She felt a weight lift from her shoulders with those few words. It wasn't so bad after all. She did it, Step 1: admit she was powerless over alcohol— that her life had become unmanageable.

Ray was right, she looked at him, and he was smiling and shaking his head up and down, mouthing the words, "good job kiddo."

She continued with her story of a failed life to the audience of other failed lives and in some cases failed livers. As she scanned the faces, she could tell some of the people in that room were long-time alcohol abusers and their bodies reflected it. A few showed outward signs of jaundice, displaying yellow skin or a golden hue in the whites of their bloodshot eyeballs. Further proof to her, she needed to clean up her act. She knew the results of alcoholism on the body and cirrhosis with liver failure were not a good way to die. She believed she may be early in the disease process, her only symptoms were a puffy face and slightly enlarged abdomen, but she thought her liver still functioned normally. She'd get some blood tests run to be sure it wasn't too late for her.

U.S. National Archives, Camp Scene, Series: Mathew Brady, Photographs of the Civil War-Era, Record Group 111, ca. 1860-1865 PUBLIC DOMAIN

U.S. National Archives, Amputation being performed in a hospital tent, Gettysburg, July 1863. Series: Mathew Brady, Photographs of the Civil War-Era, Record Group 111, Archives Identifier: 520203, ID 79-T-2265. PUBLIC DOMAIN

FIFTEEN

Summer 1864-Spring 1865

Indian Territory
West of the Mississippi

After the Green Corn Ceremony, Ben and White Hawk were joined as one. She regained her joy for life and found happiness again. They made plans to return to the east and to the war in the month of the Ripe Corn Moon when the crops ripened and were harvested in the fall. Traveling through the Midwest Forest to North Carolina in the summer months was hot and dangerous. Waiting until the weather turned cooler meant the mosquitoes, which carried fevers would be in their diapause state. The rattlesnakes and copperheads also entered a dormant period, going underground. Even so, it was still a brutal trip.

But they had given their word to Harriet to return and help her in the fight against the Confederate Army. Their marriage would make the work there difficult because they could not be together since there were laws against interracial marriages. She was light skinned passing as white and would work in the Confederate hospital as a nurse. Ben would pose as her Negro slave, tending to livestock for the camp and sleeping in the barn. Harriet was a laborer in the washhouse. All of them would work with their eyes and ears open to gather any information helpful to the North and deliver it weekly to the Union camp nearby.

Those spying were very clever; they would hide notes in the shoe soles of the slaves heading north to replenish supplies for the soldiers. Sometimes they would hollow out turnips and hide the notes inside. They used any and every tactic they could to aid getting messages to the North while evading capture.

White Hawk was unprepared for the deluge of mangled young boys and men after the battles of war flooding into the makeshift hospital. It was almost too much to bear, especially at night when she tried to sleep through the moans and screams of the injured. For a field hospital the conditions were unsanitary and little to no pain medication. Forcing her to forage the local surroundings for herbs and plants to brew or make poultices to relieve pain and try to save limbs and lives. She did not hide her native medicine. There was so much pain and devastation there was no room for bigotry in her patients. The wounded cried and begged for her help, they wanted her medicine.

One day after a brutal battle a young boy of twelve or thirteen was carried into the camp, his left leg mangled by a cannon ball. The lower half barely attached by a few ligaments and skin. He was only a child, conscious and screaming in agony. He had already lost a lot of blood, and his lips and fingertips were bluish gray. While tying a tourniquet around what remained of his leg to staunch the bleeding, White Hawk tried to sooth his fears and cleanse the wound. The doctor came over with a handsaw and immediately began sawing above the knee at the jagged bones sticking out from the stump. The boy screamed even louder.

White Hawk pushed the doctor away from the boy, "Stop, I need to give him something to knock him out before you do that."

"We don't have anything to give him, just hold him down and I'll work as fast as I can," the bloody doctor answered.

White Hawk refused and wouldn't let him continue until she gave the boy her special sleep tonic. He quickly became unconscious, and the doctor proceeded to amputate his leg.

She knew she was helping the Confederate soldiers, but she could not permit the suffering and pain of any living creature. She continued to work with the wounded, while secretly sending messages to the North as did Ben. She could see the devastation the North was having upon the South, wanted the pain and suffering to stop. She wanted the people to be free, but also wanted the war and the killing to end.

After a particularly bloody battle and dealing with the casualties, a commotion erupted by the barns, where Ben was working. There was much yelling and crowds gathering around, she knew there was trouble. Dropping what she was doing she ran to see.

Just as she feared, it was Ben. His hands tied behind his back and his shirt ripped, hanging off him. The whipping he endured left red and bleeding welts on his back. She walked unafraid to the man sitting on the horse, the whip still in his hand.

"What's going on here? Why do you whip him, without my permission, he belongs to me. That's my property you're assaulting."

The man responded as he held the note found on Ben, "this dirty devil is a spy, I caught him with this message. He can read and write and was smuggling this out of the camp. He's a spy and we're gonna' hang him for it."

"You will do no such thing; this is my property, and I forbid you to touch him. What do you say for yourself Ben? Who gave you this note?" She asked him to answer and point the blame on someone else.

Ben said in his best southern drawl, "Missus, I pick it up offn' the ground…I was gonna' patch the hole in my shoe with it."

"There you see, a simple explanation. I will have my property returned to me at once."

"Ma'am, I'm afraid I can't do that. Regulations say if we catch a spy, they need to go to jail, and when the captain comes back, we have a trial. Then we hang 'em. So, this spy is going to jail."

She looked at Ben, he was stoic, and he did not beg. He held his head high as a proud Cherokee and began walking toward the prison cell at the end of a soldier's bayonet. That didn't stop the Corporal from slamming him in the back of the head with the butt of his gun. He almost went down but caught himself and staggered on. The men in gray mocked and called him derogatory names as they led him to the hotbox.

The jail was not really a jail, but a small shed big enough for a man to stoop over while inside. When the door opened, Ben smelled the stench of death and feces. Flies swarmed out into the daylight. Someone recently died in this place and Ben's heart pounded with fear as the soldiers threw him through the open door into the blackness.

The rusty tin of the shed roof drew the hot sundown onto the box. The temperatures in South Carolina were sweltering and the box was like an oven by noon. He didn't think he'd survive the lockup. After they put him inside and went on their way, Ben took the sweat rag wrapped around his neck and put it over his nose and mouth to filter the putrid air, but it was of little help. He found a small crack in the door, and was able to close one eye peeking out, he saw no guard. He placed his lips around the hole and sucked in fresh hot air. It gave some relief from the smell but not much. He pushed with his shoulder against the locked door. It wouldn't budge, Ben was caged like an animal in a trap waiting to die.

White Hawk held her tears back and lifted her hand to her face to hide her trembling chin. What could she do to help Ben, how would she get him out of this mess? She couldn't stand losing another love like she had lost Isaac. She had to see Harriet; maybe she had an idea of how they could get Ben and themselves to safety.

She found Harriet boiling sheets in large round kettles over a hot fire. Her strong arms using a boat oar to push the laundry around the steaming pots. Once they had boiled and were as clean as they would become, she lifted them out of the pot with the paddle. Draping them on a crude clothesline to cool and drip until she could touch them with her bare hands to wring the water out. She then moved them to lay across bushes to dry in the sunshine. Then she would start the next kettle of boiling linens. The blood and dysentery at the field hospital made this nasty and never-ending work.

"Harriet, I don't know what to do, they have taken Ben as a spy. They found him with a note they claim he was smuggling to the Union. When the Captain comes back, they're going to hang him."

"Oh, my word, child. I was 'fraid that was happening to one of you'ins. Don't fret, we gonna' dunfigure somethin out. Let me think on it a spell. Now you go on back to the hospital tent and try to acts natural. We gonna get him outta this. Mark my word, we gonna do it."

White Hawk did her best to push the fear down inside and not show her concern. She wasn't quite sure how she should act, so she tried to pretend everything was going to be ok. She told anyone who would listen that Ben couldn't read or write; the note could not possibly be his. Hoping the word would get back to the accusers and it would gain Ben's freedom. It was a long shot, but it was all she could think of doing to help him.

The captain was due back from the field office in three days. That didn't leave them much time to find a solution to the problem. One option was to do nothing, and wait to plead their case with the captain, hoping for leniency. But she feared they would find him guilty and hang him on the spot. That left the only viable option, they must help Ben escape before the captain returned, and she would go with him. She began to prepare for their trip.

White Hawk rolled what little clothing they could take with them to fit on the back of the saddle in their night roll. She would change back into her disguise as a man before they escaped. She packed the saddle bags with dried jerky, biscuits, and a skin of fresh water. That is all they had room to carry. It would have to do until they could safely forage and hunt, or they would go without. If they had water, they could survive for several weeks without food. Now all she needed to do was to free Ben from the hotbox.

As the sun set White Hawk ran to find Harriet and tell her about the plan. She didn't know how to help Ben. But she had to try something—anything, she couldn't bear to lose another loved one. Harriet knew what was going to happen. Ben was as good as dead in her opinion, but she needed to give White Hawk hope.

"Child, we wait 'til the cover of night, then we can go check out the box and see what we can do. They won't put a guard on him, for no one has ever 'scaped from the box." Harriet knew there was little hope for Ben, but she would try to help those that helped her.

When the night came and the camp dark and settled for hours, Harriet and White Hawk snuck out of their tents and slithered low to the ground toward the hotbox. After scouting outside the shed to find weaknesses they might penetrate to gain his freedom. White Hawk tapped on the backside of the building, while careful not to arouse anyone but Ben. He was still awake, the cool night air made the box livable for a while, and he could breathe the stale air.

"Ben, it's me…..are you ok?" White Hawk asked.

"My love, you mustn't risk being here, go back to your tent before you are discovered."

"I brought you some water, there's a hole in the top of the shed, I can shimmy up there and drip some into your mouth. Look toward the sky."

Harriet got down on all fours and White Hawk stood on her back to climb onto the roof of the small shed. The structure shook with her body weight, it was rickety and not very well built. The top was rusty, and it scratched her hands and knees as she shimmied toward the largest hole in the ceiling. Once there, she took a skin filled with water and dribbled some into Ben's mouth. He received it like a baby bird taking food from its mother. He was so parched, his lips chapped, and his tongue swollen, the water was sweet like manna from heaven to him.

This might keep him alive for another day.

While she was on top of the shed, she looked for any place she might breach the roof and set him free. She put her mouth closer to the hole, started talking to Ben and trying to lift his spirits.

"I will find a way to free you, I will be here tomorrow night at the same time. Hang on for one more day my love. Be ready for us, once you are free, we will return to our people." White Hawk said.

She would never give up on him. She would do anything to free him from the torture of the hotbox and certain death when the captain returned. She lay on the roof, professing her love and her commitment to him until dawn started to break. Then they scurried back to her tent unnoticed.

Once she and Harriet reached the safety of the tent, Harriet said, "You seen the box wuz put together with rusty nails an ole barn wood. I think we pulled a couple nails outta' the back and he could shimmy outta the hole. I'll try my best to find a claw hammer today. Try not ta worry, we'll get some help. I have some frens that owes me a favor or two."

The next day was hotter for Ben in the box than the day before. But since he'd taken some water, he was able to survive the heat. That night after dark when the troops retired Harriet and White Hawk made the trek to drip water from the roof into Ben's parched mouth once again. Harriet was unable to find a hammer, so they must find another way to free him. When White Hawk climbed onto the roof of the shanty, it wobbled from her weight, she was barely 100 pounds soaking wet.

Maybe they didn't need a hammer after all.

She thought of a plan, but they would need help to carry it out. After giving Ben a drink, and uplifting his spirits, she asked him to hang on for one more day. They were running out of time to free Ben as the Captain would return to try him on the third day.

She went through the motions of work and prayed for rain so Ben would get some relief from the scorching heat in the hotbox. It didn't rain. Tonight, they would attempt the breakout, it was their last chance.

Harriet disappeared from her job at noon returning at sundown with two strange men. She would pass them off as workers who were going to do repairs on the washhouse. She introduced them to White Hawk as friends that owed her a favor and they were at great personal danger to be in the Confederate camp. They would help them visit the hotbox and try to free Ben.

At midnight, they crept toward Ben's cell. As she dripped water to him, the men got to work on the back of the shed, trying to pull old, warped boards from the studs. It was difficult, they had no tools but their hands. The nails held tight. Then they tried to rock the shed and throw it over since it was wobbly. That didn't work either, the corner posts were set too far into the hard ground.

Ben and White Hawk were devastated and began to lose hope at the failure to free him from his prison.

White Hawk refused to leave him, staying on top of the shed, whispering to him all night long about their future life together, and dreams of when he would be free. They both knew that it might never be, but she could not accept it as his fate. The men and Harriet left them to share their last moments together. They believed Ben's trial would find him guilty and result in his hanging, and there was nothing they could do to help.

The next day at dawn White Hawk went to the nearby stream to perform a cleansing ceremony and to offer what she could to the Great One for a blessing. She offered her life in exchange for Ben's. She prayed for a miracle and called out to the Great Spirit and Grandmother to help them. She prayed, asking Ben to be given a longer life.

After her time at the water, she noticed the camp buzzed unlike anything before. The usual complaints about lack of food, ammunition, and medicine for the camp's sicknesses were replaced with whispering and an almost jovial atmosphere. White Hawk didn't share in the mood or the talk, she was mourning her lost love already.

The captain didn't return to the camp as scheduled, many of the soldiers saddled up their horses with their bedrolls and rode off southward. Harriet and White Hawk didn't know what to make of the events as the camp became deserted of abled bodied soldiers. White Hawk and Harriet were left behind with the sick, injured and Ben slowly dying in the hotbox.

At sundown and with the camp almost empty, White Hawk decided tonight she would set Ben free from the box. She dressed in her disguise as a man. Going to the barn, she saddled two horses, tying a rope on each of the horse's saddlehorns. Harriet rode one horse and White Hawk the other. They threaded the rope's other end through the corner timbers holding the shed upright. White Hawk told Ben to brace himself and cover his head. They each kicked their horses in the flanks and held on to the saddle horn, as they both lunged forward. The horses strained and the ropes tightened. The horses jumped forward each time as they were prodded in the sides......the shed started to lean and then it went down, they had pulled it over and Ben was free.

She threw the rope off her saddle horn and quickly returned to Ben, he jumped upon the back of the horse behind her, and off they rode as fast as they could go westward. Harriet took off on her horse to the north.

Their escape went unnoticed by the camp, as more important news was discussed. Today General Johnston who led 90,000 Confederate troops in Florida, Georgia, North Carolina, and South Carolina, surrendered to Sherman. General Lee surrendered to Grant at Appomattox a few days earlier. For these men, the war was over, they were done killing one another.

With Ben now free from the box, the war was over for them as well. However, they needed to get away from anyone that hadn't heard the news, or that still wanted to own slaves and hadn't surrendered. Their journey home would be fraught with danger. Their course was Northwest while cutting through Tennessee crossing the muddy Mississippi river, Arkansas, and entering Oklahoma territory as quickly as possible. They hoped their horse would make it. It would shorten their trip, as they could cover more ground faster riding than walking. They also didn't just travel at night; they would not stop until they reached home. They took turns sleeping in the saddle on the horse while the one awake held the other upright, but they did need to stop to feed, water, and rest the animal or it would not be able to carry them the distance.

They had many miles to travel before they could be safe from bounty hunters and be in free territory. They kept on running.

MISS ROSE

Old Aunt Julia Ann Jackson, age 102 and the corn crib where she lives. United States Library of Congress, Arkansas, ca. 1938. [Between 1937 and] Photograph.

SIXTEEN

1865-1866

As White Hawk and Ben reached the north Georgia line, they heard the dogs baying in the distance. It was almost like singing, but they knew it meant the hounds were hot on their trail. They tried all the maneuvers they knew to escape, wading through water, putting deer urine on their tracks, wiping their footprints clean with branches, and turning the horse free to lead the hounds astray. As a last resort, they climbed to the tops of the cedar trees and hid high on the mountain. The sounds of the dogs kept drawing closer, growing louder and louder, and then men's angry voices became audible. White Hawk and Ben were about to be caught and terrified at what would become of them in the hands of these strange men. They had heard stories of what happens to runaway slaves.

Their capture came at dusk, in the faint light as the sun set behind the pine trees hiding them in their shadows. They valiantly fought back at the hands grabbing at them, but there were too many. The bounty hunters punched and kicked them until they could resist no more, bleeding and bruised with their wrists bound behind their backs. Heavy metal collars draped around their necks and connected to log chains at the wrist and ankles. Ropes tied the two of them together, so they could not run. The men believed White Hawk was a young man and treated her as such, if not they all would have raped her.

The men on horseback walked them all night without stopping, when they couldn't walk anymore, they tied them to the horses and drug them. The slave hunters took them to the nearest plantation and sold them for $500 each to the owner, Mr. Ward. Unbeknownst to White Hawk and Ben, the Ward farm had a reputation in the county as the place where the unruly slaves or the runaways were sent for rehabilitation. The overseer Mr. Thomas was known as 'the slave breaker' for a reason, the other plantation owners brought their uncontrollable slaves to Thomas, and he would literally 'whip them into shape.' He would work them in the fields and woods for up to a year, free labor in return for his harsh method of training. He took pleasure in the weekly beatings of the men and women sent to him for rehabilitation, he would break their spirits and return a docile, defeated, and broken-down body to the original owner.

When Mr. Thomas first took possession of the two runaways, as an example to the others, he tied them to a 6" square whipping post sunk into the center of the slave quarters yard. They stood without food or water all night. The next morning when the sun was hot upon them, White Hawk, still disguised as a man—or Mr. Thomas would have stripped her naked to the waist revealing her breast as extra humiliation, awaited their fate. He ripped their clothes to expose their bare backs, allowing her identity to remain hidden. Fear gripped them for they knew what was coming next. Mr. Thomas assembled all the field hands around the captives, and he then gave White Hawk and Ben 50 lashes each with the bullwhip. It cut into their hides leaving bleeding gashes until they passed out from the unrelenting beating. The metal restraints bit into their wrists from the dead weight of their unconscious bodies. The purpose was two-fold, to warn others not to run and to break these two who had dared try.

They awoke in a shack dumped on the floor with four others already living there. The next morning, the overseer, Mr. Thomas, put them to the fields to work the crops, without any food or water. They were near collapse, but no one cared. They were property, not people. The workhorse shackled to the wagon at the end of the row had better treatment than the two of them.

In the field, Miss Rose, a woman of at least 80 years old and permanently stooped over from years of hard field work, approached White Hawk with a bucket and a dipper to offer a drink of cool water.

Miss Rose tied her wiry gray hair up in a kerchief, covered by a frayed straw hat and wore a faded apron over her tattered clothes. Her face was rugged and wrinkled from years of sun exposure and her hands were crooked and scarred, when she smiled a black hole appeared where teeth were supposed to be. Mr. Thomas sitting atop the horse in the next row didn't stop her act of kindness. Miss Rose then went to Ben and offered him a drink of water from the same dipper. The sips of water proved enough to keep them going until sundown when Mr. Thomas, sitting high on his black stallion, escorted them all from the field to the shanties that served as homes. They survived one more day. This would become their mantra, 'survive for one more day.'

As far as the eye could see there were acres and acres of tobacco planted in perfect rows, still too young for them to cut, but now at the growing period needing topping and suckering. The fields were beautiful but disheartening to look at if you had a hoe in your hands. Tobacco work is one of the most labor-intensive crops to grow, but abundant in the South. The rule of thumb was generally seven thousand plants per acre and this field was about three acres. The plants were 'set' 100 per row, which meant that getting the plant to maturity would entail weeding, suckering, cutting, hanging, curing, and then stripping 210 rows.

When the harvest began, they would stoop and chop low at the stalk with a hatchet-like, long-handled ax, and then 'spear' the stalk with the leaves onto four-foot-long sticks. The spear was a conical shaped metal cap that would fit onto the sharpened stick, removable and placed on each new stick used. The sticks made of rough oak, squared about 2" x 5' in length. These were dangerous jobs, many had scars on their arms and legs where they missed with the axe or had speared a hand.

After threading six or so stalks onto a stick, it weighed between 40-60 pounds. These were then loaded onto a wagon and carted to the tobacco barn. The tobacco barns designed with three to five levels of wooden rail frames, usually beginning six feet from the floor, and reaching to the top of the barn 30' or more. The laborers would hoist one stick at a time to hang on the rail by someone else standing splay-legged on the rail below, lifting high overhead. This job usually fell to the smallest boys that could climb high and still be able to manage the weight to get the tobacco to the hangers.

After completing the hanging, small fires were set down in the center of each barn, covered with sawdust and left to smolder. Then the barn doors shut tight so the smoke would cure the tobacco, which preserves and gives it the desired color and texture. If the farmer were lucky, the barn would not burn down with his crop, as many did. In the fall after drying was complete, and on a wet day so that the leaves wouldn't crumble, the sticks were removed one-by-one from the rafters and stripped of their leaves. Each leaf sorted into a stack, then bundled by grade, loaded on wagons, and taken to auction. Money collected, seeds bought, debts paid, and the entire process started again in the spring.

After the first day of field work, White Hawk and Ben's hands blistered from using the hoes breaking up the hard clay dirt clots, uprooting weeds and suckering the tobacco plants. The topping and suckering process done by hand, as the overseer did not trust the slaves with knives. The sucker, or useless set of leaves from the top of the plant, diverts resources from the rest of the plant and by removing it the yield improves. Topping snaps off the bud or flower and promotes nicotine production in the roots and sends it to the leaves.

Ben had trouble getting his big hands and fingers into the space between the tender stalk and the sucker. If he broke or damaged the plant, more lashes would fall on his sore back. Their backs already shredded from the whipping, by the end of the day the sticky nicotine residue covered them as well, mingling with their blood from the plants in the tobacco fields. The juice from the plants soaking into their skin all day made them nauseous and their heads pound.

Their blisters throbbed and were so sore they couldn't make a fist, and their backs ached from the whipping and bending all day. Miss Rose took them into her cabin and sat them down in wobbly chairs at a bare homemade table. The cabin, one big room with a dirt floor, contained a bed, a table and a worn rocking chair facing a stone fireplace. Most of the cooking done outside in the summertime, on a barrel turned sideways with the end cut out for stoking with wood. The round shape flattened on one side, where she lay her food to cook. In the wintry weather months, what little she had to eat she heated over the fireplace which she also used to heat her shack. In the center of the room was a hole dug into the floor and inside she had stashed some provisions. There was a head of cabbage, some sweet potatoes, and a jar of bacon fat. The aroma of the room was stale and smelled of smoke and dirt, but it was clean, dark, and cool. The walls papered with old newsprints to keep out the cold drafts in the wintertime had brown stains from where the rain seeped in through the cracks. Miss Rose went to the fireplace mantle, retrieved a small jar of cream, and handed it to White Hawk.

"Here child, rub this on your fingers and each other's backs, it'll help the throbbing, and you'll be able to work tomorrow."

White Hawk rubbed the cream gingerly on her blisters, it burned and stung and brought tears to her eyes, but she would not cry. She wondered what ingredients the magic cream contained. She smelled bacon grease with herbs in it. After she doctored herself, she then applied it to Ben's wounds.

"I'll help you get started here but you'll have to soon be on your own, we all take care of ourselves here on the farm." Miss Rose said.

"We appreciate it ma'am," Ben said.

"What's a matter with you, cat got your tongue," she said to White Hawk.

"No ma'am, I just don't talk much," White Hawk said in her best male voice.

"I know your secret, it's safe with me honey chil.' I can tell by your hands, your features, and your voice. It would be to your benefit to keep pretending you're a gent. This farm ain't easy on a woman for many reasons, especially a pretty one like you under all that dirt." Miss Rose said.

Miss Rose looked downward with shame on her face, as if she knew from experience what atrocities a new young girl would suffer.

White Hawk was relieved that someone else finally knew her secret. It was hard for her to portray a man, her voice was too high, and she was physically weaker than Ben. She didn't know how long she would be able to keep her identity hidden, especially in the fields and when the tobacco cutting began.

Miss Rose pulled a ratty cardboard box from under her bed and gave each a flannel shirt to replace their torn clothes.

"I have these left over from my son, Joseph, you can have 'em. He ain't gonna be coming back no mo. He was sole last year by the 'massa'." Her eyes welled up with tears as she spoke.

Miss Rose went on, "there's bout a dozen of us still here workin.' Six of 'em hightailed when they heared the war was over. The 'massa' don believe we is free and say anyone else caught runnin, he'd shoot 'em hisself. He would too, he's a mean man. So, we be cowards, I'm a guessin, and here we stay put."

"Ma' am, I think what you did today, offering us a drink of water and working hard here everyday is very brave. You are a warrior; you will live to see your freedom. I am sure of that." White Hawk said.

Miss Rose smiled her toothless smile and said, "Honey chile I'm a hopin your right, but I don't know what I'd do or where I'd go. This is the only life I know'd since I was a lil gurl. I been bot by Masser Ward when I goin' on 15, and he done sole off'n my husband and all my chilun."

White Hawk said, "Let me tell you a story of a place you could go. In the direction of the setting sun there is a place called the Cherokee Nation, there we have pure streams that run deep and pure and filled with fish that practically jump into your canoe. We have trees that grow high into the sky, and fields of corn are so tall you can get lost in the rows. There we are free; we are one with each other and one with nature and the Great Spirit. You can go with us when we leave this evil place."

"Chile don't let anybody hear you talkin' like that, they'll hang you as a 'sample," she had tears in her eyes as she spoke. "But that place do soun' like the Promise Lan. I ust ta pray I'd get there someday and live free. Maybe I'll see it when the good Lord calls me home."

Miss Rose became their teacher on the farm, helping them to learn how to survive as a slave in the scorching summer fields. She gave them each a strip of cloth showing them how to dip the cool water on the rags and tie them around their brows. This kept them cooler and prevented the salty sweat from dripping into and burning their eyes. They bid their time, working each day, and staying out of trouble while saving rations for their escape but it was hard to do on their meager servings. Food was always in short supply, they were always hungry, and relied on the kindness of others for most of what they did get to eat. They were constantly scoping the direction to the west from the rising and setting sun and they watched the cycle of the full moon while growing impatient.

They felt themselves getting stronger and more prepared. They shared their plans to run with Miss Rose, trying to persuade her to go with them. They told her the story of their life as a Cherokee and their work in the war. A deep friendship bloomed between them.

Miss Rose would sing songs to them in the fields, which later at night she would explain their meaning while resting in the coolness of her shack. One she sang everyday as their time to run drew closer was "Wade in the Water[*]." The words of the song remind them the water hides the scent from the hounds set loose on them and symbolic of the Israelites fleeing captivity while God intervenes on their behalf.

That night she sang to them. Her voice was low and soulful bringing on homesickness and etching the memory of Miss Rose in their minds forever with the old Negro spiritual.

"Wade in the water Wade in the water, children

Wade in the water God's gonna trouble the water.

God's gonna trouble the water.[1] *"*

When she finished singing the chorus over and over she said, "Honey, I 'preciate you offerin me a way off'n the farm, but I be too old. I'd slow you down and get you caught and a whippin or worse mabbe hung. You go and get outta here while you still young."

The night they planned to run, Miss Rose offered the overseer a jug of her home-made blackberry wine. White Hawk mixed in some sleeping tonic made from plants she had gathered beside the fields, to help knock him out for a while. Miss Rose told them the lay of the land, what farms were nearby, where the best woods were to hide in for their escape route, and how far they must go before

---

[1] Wade in the Water, PUBLIC DOMAIN

stopping to rest. They owed her so much and had no way to repay her kindness.

On the night when the moon was full, they ran. They didn't stop until the next night when they were a good 30 miles away from where they started. Hiding deep in the woods and off the trail, they kept running until they were out of Georgia and into Alabama. They didn't stop to sleep but for a few hours each midday when it was too dangerous and hot to be moving. They avoided towns, as many Confederate soldiers were coming back from war, and still capturing runaways selling them for the rewards.

They ran through northern Mississippi, into middle Arkansas. Home was within reach, and they were almost there. Oklahoma territory was in sight. After 40 days without stopping except to forage or steal food from the locals, they finally made it to the safety of Indian Territory. They were exhausted and returning home older, weary, and changed forever.

In the time they were gone, they had seen and experienced a lifetime of sorrow and pain. They drank from the well of deep despair and left others there to drown, guilt consumed them. They were not sure if they had made a difference in the war, but they returned home with new insight and a vision for the future. Experiencing firsthand the unbearable conditions of captivity and slavery, they were even surer of their desires for freedom and equality for all their people.

Since their return, restful sleep evaded White Hawk. Her dreams were vivid, resulting in fitful nightmares. She and Ben were always running or hiding from someone, or blood of others drenching her on the battlefields. Each dawn ended the terror of the night. For weeks after her return, she would go to the water in the morning cleansing her body and mind hoping to rid herself of the plague of war to no avail.

Mother saw her weariness from lack of sleep, and the deep depression she carried like a battle scar. She worried about her daughter and proposed a solution.

"White Hawk, my child, I see those memories of the war burden you, along with Ben's captivity. Let us join with the elders and have a cleansing ceremony to help both you and Ben heal your minds."

White Hawk and Ben readily agreed, and the ceremony planned for the new moon in a few days. The men started gathering wood for the fire that would welcome the Lady of the Eternal Flame into their midst. White Hawk would wear her tear dress, made of calico and in remembrance of the Trail of Tears. Mother would prepare the black drink to use in the ceremony. White Hawk hoped and prayed for this to work helping her and Ben's return to normal. She didn't realize they would never be as they were before the war. The horrors of war, captivity and slavery changing them forever.

The morning of the ceremonial dance, White Hawk prepared by going to water for a cleansing, and while in the river she dumped water over her head seven times and prayed to the four corners. Ben did the same apart from her. Afterward, she dressed solemnly in tear-dress, remembering the walk of her youth. Her hair had regrown to her shoulders, and she wore braids with black ribbon streamers hanging down to her waist. She was ready.

The mood of the dance was strange and unlike any she had attended in the past. Mother gathered the elders, and those spiritually clean to help White Hawk and Ben. The People were seated around the fire, chanting, and praying to the Great One. White Hawk taking Ben's hand in hers dancing clockwise around the fire asking for blessings from the Lady of the Eternal Flame. As they circled the fire, she began to feel different. She felt the prayers of the people surrounding her and lifting her spirit up to the heavens. Mother sat them down, facing the fire and offered the smoking pipe to the four corners. Passing it to them, they did the same, giving thanks. Mother handed them a cup and instructed them to drink the contents and pray for peace. She told them to look inward to see the bad spirits that had invaded their minds. They must recognize them and tell them to depart.

They nodded off into a trance from the contents of the cup. White Hawk found herself in a dream and suddenly transported to a great smoky battlefield where cannons and guns fired relentlessly. She heard the screams of men as they fell in front of her. The cannons boomed continuously, and she stood on the sidelines unobserved, watching as the large metal balls took out entire regiments one-by-one. Many men and boys shot in the head with wounds gaping and blood dripping down obscuring faces. These bloody men carried from the battlefield and placed into her arms. Eventually she was in the center of a great pile of injured and dying men, covering her with their blood. Overwhelming her with the pain and suffering and little she could do to help them. She could only watch them die. This was her demon, she commanded it to leave her mind and give her rest. As she uttered the words, she immediately awoke sitting beside the fire with Ben.

Staring into the flame, still drowsy and in a dreamlike state, she began to see uninvited visions of the future. She saw Mother get sick with the fever. After many days of suffering, while White Hawk held her in her arms, Mother died, and her spirit departed her body. She also saw Ben's spirit leave him too, while sitting on his horse, he fell and then was gone.

She continued to stare into the flame, as the spirit ministered to her soul and revealed to return to the ancient ways, go back to the original teachings, to love and care for one another.

The spirit spoke, "Our people who are connected to everything, we are all one with the plants, air, water, land, and fire. One day someone will come and tell the truth to the world of how we are, we must stand as one."

Qualified as a healer and connected to the Great Father, she realized at that moment she was not just a healer of the body, but also of the spirit. She was to use her gift to help all and to bring unity to her people.

She knew in the future she would lose the two great loves of her life, revealed in the vision. She dared not tell them but vowed to live each day full of love and life with them while she could. She had also changed. Her mind would mourn no more for those she held in her arms and watched die. She would rejoice for their lives as she led them on to their Father in the spirit world. She now knew she must return to the ancient ways, and her vision showed her she would become a spiritual leader of the people. She was destined to become a "Beloved

Woman" of the Cherokee Nation and a healer of her people.

As a Beloved Woman, she would join the war council. The women of the tribe and this council of powerful women led the Cherokee, they decided the question of war and peace, the fate of captives, and chose the important leaders like the War Chief. The leader of this council was the "War Woman" or Ghighua: Beloved Woman of the Cherokee and they believed the Great Spirit spoke through her. This was a great honor not given to many. The instruction from her vision was clear and she knew she must achieve balance: spiritually, mentally, and physically to receive this recognition. But she knew this would rile the medicine man even more and he would try to invoke evil spirits and place spells upon her. This didn't matter, as she was called to action, and she must respond to her call.

SEVENTEEN

Current Day

Annie wasn't sure where to begin in the search for her birth mother. She talked it over with Miranda and they devised a plan to begin a DNA search. Maybe they'd get lucky and find a relative in the online database. She ordered a test kit, a non-threatening and easy thing to do. She also wrote to the Catholic Adoptions organization for information and to open her birth records. Now, she waited impatiently for answers.

In the meantime, the divorce process seemed simple and moved forward. The papers filed, and the court date scheduled. The filing's cause attributed to irreconcilable differences, and they mutually agreed on a financial settlement. All she and Tom had left to work out was who would get to keep the house. She didn't really care as it carried a hefty mortgage with little equity, or so she thought. Her attorney ran some routine checks at the courthouse and called her with his findings.

"Annie, I'm afraid I have some bad news for you. There was a second mortgage taken out on your house last year, equal to the first one. To get Tom's name off the deed, this needs to be paid and then remortgaged. Unfortunately, your home won't appraise the amount to pay off these loans, you're 'upside down.' Plus, you'd need 20% down payment on top of that. It looks like you might need to file bankruptcy to get clear of these loans."

"So now I'm broke, homeless, and bankrupt? This just gets better and better, doesn't it? If I weren't already an alcoholic, I'd probably become one," she said.

After a few terse letters exchanged between their lawyers, Tom agreed to bankruptcy, since his name was on the loan and deed as well as hers. The good news was that at the end of 60 days it would all be over legally. She still grieved her marriage, had no money, no house and felt like a failure, while struggling to avoid alcohol. She didn't know what the future held for her, but she knew she had one.

To stay sober, she kept her weekly appointments with Carol working on understanding why she relied on drinking to self-medicate and learning about co-dependent relationships. She continued to attend the AA meetings as often as she could. Ray agreed he would be her sponsor, and he cut her no slack. He held her accountable, and even though there was an age gap, a friendship bloomed between them. She started to work on her 12-Steps and received her 30-day sobriety chip. She always carried it in her pocket and when the urge to drink overtook her, reached in rubbing it until her desire subsided. She liked the feel of the round wooden coin's raised engraving as she rubbed it with her thumb. She was sure she was rubbing the paint off she stroked it so much.

Still unemployed, the hospital was paying her severance, and her car insurance was kicking in some disability money. She was making it, barely. She stayed sober one day at a time, some days were harder than others. Today was a good one, until the mail arrived.

There was a letter from the DNA service, with results in the envelope held in her trembling sweaty hands. She placed the unopened letter on the kitchen table, walking around and eyeing it from different angles. She knew it was a Pandora's Box and once she opened that envelope, there would be no going back into darkness and unknowing. The thought made her belly knot up. She reached into her pocket and rubbed the chip. She called Miranda to come over to open the letter together.

They sat before the computer together and everything within her screamed not to open the letter, but she pushed her fear aside and did it anyway. The instructions inside led her to open the DNA company's website on the computer, and enter a code provided in the letter, which would pull up the findings visually onto the screen. She purchased the full sequence level including the mitochondrial DNA and Haplogroup kit, which would trace her ancestry on her birth mother's side to the region of the world from where they migrated. They stared at the screen trying to make sense of the data and graphs, Annie read something and sharply inhaled. Her mitochondrial DNA and Haplogroup, which passes from the mother to child, showed she was of Native American ancestry, connected to her mother's, grandmother, and great-grandmother's line. She wasn't sure how to process this information or what to do with it. However, she realized it explained a lot about her looks, her skin tone, black hair, and brown eyes.

The next screen showed links to individuals and descendants of a shared family tree. There was one woman listed and linked to her—a distant cousin. Annie's eyes widened, was it this close—this was almost too much to grasp at one time. She read the name written there in black and white, Sarah Healer.

"That's enough Miranda, I can't go any further…..I need time to process this." Annie said.

"Wow, I can't believe it. You're Native American, I can see it in you. What do you think we should do?"

"I'm not sure, I've got to talk about this with Carol. Try and wrap my head around it—this is a bit much to take in all at once. Wow, I have a real cousin. I wonder if she is still alive, where she lives? I have so many questions, now maybe I can get some answers?" Annie said with a broad nervous smile.

She could hardly wait until the next appointment with Carol to tell her the results. Their weeks of therapy had been helpful. Carol didn't push, but let Annie talk and cry when she needed to, only asking questions that would necessitate digging deep inside to find an answer. Sometimes this was painful, and she developed new ways of thinking about things. She understood her adoptive mother's insecurities, which lead to the secret about her adoption. She knew her mother and father loved her very much, eventually forgiving them for their deceit, and she came to realize she was not some dirty secret they kept hidden away.

Carol's non-judgmental ear was cathartic for Annie. She helped her recognize that drinking was a symptom of depression, an attempt to numb her feelings of abandonment by her birth mother, fueled by a co-dependent marriage. She also realized she should have ended the marriage long before Tom strayed, but she had not been strong enough on her own.

In their next meeting, she told Carol of her ancestry search and finding a cousin in her family tree. The adoption agency also responded and agreed sufficient time had passed and they could release the name and location of her birth mother, who also agreed to open records. All she had to do was fill out a form, submit a small fee, and the records were hers. Before she did anything, she wanted Carol's opinion.

"So, Carol what should I do?" Annie asked.

"Depends on what you want to know. You're so close to finding out answers to questions that have hung over you for a lifetime, do you think you should deal with this or hide it away again? Where did that get you the first time?" Carol asked.

That was Carol's way, she always answered a question by asking another question to get Annie to find the answer herself. She never told anyone what to do, that's one of the reasons Annie liked her so much. Carol sat patiently waiting as long as it took for Annie to find her voice. Awkward silence didn't rush Carol into speaking.

Annie felt nervous at the silence and finally said, "I guess you have a point. I need to deal with this splinter once and for all. I'll begin tomorrow, starting with Catholic Adoptions, which seems the most logical place to begin."

Carol nodded her head in agreement and smiled.

Then Carol started asking questions about Miranda and their relationship.

"How often does Miranda come over? Does she just talk on the phone or show up in person? What's her last name? Where does she live?"

"What does Miranda have to do with anything? I don't want to talk about her." Annie was miffed. However, not for long, Carol dropped the subject.

A few weeks later after submitting the form with as much information as she had to Catholic Adoptions, a large brown envelope arrived for her with their return address. This time she didn't need Miranda holding her hand as she opened the seal, she felt proud of herself. She had beads of perspiration on her top lip, felt flush, and her heart pounding. But she could do this. Inside was a letter and the name of a contact person at the agency, should she have any questions, along with a handwritten note wishing her blessings on her journey to find her birth parent.

The second document in the envelope was her original birth certificate from 1978, and written there was her birth mother's name, Byrdie Healer. Annie didn't know what to say or do. Her eyes moved downward scanning the page.

Byrdie's age was 16 when she gave birth. Instead of Annie's name in the block, it merely said baby girl—she hadn't even named her, that was jarring. In the father's space written 'unknown.' The location of her birth was the county hospital in Tahlequah, Oklahoma. That made sense, as there is a large native population there. It was a starting place to begin her search for answers and her lost family. Also recorded on the certificate was her maternal grandmother's name Polly Healer and her grandfather Charley Bearpaw.

Annie realized she was holding her breath, and she let it out all at once. She wasn't sure how to feel about this information, but she was finally finding herself and it felt good but scary at the same time.

As she ran her fingers across the name of her birth mother on the certificate she whispered, "Hello, Momma….it's been a long time coming. I'm your daughter, I'm Annie Healer."

"I am Annie Healer." She yelled out to announce herself to the world, as she spun around in a circle with her arms raised, and then she cried.

She called Miranda with the news, "When can you come over and help me find phone numbers or addresses for my birth mother and grandparents? It sounds so strange to say that."

Miranda showed up after dinner and they opened the laptop searching for names and social apps to try to match someone, without success. Annie also sent an email to the family tree site to try and connect with her cousin Sarah. Now they waited again for answers. This was not an easy or fast process. She needed to learn patience.

While waiting for the snail mail response, the hospital HR department replied to her inquiry as to whether the medical board was going to pursue further actions against her. This could result in her losing her license to practice medicine. Finally, after several days, the hospital advised they were closing the investigation and would not pursue any further legal action against her, since no one else suffered injuries. Also, they had no charges for malpractice against the hospital from her patients. But they would not rehire her. She felt relieved, but realized she needed to find another job and fast, as her money was getting tight.

That night she had the same dream encountering the woman on the plains again. This time the woman spoke to her.

"My child, you were lost but now you are found." She drew near and placed her hand upon Annie's head, blessing her.

When Annie awoke, she had peace in her soul unlike anything she had ever known before, and she could not forget the woman in the dream. This was her first day since being sober that she didn't crave a drink.

Today would also be the day she would start looking hard for another job. Medicine was her calling, she knew she must get on with her life's work, and she needed income. She accepted a part-time position at the local grocery store walk-in medical clinic, doling out flu shots and doctoring other minor illnesses. Her new office consisted of a hastily erected box beside the pharmacy, right next to the antacid and anti-diarrheal aisle.

Wonderful.

It was beneath her credentials, but it was a steady job with a paycheck, and she was grateful for the pittance of a salary. She would work on this until she found something else more permanent.

In her next therapy session with Carol, they discussed her job situation and probing questions about Miranda and her absence lately.

"How many times have you seen or talked to her this week, and what was she telling her to do? Did she ever tell you to harm yourself or others?"

Shocked Annie said, "No of course not, she's my best friend. She'd never do anything like that.

But she is not coming around as much as she was; I think she's been busy."

She then changed the subject, and they talked about her job situation.

Carol asked, "have you ever thought about joining the Peace Corps or Doctors Without Borders or something like that? They are always looking for medical help. Sometimes the best way to heal yourself is to look at helping others."

Later that night she thought more about Carol's suggestion, after all, she didn't have anything holding her back. She investigated the Peace Corp website. Most of the positions required a two-year commitment in some God forsaken land. She nixed that idea. Next, she searched Doctors Without Borders, but they were looking for specialty practitioners, not generalists, and these positions were on foreign soil also. She didn't feel like her leg was well enough to carry her that far away from home yet.

On a whim, she googled the Cherokee Nation Medical Center in Tahlequah and found a beautiful facility, a teaching hospital, and Medical School in conjunction with Oklahoma State University. They needed staffing for the summer session medical clinic and hospital, June through September. She attached her resume and received an immediate response and since the pay was less than a large city hospital they provided free room, board, and a travel stipend.

In the upcoming days, Annie exchanged notes and phone interviews for the coming summer session clinic starting June 1. They offered her one of the positions but would need her acceptance in the next week or they would go to the next qualified candidate. If she agreed to go, she would have a month to prepare. This would be a major step taking her closer to her birth location, to possibly uncover more of her story. She had mixed emotions, facing her fears she made the commitment to go, she didn't really have anything holding her here.

It wasn't long afterwards she received an email from her cousin Sarah on the ancestor site. Sarah lived in downtown Tahlequah. They exchanged messages and Sarah was surprised to learn of Annie's existence, she had never heard the story about the baby given up for adoption from anyone in her family. Annie told her the names of her mother and grandmother shown on the birth certificate, and Sarah recognized them both.

She knew Byrdie very well when they were younger, they used to play as children and run around together in their early teens. Unfortunately, their paths parted when Sarah went to a different high school and then on to college leaving Byrdie behind in the Nation and she didn't see her for the next 30 years. However, she knew Byrdie had lived a tragic life and died from chronic alcoholism in her mid-40's. Sarah remembered attending the funeral and burial in the Ross Cemetery in Tahlequah, across from the W.W. Hastings Hospital.

She had lost track of Byrdie's mother Polly, but she offered to find contact information from others in the family. Sarah agreed to meet Annie when she visited The Nation in the next month and would bring family photo albums of shared relatives. She seemed happy to know she had a newly discovered cousin, and Annie would finally meet a blood relative. She was excited and apprehensive at the same time.

What if…..she stopped mid-thought—what if what?

She corrected herself, using the tools Carol had been drumming into her for the past months—ask yourself what is the worst that can happen to you? She can't eat you, Carol would say. Reminding her she was not a little orphan girl anymore, or afraid of alienating her adopted mother and being given away again. She was an adult, and it was high time to behave like one. However, these thoughts and emotions always came with company; her desire to drink was strong and her resolve was weakening.

After all, what would one little drink hurt?

Craving a drink and wanting to head to the nearest liquor store, she reached in her pocket and thumbed the coin whispering, "I can do this for one more day."

She didn't believe it this time, she dropped to her knees and recited Step-2.

"I am calling on a Power greater than my resolve to restore me to sanity. Please help me to not drink." When the urge subsided, she called Ray.

She told him her thoughts about having one little drink and going to Step-2 when she was about to give in.

"But, after thinking about it, what harm would just one do? I think I can manage it now." she asked.

He said, "it's not the one drink, it's the whole bottle you drink after the first one…kid, face it. You're a drunk, you become a different person after you drink, and you have a proven track-record you can't drink just one. But I'm proud of you for accepting help from your greater Power. Just keep working the program, that's two steps already."

She vowed to hang on, but knew the next step would be the hardest for her. She was to make a moral inventory. Admitting to her higher power, herself, and another human being her wrongs, and ready to have her higher Power remove her shortcomings. Then making a list of all the people she hurt with her drinking, and making direct amends, except when doing so would injure them or others.

She started her list after hanging up the phone, and at the top was Tom.

EIGHTEEN

She started her amends list, assuming there would be relatively few names on it, because she hadn't a lot of personal interactions over the years. Of course, the first would be Tom, the one she hurt the most. Then her boss at the hospital, he counted on her and she let him down miserably. She even contemplated adding Dr. Green to the list, but nixed that idea, there was a limit to her repentance. The more she thought about it, her list grew. There was the bartender who took her carkeys one night, she had unleashed her fury on him for that. The girl at the bank couldn't understand what she wanted one day because she was drunk, so she made a scene. She added the dry-cleaner, the grocery clerk, and her hairdresser. This assignment was eye-opening to her. She was ashamed of what she had done and who she had become. She would begin with the hardest one to make amends to and that was Tom. She ruined their marriage and both of their lives.

She dialed his cell leaving a voice message, "Hi Tom, I was wondering if you could drop by tonight, I have something important I need to say to you in person. Don't worry, I'm sober and mean you no harm. I'd really like to see you, if so around 6 would be great for me."

He immediately texted her right back and confirmed he'd be there. She had four hours to prepare for the meeting, to calm her nerves she began cleaning the already spotless house.

Tom arrived promptly and she welcomed him into the house they once called home. He was fidgety and nervous, and it showed in his body language. He shoved both hands into his jeans' pockets, clearly apprehensive about being alone with her.

She started, "Let's sit down in the living room, and get comfortable shall we."

She noticed him glancing around the room, taking an inventory of what she had kept or trying to determine what else she had thrown away of his. He sat down facing her, hands resting in his lap.

"So, Annie, what's this all about? As far as I know the divorce is on track and should be final in a couple of weeks…all the financials agreed upon. What's up?" He sounded a little hostile.

"Well, since you've been gone, I have been seeing a therapist and joined AA. Working on myself and my sobriety," she said.

He nodded his head, and she kept talking so she wouldn't lose her courage.

"And I'm now aware that I played a large part in our failed marriage by drinking and co-dependent behaviors. I owe you an amends."

"What's that?" He asked cocking his head to one side.

"Part of my 12-Step recovery entails making a list of all the people hurt by my drinking, apologizing, and asking for their forgiveness. Lucky you, you are at the top of my list." She paused while rubbing the coin in her pocket.

"At first, I blamed you for cheating, now I realize that I was as much to blame as you. I cheated with a bottle long before you cheated with her. I drove you away, before you could abandon me like everyone else I loved in my life—starting with my birth mother."

She sat there stoically, waiting for a reaction, ready for him to unleash his wrath on her, wondering how this was supposed to work.

Tom reached over and took her hands; she had been wringing together in her lap.

"Annie, of course I forgive you, but I feel like I need forgiveness too for what I did to you. I have always loved you and I am sorry I hurt you. But I was so angry with you, we had it all and you were throwing it away. I couldn't take it anymore; I couldn't stick around and watch you drink yourself to death. That's why I started gambling, at first just trying to escape this place and you. I guess I should have tried to get help for you, dry you out. But I didn't know what to do for you, so I ran. I ran straight to a casino and then into another woman's arms. Which turned out to be another huge mistake. It seems we were in lust, not love and that doesn't last. So, I'm moving out soon, I think it's over between Judith and me."

He shocked Annie with his truthfulness, but she didn't offer to let Tom come home. She was not sure he was asking, but she was not ready for that. She removed her hand from his; no contact for now would help keep her resolve.

"I don't suppose you'd let me come back home, try to work things out between us? I'm so sorry I hurt you, I have always loved you, Annie. There's just a lot that got in the way. I'm a jerk and don't deserve another chance with you, but please Annie. Please."

"I'm sorry for you Tom, I really hope you find happiness. That's what I'm hoping for me too, I think it's out there, somewhere."

She stood up crossing her arms over her chest. The signal that this conversation was over, and it was time for him to go. There would be no reconciliation, she wasn't the same person he walked out on. She couldn't go back to the way things were, she was starting over.

As she walked him to the door he said, "Would you mind if I called you every now and then? Just to see how you're doing and keep in touch. We might not be married anymore but I'd like for us to stay friends."

"Sure, can't have too many friends, but I plan to be out of town for a few months starting in June. I'm taking a summer position at a teaching hospital clinic. I'm putting a few things in storage, selling everything else, and vacating the house, so the realtor can try and sell it before foreclosure," she said.

Wishing she hadn't shared all of that with him, he had no right to know anything about her private life now. It was a surprise to her that she made the decision in that instant to do the clinic in Oklahoma and move out. She had been wafting back and forth about these decisions for a while. Tom was the first person she told, and there was no turning back now. At the door, she offered a handshake, but he pulled her to himself and hugged her tight. It felt good, too comfortable, and dangerous. She stood stiff and after a moment, he pulled away with downcast eyes and looked ashamed.

Good.

She watched a tear rolled down his cheek, then he turned and left.

She pulled out the list of names, drew a line through Tom's.

"One down, six to go," she said.

As she worked down the list, she was surprised at how gracious and forgiving everyone treated her so far. She had started with the easy ones, and they truly seemed to be happy for her and wishing her well, until she got to the hospital to make amends with her old boss, Dr. Warren. She's purposefully saved these two for last—her boss and the bartender. Because Dr. Warren was a hothead and she was afraid of his reaction, and the bartender since she wasn't sure how walking into a bar full of all that liquor would affect her.

She found Dr. Warren in the doctor's lounge, and it was just the two of them. After explaining what she was doing there, apologizing, and offering her amends, he became indignant and rude, berating her for her failure and a disgrace to the Hippocratic oath. She waited until his tirade was over, letting him unleash and heap it like hot coals upon her head. She deserved it. She then sucked up her shame, thanked him for his time, wished him well and raced to her car before anyone else saw her. She did not cry, she put the car in gear and headed to the bar.

When she walked in the bartender recognized and nodded to her, as she sat on her regular stool, it was rote behavior.

"Hey, where have you been and what'll you have?" He asked.

She started to say nothing, then she said, "How about a tonic water and wedge of lime."

"Don't you want some gin in that?"

"Yes, I do, but I'm sober and trying to remain that way. I'm in a 12-Step program, that's why I'm here. One of the steps is to make amends for those you have hurt. I came here to make amends to you," she said.

"Oh, I see, yeah, I get that all the time, and I appreciate it. You look great. Why do you need to make amends with me?"

She apologized for all the terrible drunken behavior and viscous words hurled at him for taking her keys and sending her home in a taxi, more than once. Along with all the other times she was so drunk she passed out at the bar leaving him to deal with her by calling Tom to come retrieve her. It felt good to get this off her chest and to realize that it was the old drunken Annie, not the sober one sitting here right now.

"Thanks, but it's a hazard of the job. We get lots of customers like that, it's no big deal," he said shrugging.

"It's a big deal for me, so thanks and I'm going to get out of here before I get too comfortable and my resolve fades. Oh, I hope I never see you again," she said with a smile as she slid a $20 across the bar toward him.

"Me too, good luck and don't ever come back," he laughed with her.

As she sat behind the steering wheel with Step-2 now complete, she felt proud of herself. She could hardly wait to share her success with Ray and Carol. Then her mind drifted to Miranda, wondering where she was lately. She had not called or dropped by, and Annie missed her. She had a session with Carol the next day and she'd try to reach out to Miranda afterwards.

The meeting with Carol started as most of the others had, Annie would share what transpired during the week and how she dealt with problems or intrusive thoughts that brought her down. She shared her amends stories, and Carol congratulated her for completing the list and working on the program.

Then she changed the subject, "Annie, have you seen or talked to Miranda this week?"

"That's strange you should ask, I was just thinking yesterday that I have not heard from her lately.

I wonder if she's mad at me about something."

"Annie, do you have your phone with you? I want you to go to your contacts and pull up Miranda's name." Carol said and then waited.

"Ok, now look and tell me what does the contact details for her show?"

"That's strange….it's blank, it just has Miranda's name. No address, no phone number, what…how can this be? I've called her on this phone, she's called me." Annie was wide-eyed and looked as if she was going to bolt from the room.

Carol placed her hands on Annie's to steady her and spoke very softly. "Calm down Annie, I want you to think about this with me. Just close your eyes, breathe deeply, exhale and relax a bit. There that's better."

It was quiet in the room; the only noise was the diffuser and flute music playing in the background. She steadied her mind.

"Remember something with me. I want you to go back with me, see yourself in the rehab facility. How lonely were you, how hurt, and suffering from alcohol withdrawals? Do you see Annie lying there in bed? I want you to look around you. Remember, Annie? You were in a private room, there was never a roommate there? Can you see it in your mind, still see Annie all alone in her bed? Is she crying? I want you to comfort her, go to her and tell her how you are a sober adult and will take care of her from now on, she doesn't need Miranda anymore. Can you do that Annie?"

"Yes, yes…" Annie sobbed as she realized it was true, and she didn't need Miranda anymore.

She would take care of Annie. No one would hurt her anymore, least of all herself.

She opened her eyes and grabbed Carol, holding onto her like a drowning man to his rescuer, sobbing.

"Am I crazy? How could I have imagined her; she was so real." Annie cried.

Carol spent the next few minutes reassuring Annie that she wasn't losing her mind, this was a natural response to trauma and usually seen in abandonment cases with children. They have a break with reality. Imaginary friends occur in the mind to serve a purpose, when the psyche can't manage the stress of a situation. When you sever co-dependent relationships your mind's first response is to create new ones, it's learned behavior. You must be on guard for relapse with other co-dependent personalities or Miranda—or someone entirely new may show up.

"This is not concerning to me; you just needed a little help to come back to reality. Now the real work of healing your emotions can begin. You recognize that you are in control now, you have all the power over Annie, no one else." Carol said.

"To end our session on a positive note, tell me about this position you told me you're accepting in Oklahoma. I think it's a great idea and I am proud of you stepping outside of your comfort zone. When do you leave?" Carol asked.

They chitchatted and when she left the office, she felt relieved and a little sad. She really liked Miranda, and she would miss her friend.

When Annie got home that afternoon, her phone dinged to alert her to a new message. She had seen her primary care physician a week ago and revealed her alcohol abuse with concern for her liver health and other ill effects. The doctor ordered a full panel of liver function test, and the ding signified the results were now available for her review. Annie logged onto the electronic charting system and into her private account. She was unprepared for what she saw.

Almost every one of the levels was outside of normal range, most of them extremely elevated. Especially the ALT, AST, ALP, and Bilirubin all indicative of liver damage, she self-diagnosed most probably early stages of cirrhosis. The Albumin test was lower than normal, also a marker for cirrhosis. She needed further testing to see how badly her liver might be damaged and a liver biopsy to stage the cirrhosis. She tried not to dwell on it, but her drinking may have done irreparable harm. This could be a life-or-death situation.

One more item she could add to her list of failures….she could hear her mother now, *'don't' Annie.*

NINETEEN

1866

Indian Territory
West of the Mississippi

White Hawk's nightmares ceased after the cleansing ceremony. The atrocities of the war dimmed and became a distant memory for both her and Ben. Her life with Ben and Nan became all she had ever wanted for a family. He was a good father to Nan, loving her as his own and life slowly returned to normal for them in Oklahoma territory.

However, her desire to help the Freedmen did not wane. She knew there was more to do for Isaac and Ben's people, and she vowed to keep fighting against the damaging racism, bigotry, and slavery.

The world their daughter grew up in would not be the same one she had experienced. Nan was of mixed races and her life would be more difficult because of that without the added threat of slavery hanging over her head. White Hawk wanted Nan, and other young men and women in the tribe, to get an education and pursue their dreams in life. There was still much work to do to accomplish equal opportunities for them in the white man's world.

The medicine man continued to vex her and her family by casting spells and conjuring evil spirits. He spread lies and gossip amongst the people to turn them against her and her plant medicine because of his jealousy. However, he was not successful, the people knew her heart, and it was pure and full of light and love. This made him hate and curse her more and cast bad medicine for more evil spirits to attack her. No matter what the medicine man invoked against her, she remained in the light working to heal her people the only way she knew, with plant medicines and offerings to the Great One.

She accepted gifts of healing and nurturing the spirits while passing their words on to those in need. She embraced her uniqueness, welcoming the visions and visits of the spirits. The spirits would come in the calm of the night when the bullfrogs come from the underworld. Legends say they croak to make their presence known, going to the moon to take a bite out of it each night until the moon was gone and then it would be full again. Then the cycle would start over again.

The fireflies flitted in the night around the campsite. These were the friendly spirits in a spark of light, an orb that flew around her, and she could feel love for her. Both were the ancient ones giving her signs and strength to keep going and educating her people in the old ways. Occasionally she would walk in the 'land of no time.' She cherished the visits with her departed loved ones and the ancient ones she would meet there. They told her what she yet needed to accomplished in this life and showed her the future. She vowed never to leave her home and family again, this was where her life was and where she needed to be to help The People of The Nation.

Each healing she performed drained a little bit more of her strength, and the visits into the spirit world 'land of no time' replenished her mentally and spiritually but were difficult on her physical body. As she grew older, the healing and spirit walks became more difficult for her to recover from, feeling the effects for weeks. But she would never stop until she could do it no more. She continued to train Nan in sacred ways, just as Grandmother and Mother had trained her. Nan would continue the legacy of healer in the paint clan, and eventually found herself to be even more gifted than White Hawk.

Many months after Ben and White Hawk returned home from the war, Nan came home from school feeling sick. She started with a slight fever, headache, and a cough. White Hawk began treating Nan's fever with tonics, potions, and rest while lying down on the skins. As the day turned into night, Nan got sicker, and her fever went higher. White Hawk feared the medicine man cast dark magic and bad spirits were attacking sweet Nan, for there are good and bad spirits roaming the land. The good ones become eagles, hawks, or birds in the sky. The bad ones turn into wolves and show their pointed teeth, waiting to devour and bring death to your earthly body. She had Ben stoke the central fire outside so that the wolves would not come closer.

Nan's brow got hotter, sweat broke out and her face flushed as the evening wore on. Then Nan drifted into jerking fits, that would not cease. Her body would grow rigid, her back would arch, and foam would come from her mouth. White Hawk was frightened and sent Ben to fetch Mother to help her doctor Nan.

Mother entered the cabin, immediately smelling the sickness in the air—she knew it, she had smelled it before. Rather than the stale smoky air of the cabin from the stone fireplace they burned in the chill of the night, this odor was different, it was putrid. As she drew nearer to Nan, she noticed her body smelled like baked bread. The sweat beaded up Nan's young face, plastering her hair to her forehead with wet curls on the nape of her neck. Her eyes rolled back into her head showing only the whites sunken deep into their orbits. She didn't rouse when Grandmother spoke to her. The fever muddled her brain, and her breathing made a whistling sound when she exhaled.

"How long as she been like this?"

"Since returning home from school, about four hours now, she grows worse by the minute. I have tried all the tonics I know. Nothing works to lower the heat in her body. She grows sicker and now has a foul bloody flux. I see her spirit drifting out of her." White Hawk said.

Mother pulled up the sleeve of Nan's shirt to look at her arms, and the waist to look at her belly. Small flat rosy spots covered her lower chest and abdomen.

"Oh no, this child has typhoid fever," Mother said.

White Hawk gasped, she knew this was bad, and she admonished herself for not recognizing it sooner. Not just for Nan, but this could spread amongst the tribe and the people in the room were in grave danger. Nan's life hung in the balance. She knew they needed to do all they could to break the fever, if Nan had any chance of survival.

White Hawk asked Ben to listen for the drumming in the far-off lands of the Yunwi Tsunsdi. The ancient ones told stories of these short people, no taller than your waist that hid in the mountains. They had crooked teeth; their hands and eyes were on fire. They swallowed the sun to make darkness. The 'little people' were night travelers, who never wanted to be seen, but you could watch the weeds sway at night as they moved through them. They would beat their drums and sing warnings of things to come. The ancestors told stories that these 'little people' could cure sickness, and if one could be caught, it might cure Nan. She was desperate and would try anything.

Mother began chanting to the four winds to rebalance Nan's life force and purifying the lodge of evil spirits. She smoked sage in the room and rubbed the burnt ashes on Nan's forehead, then took the sacred eagle feather and fanned the smoke all over her body. They opened the door wide to let the night air in to help Nan breathe. Mother also smoked the room with cedar boughs on the fireplace. She removed Nan's clothes and burned them in the fire. She lay naked as a newborn without anything for the evil spirits to cling onto. As Mother tried to cool her body, Nan shivered from her fever in the cool night air.

"Ben, I need you to go to the icehouse to get a block of ice. Pound it until it breaks into pieces and then we will pile it around her little body to lower the heat of the sickness," Mother said.

The men had harvested blocks of ice last winter from the river when it froze solid. They stored them deep underground, insulated with straw and sawdust, in the community icehouse for needs such as this.

All day and night Mother and Grandmother would bathe her in cold water, try to feed her slivers of ice, and place cool towels on her head and torso. Her teeth chattered as she lay in the pool of cold water and ice, and her lips turned blue, but the fever raged higher.

After Ben delivered the pounded ice to the lodge, he took red paint, put an x around the door, standing guard outside so no one could enter. Then he sat outside and prayed for the Great Spirit to heal his daughter.

When White Hawk wasn't tending to Nan, she was praying, offering smoke to the four corners, and asking Great Spirit to allow her the gift of healing for Nan. She nor Mother would venture outside nor let anyone inside the cabin for fear of spreading the contagion.

They fought the fever for three days as it got higher. Nan would not eat or drink and made no water. She grew weaker, falling deeper into her sickness and growing closer to the spirits of the upper world. The red rash covered most of her body, she turned yellow and became delirious fighting the hands that worked to save her. Nan spoke to spirits no one could see but her. This was painful for White Hawk to watch as her child struggled to hold onto this life. Her hands reached for the heavens and mimicked climbing a ladder—a sign of trying to get to the upper realm. Nan became agitated from the high fever and White Hawk's medicine could not sooth her. She knew this was Nan's spirit fighting to leave her earthly body. She tied a red string to Nan's wrist and the other end to the healing stick to hold her in this world. White Hawk and Mother used every herb, medicine, and amulet they had to save Nan, but nothing worked to help her.

As a last resort, she sent Ben to the lodge of the medicine man to seek his help for Nan. He agreed to try his medicine because Nan was just a child. He gathered a group of elders, painted their faces and bodies. The medicine man would sup a liquid into his mouth, and then spew it onto the fire which would explode upward to the sky. They sang and danced around the fire in the center of the village all night.

Nan died on the fourth day of her suffering. She just stopped breathing and the fight was over.

Her body finally grew cold, gray, and stiff as the fever lost its host.

White Hawk was desolate and felt her heart break once again. Her beautiful, smart, gift from

Isaac was now gone from her and this world. She mourned the death of her child and her dreams for the future she carried in her heart. Ben and Mother were inconsolable as well. The tribe braced for the illness to strike their loved ones while mourning the loss of the young girl —the healer's only daughter. If she couldn't heal her own child, they surely had no hope.

After preparing Nan's body for burial, she was placed her on top of her father's bones in the burial mound. The last bones to lay in this mound would be the priest, and then they would start a new burial mound elsewhere. White Hawk prayed that she would soon lay with her beloved's bones in this place.

The death of her child was different this time than when the bounty hunters had murdered Isaac. Isaac had been a grown man, had lived a good portion of his life, married, and fathered a child. However, Nan was young, innocent, and pure. She had her whole life ahead of her and important things to accomplish. She should not have died at 15. White Hawk did not want to go on living but knew she must, and the entire tribe mourned Nan's loss.

The contagion spread throughout the camp, and the healers were unable to do much of anything to save those that contracted sickness. All they could do was treat the discomfort of symptoms and fevers and pray for healing to keep it from spreading. Most of those that died were adults and elders. Those that survived were sick with the fever for a month or more and suffered weakness for a while. After a few months, the disease ran its course in the camp and left as quickly as it came upon them.

The weeks turned into months and yet White Hawk's pain didn't diminish. She and Ben missed their vibrant daughter. They were lonely and turned to each other to get through the sorrow. Their love grew stronger in sadness, which they didn't think possible.

Eight months after Nan's death, White Hawk began to have morning sickness, her breast grew tender, and she realized she had not had her flow for months. She knew she was with a child and while happy, was also afraid of losing another love in her life. Ben was happy with the news of the new life they created growing within his love. He gave thanks to the Great Spirit for the blessing of this child.

After due time, White Hawk and Ben welcomed the new baby into their family. White Hawk still felt the loss of Nan, but her heart now held hope of new life and love. It was as if the birth pains drove the sadness out of her body when this daughter arrived. They named her Agali, which meant 'Sunshine.' Her brightness outshone the darkness of Nan's death and took away the sadness in their home. Agali grew strong and tall and learned the gift of healing just as Nan did before her.

White Hawk continued to provide healing to the tribe as she and Ben worked to help integrate the Freedmen into the Cherokee society. Since the end of the civil war, and over the next 10 years, seven Freedman schools were built in the Cherokee Territory. White Hawk and Ben saw the Cherokee Freedmen vote in the 1875 election. Their dreams for their brothers and sisters and former slaves were coming true; validating that all their work and sacrifice was not in vain.

TWENTY

Current Day

Cherokee Nation
Talequah, Oklahoma

The month passed and June arrived sooner than expected, her life had been a whirlwind since she made the decision to take the summer position. Annie spent the month packing up the house, getting rid of things that held no meaning to her and that seemed suddenly unimportant. Storing only the essential belongings and listing the house for sale with a realtor were her last tasks to complete. She found it very liberating to be free from all the ties and bad memories Chicago held for her. It was like a weight lifted off her. She felt eighteen again, heading off to college and a new life awaiting her, yet older and wiser.

Annie was excited and ready to be practicing real medicine again. Jabbing vaxes, treating colds and flu at the grocery store walk-in clinic was mind numbingly boring. But the good news, if you could call it that, they graciously granted her time off without pay and she would have a job waiting for her when she returned in September.

In the months leading up to her departure she continued to make progress in her 12-Steps program. The last two steps to complete were to seek her Higher Power's will for her life—the power to carry it out, and to carry the message to other alcoholics while practicing the principles in her life. She believed the knowledge of how to accomplish these lofty goals would be revealed to her in time, because she didn't have a clue how to do this on her own. She wasn't making plans or worrying about it like she normally did. She was doing her best to hang on to her sobriety while living life one day at a time all alone.

She drove 11 hours from the outskirts of Chicago to Tahlequah, Oklahoma tribal headquarters of the Cherokee Nation on the Friday before the job started on Monday. This gave her a couple of days to settle in, check out the facilities, and find her bearings around town.

On the drive, Annie called her newly discovered cousin Sarah leaving a message that she would soon be in Talequah and would like to meet in person. She also asked if she had found any information about her grandmother Polly. She had thought of little else since learning of her newly found family, wondering what they were like and if there were any family resemblances. She had never looked like anyone else in her life. She was nervous but also excited at the prospect of finding her roots and someone to answer her questions.

She stayed one night at the local motel, which met her pre-requisites of clean sheets, no hourly renters loitering outside the doors, and affordable. Early on Saturday morning she met the only full-time nurse at the public health clinic, nurse Betsy something, she couldn't understand her last name. There was no doctor, he had quit six months ago taking a job in Tulsa leaving the locals in dire need of a walk-in clinic. They advertised to fill the vacancy but received few applicants. Those that did express interest initially came for an interview and then flatly turned them down. Citing various reasons, such as too little salary (number one reason), too much poverty in the Nation, and the isolation. They usually had much more attractive offers to consider.

Nurse Betsy was a talker. She gave Annie the low-down on the state of affairs, and the other health-care volunteers arriving later that afternoon. There was one other physician, two PA's and six nurses staffing the summer session clinic, held in conjunction with the local hospital. They would work two days at the doctor's clinic building seeing scheduled patients or walk-ins, and three days in the hospital setting in a teaching/mentoring role for interns or filling in for shortages of staff. Dr. Chase Hunter was the other doctor coming from Nashville, Tennessee, where he practiced for 15 years. Interestingly, Betsy pointed out that he was born a Cherokee of the Eastern Band from North Carolina.

Betsy organized a dinner for later that evening, allowing the entire team to meet and get to know one another before beginning rounds on Monday. The team enjoyed a pitch-in dinner held at the clinic first, getting acquainted and sizing-up with one another. Annie was pleased with the talent and especially liked Dr. Hunter. They hit it off from the beginning, sharing many of the same experiences since he was about her age. It didn't hurt that he was tall, had a broad white smile—which seemed perpetual, straight teeth, thick dark hair parted on the side and slicked back with gel. He spoke with a southern twang, exhibited good manners, and was nice. The dinner prepared by some of the local women was delicious fried chicken, mashed potatoes with white gravy with sides. Many of the dishes she recognized and sampled, but the most interesting was grape dumplings. Which she never heard of or could even imagine the coupling of the ingredients as tasty. It was just what the name implied; sweet dumplings cooked in grape juice. It was an amazing recipe from the old timers and became one of her favorites.

When the evening ended, she was surprised to learn that her free room was in a local's home—not a hotel room as she imagined. Her host was elder Leotie Smith, who was 80 years old and a revered storyteller in the tribe. At first Annie was apprehensive, but then she realized what an opportunity to learn more about her heritage straight from an elder. After following a map drawn on a scrap of paper, she found the house arriving about 9 p.m. She was timid as she gently knocked on the glass pane in the front door.

"Come in," Leotie yelled, without even moving from her chair.

Annie found the door unlocked, and Leotie sitting in a cozy, dimly lit living room watching television. A colorful blanket wrapped around her legs, propped upon a worn ottoman. As if stepping back into a history book, Annie inhaled the earthy fragrance of the room and took in the well-used belongings. Pictures of native men and women, she supposed were family, circled the room hung much too high on twine looped over nails driven into the four walls. Exposing long strings of twine, suspending each frame from the nail became part of the display. The house was small, one tightly packed living room, opening to a smaller kitchen with two-bedroom doors and a bath leading off from the living room. Each bedroom was only big enough for a twin bed, nightstand and a three - drawer chest. The home was clean, comfortable and had a sweetness like a home. She felt this was where love once lived, and the specters remained. After taking in her surroundings, Annie's eyes rested upon the smiling face of her host Leotie Smith.

Leotie wrinkled from head to toe wore her long gray hair parted in the middle with two braids hanging down beside her weathered face. When she smiled her eyes smiled too, crinkling into tiny slits and her mouth opened wide, revealing pink gums. Leotie would not turn her eyes directly onto Annie as she spoke, her voice was low and had a monotone pitch. Annie knew she was in for a delightful stay with this warm old soul, and she looked forward to hearing some ancient stories from her. Annie sat down on the sofa covered by another blanket and introduced herself, she already felt right at home.

Does Leotie know my grandmother, Polly?

It was entirely possible, as she was about the same age. Annie would hold off questioning her until they became better acquainted. After a few minutes of chitchat, Annie realized how tired she was from the long drive and evening activities. She needed to find a bed and rest. She just hoped her leg didn't give out and she didn't conjure any more imaginary people. As she began to drift off to sleep, she realized the next few months would be a bit strenuous.

The next morning Annie entered the kitchen at 6 a.m., Leotie had brewed coffee, fried bacon, scrambled eggs, and baked the biggest cathead biscuits like she had never seen before. The table was set with her plate, real butter, cream, and a jar of homemade apple butter to slather on the hot biscuits.

"Leotie, I think I may have died and gone to heaven, this smells and looks wonderful. Do you do this every morning?"

"Why yes, I used to cook for my husband Dewey. He died last winter, so I can't seem to break the habit. We were married for 53 years," she said.

Her voice trailed off and Annie sensed her loneliness, and then caught a glint in her eye. It was as if she had summoned his memories into form and she saw him once again. Annie wondered what it would be like to have a love like that, to have a profound spiritual connection to another person. To have such a memory, which can cross great chasms to visit with you from the beyond. She didn't think she would ever know that kind of love.

Annie cleared her throat to bring her back and said, "You don't have to go to all this trouble for me, I'm used to eating on the run. You're gonna spoil me."

Then she ate every delicious bite and still had time to make it to the clinic by 7 a.m. ready for the day. Annie looked forward to coming back in the evening; she wanted to experience more of the life Leotie knew and hear her stories from the past.

The Monday morning rounds began promptly with chart review at 7 a.m. and the first patients seen by the entourage at 8 a.m. Four medical students accompanied her until noon, then she would take lunch and resume with another group of four for afternoon rounds.

After finishing the first day, Betsy arranged another team dinner at Mac Daddy's in the nearby town of Tahlequah. The restaurant looked more like a bar than an eating establishment, and she was hesitant to go inside. However, she wasn't ready to tell anyone about her drinking problem yet, so she went along with the group. She just wouldn't drink. She reached into her pocket to be sure the chip was there. Once inside she noticed the centerpiece of the establishment was a 15-foot old oak bar with brass foot rails, and every stool was occupied. The bar beckoned to her, but she resisted. This place had some age on it. The lighting was from an old buggy wheel suspended in the center of the room, lights wired around the top of it and covered with Mason jar shades. It was not very pretty or efficient. The bar room was dark, dingy, and held the lingering smell of stale cigarette smoke. Likely wafting from the walls which looked sticky and covered in tan nicotine film exhaled by countless lungs of days gone by. The jukebox played a whiney country song from Waylon or Willie or someone similar, and the patrons were talking loud enough to drown it out. The clanking glasses and bottles transported her back to memories of her local dive and brought with it pleasant feelings. She pushed those feelings away and steadied her resolve. She noticed toward the right side of the bar was a room and through the doorway she saw tables for dining, the group headed that way like a herd moving all together as one. Once seated at the round table, she wiped the perspiration from her top lip while trying to focus on the menu. She prayed silently that no one would order cocktails. Then she heard Dr. Hunter tell the table he wanted to buy drinks for all around to celebrate the success of the first day's clinic.

"Oh shit," she muttered under her breath.

When the server asked her order, she shocked herself at what came out of her mouth, "gin and tonic with a wedge of lime."

She had five minutes at best to get her resolve back before the drink arrived, she thought of her promises to Ray and Carol.

Afterall, what harm will one little drink do…

The internal volley back and forth continued until the drink sat before her on the table. She twirled the glass around sloshing the liquid, stirring with the plastic sword stuck through the lime wedge. She then squeezed the lime into it like so many times before, it was amazing how easy it came back to her. She could already taste the tangy gin and imagine the warm feeling of it going down her gullet.

The others raised their glasses and clanked them together around the circle of new friends, she did likewise and did not want to stand out from the crowd. Inside she was falling apart, this was bigger than one little drink, all her hard work would be for nothing. Her life was just starting to come together, and the craziness subsided, her cravings were lessening, and her mind was healing. After the group toast, she placed the rim of the glass onto her lips, smelled the familiar fragrance but did not drink from it. She sat the glass down, she had won the battle. She remained sober for another day.

The meal continued with them trading stories about their day and noting minor improvements to the process which would help the next day and future clinics. Annie remembered this feeling from med school, happiness from healing people that really needed her. She hadn't felt this way for a long time, Carol had been right again about helping others. It was good for her soul, and she was proud of herself for passing the tests thrown at her today.

Dr. Hunter regaled them with funny stories from the south in his smooth southern drawl; she liked to hear him talk. She was quiet and content just to listen to the others speak. After dinner the team broke up and headed to the bar attached to the restaurant, Annie felt uneasy but went along. She thumbed the coin in her pocket and thought about her promises to Ray and Carol, and her victory over gin. Some of the group settled at the bar, some headed to a pool table to play a round. She found herself alone with Dr. Hunter at a tabletop for two.

He ordered a beer from the server and looked toward her.

"I'll take a tonic water with wedge of lime."

"You're not drinking anything?" he asked.

"No, I may as well tell you I have nothing to hide, I'm a recovering alcoholic. I pretended to sip the drink with dinner, I don't drink anymore. I'm sober now," she said.

She pulled the worn coin from her pocket and showed it to him, like a warrior showing off the Silver Star medal.

"This is my first chip and my good-luck charm."

"Congratulations, I guess that explains your altruism of working a summer clinic on the nation for your vacation," he said.

"Partly right, I am trying to find inner peace, but I also have an ulterior motive."

"Oh, you hoped to meet an eligible bachelor and fall madly in love? I just happen to be free," he laughed.

"No, I'm off men too, not that I'm lesbian or anything, which is ok….," she stammered, and her face reddened afraid she sounded homophobic.

"But that's not what I meant. I just ended a long-term relationship and am not looking for another one. My Higher Power set this all in motion for me, I believe. I think I am here to find something lost to me for a long-time."

"Well, I'm intrigued, spill it," he said.

"I might share it with you before the summer is over, but I have some things to work out first."

She changed the subject and said, "Now tell me your secrets Dr. Hunter and all about your exciting bachelor life in Nashville."

"Please call me Chase," he said.

They talked until midnight before noticing the time. When she realized the lateness, she worried about keeping Leotie up past her bedtime. After hurrying home, she found Leotie snuggled in the big chair, wrapped in the blanket, and snoozing. Annie liked the feeling of someone caring enough to wait up for her and it touched her heart. Annie woke Leotie and helped her limp to bed, but she could hardly find sleep, eager for the next day to begin.

She found a message on her cell phone, which Sarah had left the evening before, and it brought sad news. While great Aunt Polly was still alive, Sarah talked with her, and she was not willing to meet with Annie. She relayed through Sarah that she was now 76 years old and long ago sent Byrdie to the spirit world, and never knew her baby. She was too old and sick to open this wound back up. However, Sarah would still like to meet her long-lost cousin and would call her back to schedule a dinner later in the week. Annie couldn't believe the message, she thought she had come here to meet her true family, but now her own grandmother was disowning her again. She didn't think it would mean this much to her, but it did.

She craved her morning drink of vodka and orange juice; she tried thumbing the chip in her pocket. But it didn't work today. She sat down on the bed and dialed Ray's number and even though quite early back in Chicago he answered with his usual chipper self.

"Ray, sorry to call you so early, but I need you I'm about to lose it," she shared her story and disappointment with him.

He talked her down, recommended that she find a local chapter. Almost ordering her, pay a visit, and do it soon. She agreed to find one tonight and would hold on to get through the day.

Today she was scheduled at the walk-in doctor's office, and the work was good for her, taking her mind away from her troubles and the desire to drink. She noticed Chase was spending more time around her today, she thought it was because he had a lighter load of patients. Then she saw his backlog sheet, he had more patients waiting than she did.

Is it possible he's flirting?

She tried to make herself scarce when he was around, avoiding him all day. She did not want to start anything romantic with this man, no matter how attracted she was to him. He would be long-gone in a few short months.

Nope, nada, not gonna do it.....

As promised to Ray, she found a local friend of Bill W. meeting in the First Baptist Church basement in downtown Tahlequah. She was surprised to see all the Native people there, she supposed they came from the Nation. When they shared, she found their stories like the ones heard back in Chicago. They described the same drinking, same destruction of lives, same disease, and same 12-Step Program helping them survive hour-to-hour and day-by-day. Sharing a cup of coffee and getting to know some of them afterward helped her hang on to her sobriety and strengthened her resolve once again. Ray was right.

A few days later Sarah arranged dinner plans with Annie at a local restaurant. Annie was nervous about meeting the first blood relative she ever knew existed, but she was also excited. She changed her outfit three times before just giving up. When she arrived at the Hitchin' Post steak house, the hostess seated her at a reserved table in Sarah's name. A few minutes later a woman in her mid-sixty's made her way to the empty seat across from her introducing herself as Sarah. She was average height, a little on the stocky side, and dark hair sprinkled with gray. Annie could tell that she was Native but saw no other resemblance to each other.

"Oh Annie, oh my gosh you look just like Byrdie when she was young. I'm a little taken aback by the similarity. It makes me miss her even more."

Sarah was warm and friendly, sharing with Annie details of her birth mother. Things Annie had always wondered about. Byrdie was very smart in school, and exceptionally pretty. All the boys flocked around her, and she had a great personality, always the life of the party. Annie didn't inherit those traits from her, she was quiet and standoffish until she got to know a person. Sarah also brought pictures of her and Byrdie from their teens. She made copies for Annie to have, and Annie couldn't take her eyes from the photos—she did look like her. There was her face and stature looking at her from the past, a surreal moment for her. She now had a face to go with the name in her head.

Annie shared about the wonderful life her parents gave her. Talked about her education and medical school, but she omitted any discussion of Tom, her failure at love, marriage, loneliness, and addiction.

Then the discussion got serious, Sarah apologized that Aunt Polly would not meet her. She had trouble understanding her reasoning, it had to be something too painful for her to face.

"I want to stay in touch with you Annie, after you leave. It's like I have a little piece of Byrdie back to hold onto. I loved her so much and I know how proud she would be of you, if only you two met earlier maybe things would have been different for her. If there had been any way she could have kept you and taken care of you, I believe she would have."

Sarah explained life in the nation as a single mom in the 70's and believed Byrdie did what she thought was best for Annie. She wondered aloud if that guilt was what led to Byrdie's drinking problem eventually killing her.

Sarah blamed herself for losing Annie to their entire clan. She believed that if the family had known about Byrdie's pregnancy, they would have tried to adopt her baby. Polly would be the only one who would know if they tried, and it's doubtful she would ever talk about it.

Prior to Annie's adoption there were no laws to protect the babies born in the Nation, Sarah explained. Many infants taken from their families by the courts and given to white couples for assimilation. Just months after Annie's adoption in 1978 the law was set in place to change the practices for Native babies. That law meant family members have preference to adopt before their infants can be placed with white families off the Nation. Her whole life could have been different if she had been born just a few months later. It gave Annie something to ponder.

What would have become of me….

Carlisle Indian School,
Pennsylvania
Ca. 1885

https://carlisleindian.dickinson.edu/images

The Carlisle Indian Industrial school operated from 1879-1918 as the first federally funded off-reservation boarding school in the U.S. Over 10,000 students from 140 tribes were forced to attend Carlisle. Removed from their homes by law denying Native parental rights in 1891. This practice ended in 1976 with the Indian Child Welfare act.

Approximately 234 students died, and 190 students were buried at this school.

TWENTY-ONE

1890

Indian Territory
West of the Mississippi

Time marched onward but change came about slowly and not in the best interest for the Cherokee. After the civil war new treaties between the U.S. government and the Five Civilized Tribes of Indian Territory—Cherokee, Chickasaw, Choctaw, Muskogee, and Seminole people, outlined citizenship for formerly held African slaves to be known as "Freedmen." Each of the Five Tribes dealt with the Freedmen in some manner, but the Cherokee Nation's 1866 Treaty stated that all Freedmen and their descendants have the same rights as native Cherokees.

Even though the Cherokee made this treaty in good faith, the 'settlers' and the politicians of the day still plotted to steal The People's land. The formation of the Dawes Commission in 1887 under the General Allotment Act, created specifically to bring about the dissolution of tribal governments by the allotment of land parcels to individual tribal members. The Act gave each family head 320 acres of grazing land, or 160 acres of farmland. Single adult men received 80 acres, boys received 40 acres and women received no land. Registration for anyone to get their name on the Dawes Roll was a nightmare of paperwork and bureaucracy as the burden of proof was on the applicants. The enrollment was by blood quantum, primarily through guesswork. It was a disaster for the Cherokee as it further stripped them of their tribal culture and caused many of them to lose their land by fraud and deception. These plots were deemed too small for sustainable agriculture and ignored traditional native views of land ownership. Not only did the government steal the land, but the Cherokee gained a major source of income through lease arrangements with large cattle ranches. In 1889 the Cherokee agreed to a 5-year grazing lease for $200K annually on acreage west of their lands, however, congress nullified the arrangement effectively eliminating tribal profits from grazing land.

The true motivation for the Dawes Act was greed by the whites for land. After doling out the allotments, the millions of acres remaining opened for sale to whites. This brought on the land run of 1893 and paved the way for Oklahoma statehood in 1907. The stolen land amounted to 86 million acres, or 62 percent of the pre-1887 holdings.

White Hawk was soon turning 60 years old and had been a healer for most of her life. She was tired and worn out from years of mistreatment and constant conflict with their people. One of the only good things in her life was their daughter Agali. She continued to be the sunshine of their lives, and now performing most of the healing for the clan.

For several weeks as the nights got cooler turning the leaves from vivid green to brilliant colors of yellow and red, found White Hawk plagued with a foreboding that hung in the autumn air. She knew something bad was about to happen and felt compelled to do a spirit walk and commune with the ancient ones about these feelings. The spirit walks were becoming more difficult for her to recover from physically, but she believed this was important enough to take risks to her health.

With Agali's help, she prepared the tonic and the lodge for the spirit walk. She cleansed the space of evil spirits lurking about and from each person sitting around the fire chanting for her. She tied a red string to her healing stick and handed it to Agali, and the other end was tied around her wrist. In case, she needed help finding her way back to the land of the living.

"Agali, while I am gone you will need to lead the chant of our fathers so that I can hear you from beyond. I am afraid that if I can't find my way back, I may cross the chasm of no return and be lost for eternity."

She realized this was a lot of responsibility to place on a 24-year-old, but Agali was ready for it.

White Hawk trusted her with her life and death.

Agali began the chanting and shaking the dried gourds, "oh eh ye oh"….a song to the Great Spirit rang out from her soul and the others followed in unison. Mother taught her well and she knew the words to sing. White Hawk gulped the bitter drink and rested her head downward waiting for the effects to take place. Soon her spirit was on the desert plain, the winds whipping around her and the heat radiating from the parched land beneath her feet. Her spirit guide suddenly appeared beside her. Then she saw Grandmother standing on the far mountainside, she imagined standing beside her and then she was there.

"Grandmother I have missed you so, and I long to be with you for eternity."

"My daughter, I am afraid you have many years to travel upon the Earth before you will become one with eternity. However, I want to prepare you for a great loss. You will soon see Ben's spirit flyaway.

He longs to be here with Isaac and his ancestors. His time is short to walk beside you and Agali upon Mother Earth."

"No Grandmother, I am not ready lose another loved one—please, not my Ben."

Grandmother continued, "I also see into the future of the Cherokee Nation, there is more turmoil coming again between the white man and our people. They want us to forget our heritage and become like them. They will take our children forcing them to go to white man schools to change their character or be punished. We must never do this; we must never let them forget their ancestors. Teach our young ones the old ways of our people. Keep the language and dances of our culture fresh in their minds.

The white man will spill the blood of our people over the Ghost Dance, which many believe will enable our people to go into battle unseen. Bullets will not penetrate warrior clothing, and our horses will stand strong and not fall to the bullets from the white man's guns. This will happen farther in the west, but the white man is against this dance, and it will lead to a battle between our brothers and the soldiers."

She went on, "This will come at grave cost to all native people. The Great Sioux Nation will suffer the death of their Lakota Chief, Sitting Bull. I see another battle at Wounded Knee killing many of the Lakota people by the U.S. Troops. This will anger the white man even more against us. They will steal our children from their families and be forced into white man's schools taught to deny their blood, cut their hair, and change their names. Many children will die or suffer fates worse than death, the death of their spirit. They will try to kill the native in them. They will make our young women barren to kill off future generations. They will forget their own tongue and speak only white man talk, many will lose their culture and sacred teachings. They will steal one of your own daughters to be lost to our people. But there will be a day when the lost one will come back and reunite with the ancestors. Don't lose faith, the Creator will make us whole one day, and your seed will return to the land of our people. Oh, how I weep for our people.

You must go back to your time now; you tarry here too long, and your spirit weakens to the point of no return." Grandmother said.

"I haven't seen Isaac or Nan yet, will they come forward?"

Then the large black stag appeared on the hillside and beside him stood a small white fawn. They ran toward her and as they did morphed into Isaac and Nan. Briefly reunited in the netherworld, White Hawk tried to reach out and touch them, but they disappeared from her fingertips. They became only a wisp of smoke and a memory.

"They are here together and await the day you will come, but it will be many years for you upon Mother Earth before you journey here permanently. A great many things will happen to you and your offspring, as I foretold. It will come full circle, and your line of healers will grow and prosper into the new millennium, it will be different but the same.

You will see all this and a great honor for our line of healers come to pass."

White Hawk heard Agali's chanting calling her to return to her body. The pull between here and there was getting stronger and the red string was taut on her wrist. She had to leave or risk the string breaking, losing her forever in the 'land of no time.'

"Now go from this place and do not come here again, until you walk here for eternity and with no plan to return to the other side. This ability to walk amongst the spirit world will die with you, until the special one has been born and will come here again one day in the future. You will meet her here many seasons from now. Return to the land of the living, go!"

White Hawk awoke back in the lodge. Many hours had passed and Agali was still chanting the songs of the ancestors and shaking the gourds to bring her back to them.

Agali's hair and face were wet with beads of perspiration and her voice was hoarse. She had been chanting nonstop and shaking round dried gourds to the beat of a lone drum outside the lodge. It was

Ben, sitting a safe distance away from inside a holy place.

White Hawk was not sure what to do with the messages from grandmother. After giving it much thought she told no one. All she could do was watch as the future unfolded and share the heartache that befell her people. In December, the Ghost Dance defiance occurred, and they killed Sitting Bull two weeks later. Then they killed over 300 Lakota, two-thirds of them men, women, and children at the battle of Wounded Knee. These were turbulent times for the native people, constantly at odds with the white man and the U.S. Government. Tensions were high, and there was no peace at home, as they stole more and more children from their families sending them to the government boarding schools for 'rehabilitation' from what they deemed as savagery. Their fates at these schools were abusive discipline, cultural erasure, and physical and sexual abuse, even death in some cases. The true number unknown as unmarked graves at many schools were the only proof they existed.

Yet, White Hawk and Agali persevered in the work to heal and educate her people—it was all she knew to do.

Ben died in early spring from pneumonia. She tried her best to heal his body, but he was ready to pass over and she knew it was his time. She was happy that he would finally reunite with his brother Isaac, daughter Nan, Grandmother, and ancestors. She wished she were with them at times, but she still had work to do.

The following year Agali travelled east to attend nursing school, leaving White Hawk alone in the Territory. After earning her nursing certificate, Agali met and married a Cherokee man in the East. They soon welcomed a daughter, Susan.

Tragically, Agali's husband died when an automobile collided with the carriage he was driving. She returned home with baby Susan to establish a medical clinic adopting the white man's medicine that was acceptable to her people, many were leery of the Eastern practices.

When Susan was barely eight years old, the government required her to attend the white man's boarding school established in the Territory. She would be one of the first Cherokee students to live there forcibly removed from her family, and indoctrinated, to remove the Native culture from her. The moto of residential schools was "kill the Indian in him, save the man."

Susan was lucky and allowed to go home on weekends where Agali would speak only Cherokee with her to remind her of her language. The first week at school, they cut off Susan's long braids making her hair short and dressed her in a uniform, while burning her clothes. Susan's happy demeanor changed, and she became withdrawn.

A few weeks later, on one visit home, mother raised her arm to swat a fly and Susan flinched, cowered down covering her head with her arms. Mother also noticed Susan was unable to use her hands, when she looked at them, she saw the red whelps and bruising on her palms.

"My daughter, what has happened to your hands?"

"I'm sorry Mother, I made a mistake with the teacher. I used a Cherokee word instead of English when I answered a question in class. She said she would make an example of my savage ways. She bent my hand backwards and then struck me five times on each palm with the wooden ruler."

Susan would tell mother stories of punishments for simple offenses some of the other girls had suffered. The children required to pray to white God and renounce the teachings of their people. If the teachers overheard anyone speaking Cherokee with any other classmates on the playground or at lunch, harsh punishment ensued. She had seen children put in solitary confinement for days, flogging, starvation, whipping and cuffing. Some of the children just disappeared, without an explanation for their families.

After telling her mother of these abuses, she said, "They call me a heathen, what is that mother?"

"My daughter, you are a proud Cherokee, pay no mind to their names. We will not let you forget your heritage, your language, and your purpose in life. You may have to endure this for a time, but hold onto what is rightfully yours, remember what I have taught you. Hold it in your heart."

Susan learned the language and the stories of her past and integrated her present into her culture she kept hidden while living amongst the white people. Agali kept the stories of the Cherokee alive in her daughter and saw her travel east to attend college and medical school in 1910.

However, in the early spring of 1918 the Spanish flu hit the world. The pandemic spread to the nation just as it had in the east. White Hawk used her most powerful medicines but could not stop the 'Winter Fever' from spreading and killing most of those that were infected. Agali tried to get the people to wear face masks, but they would not. Their culture believed that they were hiding their true self from their friends, and they refused to wear them.

One evening a runner summoned White Hawk to Agali's lodge where she found her lying on pelts with a high fever and unable to breathe. She couldn't stand and hadn't eaten or drank for several days without vomiting.

"Daughter, why didn't you call me sooner? I fear the grippe has you hard in the chest, like a fist that won't let go. I don't know if my medicine is strong enough to free you from it now."

Agali began to whimper, she knew her life was in the balance, and she may never live to see Susan in the territory again.

"Mother, I am not afraid to cross to the land of no time and beyond. I am sad that I won't see you or my daughter for many moons. I will be free either way, no matter if I live or die."

White Hawk began treating her immediately. First, she prayed for the Great Spirit to allow her to heal her daughter, giving her knowledge and strong medicine. She built a fire and burned sage around the room while chanting to drive out the evil spirits and clean the air. She placed fresh pine boughs on the fireplace to allow the smoke into the house to disinfect the room. She used her most powerful medicines in her satchel to save her daughter, but to no avail. Agali died as did a great many others in the Nation, Grandmother did her best, but her medicine could not save her only remaining child.

The Far West-shooting buffalo on the
line of the Kansas-Pacific railroad.
Ca. 1871

The Far West – shooting buffalo on the line of the
Kansas-Pacific Railroad/Bghs.,Great Plains, 1871
Photograph, courtesy Library of Congress.
https://www.loc.gov/item/2004669992/

TWENTY-TWO

1900-1930

*Indian Territory
State of Oklahoma*

The beginning of the new century was a devastating time for the Cherokee Nation in the Indian Territory of what would become Oklahoma. The Civil War had ended, and the country tried to rebuild and restore trust in one nation under God, while westward expansion exploded with the construction of the modern railway. From zero railroads in 1870, Congress once again butted in by

giving land grants through Indian Territory. The west experienced a great railroad boon in 1897 due to settler movement westward further encroaching upon the Cherokee lands with the discovery of coal, and oil fields and their expansion.

The impact upon the Cherokee way of life was threatening their livelihoods. For generations, the Cherokee relied upon the buffalo as their primary food and clothing source, and practiced taking only what they needed or used, and then giving thanks to the Great Spirit for every life harvested. They used every bit of the buffalo, from the skin all the way to the bones. The Cherokee watched in horror as the white hunters came from the east on the new railways. The People saw them kill the great animals for sport leaving carcasses upon the ground. The railroads advertised 'hunting by rail' allowing hundreds of men to ride and shoot buffalo from the moving trains rooftop, or open windows. Slaughtering great herds as the trains rode by, leaving the animals carcasses rotting where shot for sport.

It wasn't long until the skinners showed up and a bustling trade was born. The buffalo in the west became like the gold in New Echota, and the white man came to take it. Buffalo hides were sought after back east for belts in factories, and in the fine stores for fashion, and their bones ground for fertilizer.

To meet the demand rail cars hauled tons of hides to the east, hundreds of buffalo killed per day leaving the scattered carnage on the grasses to stink. The smell grew so bad the People had to cover their nose and mouth with rags and would gag as the winds changed directions blowing into their camps. Death surrounded them, White Hawk mourned for the animal that once provided food, clothing, and tools for them. Their food source became scarce, and they hungered.

The government promoted this to starve the People into leaving the open regions and moving onto the Indian Territory, making more room for the whites to settle. By the beginning of 1900's the majestic buffalo herds were gone from the sacred hunting grounds. White Hawk saw the railroads and the white men come into their midst and intrude upon their peace once again, plotting to take their lands, while leaving a path of destruction in their wake. There was little they could do but to survive. The stories travelled over the plains of the soldiers extinguishing the Nations in the South and West that tried to fight back, burning villages to the ground. They killed men, women, and children leaving no one behind to bear witness to their evil deeds of genocide. During this time of hardship, White Hawk turned 70 years old, the People revered her as an elder and leader. Just as she had seen in her vision many years earlier, the Tribal Council bestowed the title of 'Beloved Woman' upon her. This honor, awarded to very few over the centuries, signified the respect for her work to educate, free those enslaved, and healing for the People. The ceremony held in the community lodge in the center of the village was standing room only.

White Hawk suffered from arthritis in her knees, and it was difficult for her to stand or walk, she now used her healing stick as a cane, and the hair of those she healed long ago still dangled from it. She hobbled from her chair of honor to the center of the room and stood facing the crowd.

While stooped over, a Cherokee Nation elder prayed over her and the leader of the Tribal

Council draped her shoulders with a ceremonial blanket woven in purple especially for her. They tied beaded swan feathers around the room to honor and represent the Cherokee Beloved People of the past and the chief bestowed a piece of deer antler shaped into a star around her neck and said fine words about her. She fought her entire life for land, for rights, for ceremony, for health, and for citizenship for her People. The ceremony was humbling for White Hawk, as The People finally recognized her work.

White Hawk thanked the Chief and the Council and then addressed the room.

"I am honored to stand with the Beloved Women that preceded me, I did not work for recognition, but because it was the right thing to do. We must continue to fight to protect what is ours and stand tall as a proud Cherokee Nation. We must return and cling to the 'old ways' of our ancestors."

After the ceremony, a man pointed a square box at her and took a photograph, which would be the first one framed to hang in the great room with the others that would follow her for generations to come. The tribe named her 'War-Woman' a role of power among the Councils. She would lead the Cherokee stand against the U.S. government as they began taking away their income from grazing lands leased to cattlemen, and other rights. Losing this funding affected the schools she had worked so hard to start and nearly bankrupted the tribe. The fight was now in courtrooms and halls in Washington D.C. and Bureau of Indiana Affairs, instead of the battlefields. Treaties between The Cherokee and U.S. government signed and then broken when it suited the white man's purpose. The politicians continued to eat away at what was rightfully the Cherokee's, and the once proud people became like walking ghosts trapped on foreign lands at the mercy of the government for handouts. Her heart ached with them.

White Hawk knew the attack on her people by the white man would not stop until they had taken everything sacred from them. The land, their ceremonies, their language, and their very existence was an abomination to the whites shouting for progress. As the white settlers pushed further westward, only the Five Tribes stood in their way.

Congress clamored to grant Oklahoma statehood, but first they had to do something about the sovereign land now owned and occupied by the Cherokee Nation and the other tribes. The government solution to their Cherokee problem was to form the Dawes Commission, which created the final rolls—recording all members of the Cherokee Nation at the time. This Commission then allotted tribal land of 160 acres to head of household and simultaneously extinguishing land rights for the entire Nation, resulting in the disbandment of the tribe by the U.S. government. Over four million acres of land allocated to slightly over forty thousand enrolled Cherokee. The land was rich with oil and white land speculators then bought or swindled the Cherokee out of their allotted property, leaving many destitute. The government thought they had won, but once again, they underestimated the resolve of The People, and the Cherokee Nation stood firm and survived.

An unexpected benefit of the Dawes Rolls would make a way for many to trace their ancestry back to their Cherokee bloodlines. Recorded on the pages as full blood was White Hawk's name and that of her daughter Agali along with her granddaughter Susan. This bores a record for all time and confirmed their existence. It was in black and white and would withstand history. Denying their purge from the earth and harkening their memories calling forward to their unborn daughters and sons.

White Hawk continued to heal her people and deliver babies until she could walk no more.

Returning to the land of her ancestors in 1920, now as a physician was her granddaughter Susan. The daughter of Agali, who inherited the gift and legacy of healing from White Hawk.

Susan was destined from her childhood to be a great healer. After finishing mandatory boarding school, she traveled to the East, where she attended college and then medical school. One of the few native people and first females allowed into the male domain of medicine, she worked hard and earned her place among them. They could find no fault in her. She longed to get her degree and return to her people and practice white man's medicine alongside Mother and Grandmother's methods. She believed there was room for both. The white man had new methods of surgery and drugs, but the medicines of her ancestors were sacred and existed since the beginning of time. Susan would not abandon their use; she would supplant them in her practice.

Susan attended college in Virginia at Hampton Normal and Agricultural Institute—a Black college that also accepted Native People. Most of the students there went on to become Black educators, the most notable being Booker T. Washington. Washington had walked over 500 miles from West Virginia when he was 16 to attend this school, graduated class of 1875, and went on to become the leader of Tuskegee University in 1881.

After graduation from college, Susan attended medical school at Women's Medical College of Pennsylvania, receiving tuition support from the Philadelphia Quakers through Society of Friends.

Medical school was a challenging time for her. She was frequently the brunt of jokes while working twice as hard as the best male student to keep her place. But she earned respect as an adept surgeon and diagnostician. Things seemed to come naturally to her. She learned many homeopathic remedies from Mother and Grandmother, returning home each summer working with them and preferring to use these cures on her patients. It proved cheaper and came with fewer side-effects than the uncontrolled pharmaceuticals of the day. Quacks abounded in the East and offered cures from ingesting pure mercury to drinks laced with cocaine and frequently killing more than they cured.

Her professors did not approve of her ways, so she prescribed remedies on the side when she wasn't being observed or graded. Patients flocked to her as the word spread about her abilities, treatments, and demeanor with women. This at a time in history when male doctors usually told women the condition stemmed from their emotions. She would integrate what she learned at the university with the natural ways of her ancestors. She learned the 'old ways' along with the new ways and vowed to return home one day to deliver modern medicine.

Susan visited the territory each summer while on break from her studies to spend time with Mother and Grandmother. It was like traveling back in time when she came home. In the East, she walked down cobblestone streets in fine hooped dresses, with gloves and delicate handkerchiefs to keep the dust out of her nose.

While at school she met and married a Cherokee man named Henry Wolf. Henry received a law degree and was open to traveling to parts unknown with her, wherever she wanted to go, he was agreeable. Of course, her first choice was home to the Cherokee people. Life in the territory was still difficult, the roads were either dusty ruts, or muddy bogs. Most of the homes were shacks with dirt and poverty in abundance. Yet, home called to her spirit, and she belonged there with her people.

She vowed one day to make the trip to the territory permanent and to practice modern medicine there. She would become the healer of her people integrating what she learned from the white man with the natural ways of her ancestors. There was room for both in her opinion, which was not a view accepted by the white man or Cherokee in the early 1900's.

She graduated as valedictorian of her class and earned her medical degree. They returned to the nation, where she received a government salary of $500 per year to establish a medical practice.

Susan the daughter of Agali, granddaughter of White Hawk accepted the gift and legacy of healing and returned to the land of her ancestors in 1920. Henry could not find work and fell into a deep melancholy. She tried to help him, but he found the bottle instead.

Unfortunately, Susan would suffer more heartache as Henry fell to the call of alcohol and could not hold down a job. Susan became a staunch supporter of prohibition, for she had seen first-hand the effects of alcohol abuse prevalent within her people. Alcoholism in the nation was a leading cause of poverty, domestic violence, sickness, and death.

White Hawk could hardly wait for Susan's return to work beside her just as her mother Agali had for all her years. Grandmother was now 90 years old, still healing, and midwifing for the Cherokee people. She used the healing stick more as a cane to walk now, but she was still spry for her advanced age. She would trek stooped over leaning on her stick many miles daily to the lodges of the sick carrying her bundle of herbs and remedies or they would come to her seeking help. Working together as a healer with her granddaughter Susan would be bittersweet time for both, as Agali was gone from their sight. But they knew she was watching over them from the land of no time. She now walked with their ancestors that passed before and would visit them in their dreams from time to time.

In 1926 Susan became Mother to Fannie, Grandmother was there to assist in the birth which took place in her lodge, like hundreds of others before her. White Hawk followed the full ceremony and customs of The Cherokee, practiced since the beginning of time. Sadly, White Hawk would not live to see Fannie grow to adulthood, or the resurgence and re-establishment of the Cherokee sovereign Nation.

Susan was there to help her pass from this world and be reborn into the next, just as Grandmother had escorted her to earth. White Hawk's death was not mournful. It was peaceful and she looked forward to passing into the 'land of no time' to join for eternity those she loved in this life. Grandmother would not allow Susan to use modern medicine upon her, she would not suffer jabs of the white man's needles. Preferring teas and tonics, the recipes she used and taught to dull her pain and ease her rebirth into the new world. Susan knew those ways of healing also and honored the Beloved Woman's last wishes.

When White Hawk's death was near, as she lay covered in her purple blanket, two dragonflies visited her bed. They lit upon her head remaining there for a short while, she roused from her sleep, her ragged breath slowing and becoming steadier. The People believed this as a sign from the spirit world that loved ones were visiting and nearby awaiting her arrival. The dragonflies symbolized the illusion of time and the fleeting nature of life, as hers ebbed from her body.

Susan knew White Hawk didn't have much time left to walk beside her on this earth. She lay on her pelts unable to walk, and in the last two days stopped eating and drinking. All Susan could do was to keep her pain free and be there for her as she lay dying. Sitting by her and tending to her needs even sleeping on a floor pallet next to her.

As a physician she recognized the signs of the body shutting down. White Hawk's feet and hands grew cold and turned motley blue gray. She became incoherent, seeing and speaking to beings that were not there—at least not that Susan could see. Then on her last day, the death rattle came. The phlegm started to build in her throat, and she was too weak to expel it. Each breath brought a crackling, wet sound, sometimes like soft moaning or snoring. Her eyes stayed half-open, glazing over, and her jaw sagged, which made the sounds worse as she labored to breathe. The inhales and exhales grew farther and farther apart and became unpredictable. She took one ragged breath in, then out, and no more. It was over. When the dragonflies flew upward into the sky, she breathed her last breath upon this earth. This brought great comfort to those waiting with her, recognizing that loved ones from beyond visit and bringing signs to the living, and were there to receive her spirit.

Her beloved grandmother, the one that helped raise and shape her into the person she was today, had left her.

Susan felt like an orphan, she had no mother, father, or now her beloved grandmother. But she did leave her a legacy, she taught Susan the healing ways of the Paint Clan. She would mourn her loss and miss her until she walked with her again in the upper world.

The village held a large feast in her honor at the community lodge. Her internment was in the nearby cemetery where Chief John Ross's bones lay. The entire village mourned their loss.

Susan placed a large tombstone over White Hawk's grave plot so that no one would ever forget who this 'Beloved Woman' was and would remember all she did for her Cherokee People.

The stone read:

White Hawk

Healer

Beloved Woman of the Cherokee Nation

1830-1930

Daughter of Running Deer,

Mother of Nan & Agali,

Grandmother of Susan

Henry succeeded in finally drinking himself to death leaving Susan and their daughter Fannie to continue alone.

TWENTY-THREE

1930

The Cherokee Nation
Talequah, Oklahoma

Susan held White Hawk's hands in hers and kissed them as the Beloved Woman took her last breath. Her spirit rose upward, leaving the bounds of earth behind. She was light and felt no more pain, finally free of her earthly shackles. Her heart soared with her spirit to the upper world, to join her loved ones.

This is what death is like? Why is man so fearful of the rebirth onto the realm of no time and beyond?

Suddenly she was on the great plains she had visited long ago in her spirit walks, the 'land of no time.' But now it looked different and felt different to her. She saw with new eyes; the veil lifted, and she could take in all the beauty that surrounded her in this place. The light was brighter than the sun and without the spirit eyes she could not have looked upon it. Even the colors had motion to them, vibrating and swirling over and around the land. She could see and feel the constant movement. The internal workings of the trees and plants were visible to her: the sap throbbing through their stems in tune with a heartbeat she never knew they possessed. It pulsed from under the earth, up to the tips of the leaves and outward and into the air. Everything was fully alive and emitted emotions. The visions before her were too much to encounter and still live in human form.

Her feet were on the ground, but she could not feel the dirt under them. She held out her hands and looked at them. They looked the same shape, but they appeared to swirl in waves. When she tried to pick up a rock, the stone passed through them for their form had no consistency. The sun shone brightly in a vibrant blue sky, but it was not hot. It was silent and peaceful.

Everywhere she looked streams of crystal water were flowing across the land fed by great waterfalls coming from within the rock walls. The water had no beginning and no end and was a color she had never seen before. It was unlike anything known to her, and she was eager to drink it, for she knew that whoever drank of this water would never thirst again. But that could wait, she wanted to see her family first.

She met her spirit guide, the red-tail hawk. He greeted her with a piercing cry and was the first to greet her, announcing his arrival with a piercing cry. Outstretching her arm for him to light upon it, and then he morphed into one with her, his abilities now within her being. Her vision now was with his eyes, and she saw vast distances. There she saw the paint stallion running toward her and recognized Nan upon his back, laughing, and her hair flowing in the wind. She was healthy and pure love and joy emanated from her being.

Nan shouted, "Mother, Mother, it is I Nan. Stand there, I will come to you."

Down below on the canyon floor, where Nan first appeared she saw the black stag—Isaac, and her horse with Agali seated upon its back. There too was Benjamin, and her mother Running Deer. She knew them all by their presence as they had no human form. She knew them by the love they pushed her way.

Instantly Nan was beside her, took her by the arm and they were with those gathered below. White Hawk didn't sense the movement, one minute she was here and the next there. Suddenly, there were hundreds more spirits surrounding her, waiting to greet her. These ancestral spirits communed without words. They were ones that had gone before and now joined again with her in the land of the Great Spirit. They glowed and sparkled in the sunlight, and one-by-one made their name known to her, she remembered each of them, as she joined with them forever. They were her brothers and sisters, and together they were all children of Earth Mother and the Creator.

After greeting her family, she moved to the nearby waterfall. There was no quarry or lake hidden behind the rock feeding the flow. The water was coming from nowhere and going to nowhere, the unending living water.

The Great Spirit said to her, "I am the living water, partake of me. Give thanks, like all the times you did in your human form for Earth Mother's blessings, and when you consumed her goodness, I am well pleased with you my blessed one."

She was not afraid, she let the water fill her cupped hands and then sipped. It tasted sweet like honey but clean like water. Nothing like this existed on earth, the feel of it on her hands was not wet like water or sticky like honey. She gave thanks for the living water, and as she drank it, her spirit became more knowing, and strength returned to her.

She felt such deep love, and excitement. Everything was more vivid than she recalled in her previous spirit walks. Now her new spirit body reflected the light of a hundred stars coming from inside of her shining outward brought to her from the living water.

"Nan, how do I soar like the birds of the air, or run like the horses in this place?'

"Simple, you just think it, if you want to fly believe you can, envision it and you will," Nan said.

She closed her eyes and thought of soaring like the eagle, and she could fly anywhere. Her eyes were sharp as the hawks. She could see rodents on the ground from high in the sky and fish in the water as she glided over the lakes. There were no restraints on her physically in this place—for there was no body only spirit. She knew everything that was, and is, and yet to be. Here there was no death, no hunger, no wants…it was paradise, where all good things resided, and from where blessings to the living come.

She could also see forward in time. She saw Susan in the physical world and felt the grief she carried over her and Henry's death. Susan's daughter Fannie would continue the healing tradition, finding true love and becoming mother to future generations in the Nation.

White Hawk left the air and made her way back to her circle of loved ones on the ground, when the thunder clapped loud, and she saw lightning flash.

What does this foretell?

"Don't worry Grandmother that is just the two Thunder Boys coming to greet you, wait until you see them. The stories told by the elders were true, they are always plotting mischief."

The Thunder Boys appeared from the west dressed in lightning and rainbows. They were loud and brought the rain and blessings with them. Staying only for a moment, they flashed lightning and told her they would travel back to the physical world. There they live in the cliffs, mountains, and waterfalls, where priests pray to them to bring rain upon the land for the people. In a flash, they were gone from her, but she could still see their lightning strikes in the distance.

In the distance she saw her eternal beloved Isaac, his spirit was strong as he morphed from the black stag into his old body image. Ben standing beside him, she loved Ben, but not like her first true love Isaac. Ben knew this, for he loved Isaac too. Of all the things she had longed for on earth, this was her most fervent hope, to be with Isaac again.

She willed herself to be near Isaac and in an instant, they stood face to face. They raised their hands to touch palms together, and she could feel his emotions. Her insides tingled and she cried out his name. He glowed from within, and his new body bore none of the scars from the earthly life and tragic death. The red gouge around his neck from the hanging was gone. She couldn't even remember any bad things that she witnessed in her old life—those memories erased. She knew him as on earth and the purity of his new body seeped from his pores illuminating all that was around him.

"My beloved, I know all of this is new to you, marvel at the beauty that surrounds you, drink it in. While here you can see into the realm of the living, you may visit them in their dreams, and they may visit here and commune with us if their power is strong enough for them to control their minds for the journey. Just as you once did, but they must possess the special power to do this walk. However, soon we will depart to the upper realm to reside in our eternal home with the Great Spirit. The upper realm is a sacred place where the living cannot visit, and even more magnificent than here. There all things revealed unto you but kept sacred and secret from those who are not one yet with the Creator. With our new spiritual bodies, we traverse through the three realms, but the living can go no farther than this place, or their physical bodies will die. You must warn those that come here to go back to the earthly realm before they weaken to the point of no return.

Because once you taste the nectar of this place, the mind craves to remain."

"You mean there is more for me to discover of secret places? I am already in awe and filled with happiness like I have never known before." White Hawk said.

"Come my beloved, let me take you to the upper realm. There the Creator waits to welcome you and where you can look upon His Spirit and not die."

In a moment, she was in the unknown place, where one year was like one second on earth. In the sweetness there are the secrets and answers to all life's great mysteries revealed to her. Her time on earth displayed to her, the good and the bad. She saw the way others responded in the future by her slightest actions of her past. Her actions revealed to her were like dropping one small pebble into a vast body of water. The ripples were still moving outward, bringing change throughout the centuries. She saw her impact on education, now open to all races. The horror of slavery abolished. The great buffalo resurrected—brought back from extinction and protected in National Parks, women freely admitted to colleges and medical schools, even the right to vote in U.S. elections for all people—Freedman, native people, and women.

This love from the Creator was unlike any other bestowed on her. Even when shown her shortcomings, an unquantifiable love that knew no depths enveloped and bathed her in His light. There was no guilt or shame. What transpired there was sacred to her, and she would hold to these memories, which would never leave her.

While in the 'land of no time,' she would occasionally walk in the first realm of earth to reveal in dreams and drop thoughts into fertile minds like planting a kernel of corn into a row of fresh dirt. When dreamers awake from dreams, they will reap the harvest of the seeds planted. She also gave encouragement, truths, and visions to her descendants. They honored her life by keeping the stories of the 'old ways' alive. The remembrances of a People from thousands of years ago, called 'The Real People' and recorded in the text of the medicine men passed down through the eons, on to the future generations. Still communicating with those who are teaching their culture—a culture that the white man tried to stamp out and yet it lives on, customs, memories, and language to the young ones so that they never forget the sacred teachings.

Unless one has the special power to recognize these nighttime visitors, they will not know it is White Hawk and others like her, protecting and carrying forward these memories. These are the spirits alive for eternity, traversing the three realms to help the living balance the physical and spiritual with earth's harmony.

The living will have visions, catch snippets of memories, recall faint smells drifting from the recesses of their minds, or the spirits that reside in the animals and birds bringing the messages to the living. These things trigger memories of when the ancient ones walked beside them, and the sayings will go forward to the next generation and on to the next. The Cherokee people will not die.

TWENTY-FOUR

Current Day

Annie was exhausted after the first week of clinic but felt more fulfilled with her work than she had been for a long time. The nurses and interns were professional and fun to be around, but she especially liked Chase. He was polite, always smiling, an exceptionally good doctor, and all the patients loved him.

Work kept her busy, which diminished her urge to drink during the day, and she was too tired at night to even consider it. She was putting more sober days into her bank account, and it was getting easier for her day by day. She made sure to be available for the local AA meeting, at least once per week and became a regular with the group.

Each night after work Leotie would prepare a small meal for them to share, and Annie would recall the events of the day as they ate together. Afterward, they would sit in the living room and watch gameshows. Tonight, Annie planned to share her adoption story, maybe Leotie knew Polly or Byrdie. She was nervous and her voice gave it away as she started to speak.

"I want to tell you a story tonight….about me, about my past," Annie started.

She relayed how she found out about her adoption, the record in the family bible and doctored birth certificate, the DNA test and finally the records from Catholic Adoptions. She looked at Leotie's face to gauge her reaction. Her eyes reflected sadness as she looked anywhere but directly into Annie's eyes. After all these weeks in The Nation, she realized that was the Cherokee way.

"I know all about those adoptions. It was a troubled time for my—our people, they took our babies. The white judges in the state courts would not let other family members keep the children with the families; they placed them with white couples that could not have their own. They said they were giving our children a better life. What is better than a child being loved and cared for by their own people?" Leotie said.

Pausing and shaking her head at the memory, trying to erase it.

Annie felt Leotie probably knew and remembered families personally affected. Annie waited for her to say something.

"Do you know anything about your people, who are your clan?" Leotie asked.

"Yes, I have some names. I was hoping maybe you knew them. Byrdie and Polly Healer, Polly is married to Charley Bearpaw and Byrdie is my mother. Charlie and Polly are my grandparents and supposedly lived here in The Nation at one time. That's one of the reasons I came out here this summer, to try and find them. Does any of those names ring a bell?" Annie asked.

"I don't recognize them. But if you want, I'll make some calls tomorrow and see what I can find out?"

Annie nodded. It seemed that Carol was right again, when secrets become exposed, they aren't so frightening, and they lose their power over you. Her birth wasn't a secret anymore. However, she felt ambivalent, on one hand sadness that she had been ripped away from her family and culture, resulting in always being a lone outsider, somehow different. On the other hand, guilty at the opportunities she gained through her birth parents, ones that she may not have afforded to her if not adopted. This was not an easy thing to wrap your head around, placing blame of right or wrong. But she wanted—no needed, to find out who she was and where she came from. Why was she given away, why wasn't she wanted?

They became quiet, both lost in their own thoughts and ghosts of the past. After staring at television together for a while, Annie excused herself then fell into bed. She could tell by the aches and pains she had not totally recovered from her accident. Her head and leg throbbed most nights, and tonight it proved relentless.

She tossed and turned in the bed for a while because of the pain and overtiredness, but then drifted into a deep sleep. Annie suddenly woke-up and the woman from the plains was there in the room with her. The apparition didn't evaporate this time, but Annie had no fear. She was stroking Annie's head and whispering to her. She was soft and gentle and had a glow that emitted loving tenderness outward toward Annie.

Was she still dreaming, or was this another hallucination like Miranda?

The woman spoke and sang to her in unknown words, yet Annie understood her. It was melancholy but a beautiful soulful sound. She was chanting, praising, and thanking the Creator for the lost soul, now found, and returned to her People. Then she spoke directly to Annie.

"My daughter descended from generations past, my beloved, we have found you and you have found us. You are of my blood and possess special powers to use for your People. You have a gift that you have not yet realized, that is why two spirits fight in your mind. The evil one wants to hold you prisoner and take you and your gift from us. You must ask the Creator to reveal to you the ways to use this special gift and give thanks for it. He will then guide you to the place you are meant to be and where you will find your place. There also you will find your peace and love."

She stroked Annie's hair once more, kissed her on the forehead, and then she was gone, just as Annie's alarm roused her from the warm bed. She remembered her dream, it felt so real.

Was it a dream? Of course, it was, but it felt so real.

When she sat down for coffee and breakfast with Leotie, she shared her crazy dream and chuckled.

Leotie was indignant that Annie was laughing at the encounter, and she made it known by rattling the dishes in the sink.

"Daughter, this is not something to laugh about. Our people believe the spirits of our ancestors come to us in our dreams, or with signs or animals, to share important messages from the Creator and the spirit world. You might want to listen to what the wise one revealed to you."

Annie felt scolded, thanked Leotie for the meal and left for her shift at the hospital. She was early as usual, and as she sat in the car in the parking lot, she contemplated her dream and Leotie's words.

"All right, I'm game….Oh, great Creator, reveal the message you have for me. What is my purpose in life? If you help me figure that out, I'll owe you one."

She smiled and shook her head after she spoke the words aloud, feeling foolish, and then she walked into the hospital to start another day not giving the dream another thought.

As she got off the elevator, the floor charge nurse met her with her list of patients for the day, and a stack of medical charts for each of them. Handing them to Annie to review the caseload for the day before seeing her first patient. Chase was next to arrive, the same nurse handing him a stack of charts as well. He plopped down beside her at the nurse's station.

She tried to focus on the patient's charts, but Chase made it difficult to concentrate. He did smell good, not perfumed like some men, he smelled rugged and fresh like the outdoors or something she couldn't readily identify. Pretending to read, she kept thinking about his smell.

Like soap. That's it soap, good clean soap.

Then she imaged him all soapy standing under the shower rubbing the suds all over his muscular chest and body…..

Stop Annie, stop right now….focus on Ms. Smith's heart disease. What has gotten into you?

She was sure she was blushing at the thoughts.

Chase caught her eye and said, "good morning," flashing his flawless smile and bright white teeth, magnified by his dark skin.

She nodded back at him, unable to speak coherently and glad he couldn't read her mind.

"I was wondering if you'd like to grab dinner with me tonight, maybe we could go listen to some music or even dance after?" Chase asked.

She was dumbstruck, and did not know how to answer him. She needed to think about this before deciding.

"Let me check and see what Leotie has planned for tonight, I'll let you know by lunchtime, ok?"

She was trying to act nonchalant so her nerves wouldn't show. She didn't need to check with Leotie, she just needed to stall and decide if she should do this. By lunchtime she had talked herself into going to dinner with him, after all it was just eating together. It wasn't like it was a date or anything, there was nothing romantic about it and she was not looking for a relationship. It would be the cordial thing to do with a co-worker when both of you were from out-of-town with no friends or family around, and she could only watch so many game shows with Leotie before she maxed out.

They agreed to meet at the restaurant rather than Chase driving to Leotie's house to pick her up, because this wasn't a real date. It was just two work colleagues having dinner and talking about their careers. That was her story, and she was sticking to it.

They arranged to meet around 6:30 at King's BBQ in downtown Tahlequah. Chase had been there before and recalled they served tasty food. He sounded excited when he shared one of the wonderful things about this place. Next to the dining room, there is a bar with a dance floor, featuring a live band tonight. She smiled all day and didn't think 5 o'clock would ever arrive. She had just enough time to get home, shower, change and get to the restaurant for her 'not a real date.'

What does one wear to a BBQ dive-bar with a dance floor in Oklahoma with 'just a friend'?

She decided on casual, Oklahoma casual. That meant her good ole, tight jeans with holes in the knees, black T-shirt, and well-used cowboy boots. She had splurged on the boots as a souvenir last weekend while shopping downtown at thrift stores.

She paid $30 dollars for the well broken-in boots that fit her perfectly. She even found a black round-brim felt hat for $5, which was in style.

When Leotie saw her walk out of the bedroom, she said, "Wow, you look like a Cherokee. I love it."

"You don't think the hat is too much do you?" Annie asked.

"Not at all, you look great. But wait, I have something you can borrow that will finish the look for you."

Leotie went into her bedroom, and Annie could hear drawers opening and closing. After a few minutes she brought back a necklace that was large pounded-silver circles, joined together accented with pieces of carved abalone shell and copper. It was a work of art, hand crafted, and beautiful.

"Here, wear this," Leotie said as she fastened it around Annie's neck. "It'll bring you luck, not that you need it. My great grandfather made this for my great grandmother as a wedding gift. It's been handed down to me. I never have occasion to wear it, I'd love to see you use it tonight."

"Thank you, it is so beautiful. I promise I'll take good care of it."

The silver stood out against the black shirt with her long dark hair.

Annie turned to walk out the door, smiled and said, "But I don't need luck, 'cause this is not a real date."

Now she just had to keep saying that to herself on the car ride to the restaurant, because it sure was beginning to feel like a date.

She found Chase already seated when she walked into the restaurant. There must have been some telepathy between the two of them, because he had on a black T-shirt, jeans, boots, and a black hat. They looked at each other and started laughing and pointing at one another. Almost everyone in the room turned to look at her, to see what table she walked toward. They kept staring even after she sat down, some nodding their approval at her choice. They made a striking couple.

She was a little uncomfortable with all the attention.

"Do I look stupid or something, are people staring at my hat?" she asked.

"Hardly, in case you don't know, you are gorgeous. Your outfit, your jewelry, that hat—just everything about you tonight, it fits together perfectly," Chase said. "Beauty and brains, how lucky can one guy get."

Annie blushed; she was at a loss for words, as she was unaccustomed to anybody complimenting her and wasn't quite sure how to respond.

She just said softly, "Thank you."

They chitchatted about work, the weather and then ordered dinner. Things turned serious when Chase asked her the big question that had been on his mind since the day they first met.

"So, Dr. Hayes, what brings a young woman to the middle of The Cherokee Nation in the blazing summer? It sure as heck isn't the vacation hotspot of the world, and can't be the weather, 'cause it's hot everywhere....so what's the deal?

"You sure you want to hear this? It's a long story?" She said.

"Try me."

"I'm here to try and find me," she said.

Annie proceeded to tell him the whole story, even the part about Tom, the accident, divorce and losing her home. She held nothing back and really didn't care what he thought about her because of it. It was life and life wasn't always pretty, besides this clinic would be over in a couple of months and they'd never see each other again. It was cathartic to be able to talk so openly to someone.

"You do look Native, adoption explains a lot," he said.

"Now, your turn. What's a young man doing in the middle of The Cherokee Nation during the blazing summer? Like you said, it's not the vacation hotspot."

"My story is not nearly as interesting. I am here to see what it's like. I'm from the Eastern Band of

Cherokee, bred and born in Cherokee, North Carolina, but now working in a Nashville hospital. I'm contemplating a job offer, moving out here and taking a position at this new medical facility in Talequah. It's kinda like a try before you buy experience," he said.

"So, what's your impression so far?"

"I really like it, brand new facility, state-of-the-art equipment, friendly staff. I'm leaning toward a yes," he said.

"You know Annie, from the story you told me, you've got nothing holding you to Chicago. Maybe you should consider doing the same thing, especially since this is where you were born. Perhaps you should think about it. There is a shortage of good doctors here," he said.

She hadn't even considered that before. "I will," she said thoughtfully. "I really will."

The BBQ meal was delicious as promised, and afterward they went to the bar side of the restaurant and grabbed a tabletop for two and waited while the band warmed up. Chase ordered a beer, and she had tonic water, which she would nurse all night. She didn't even crave liquor tonight, but just in case, she carried her chip in her pocket. She didn't rub it once.

The music was country western, and Chase pulled her to the dance floor when the boot-scootin' boogie music started to play. He held her by the hand, refusing to let her sit back down. She quite liked the feel of her hand in his. It fits well, the perfect size.

She protested, "I don't even know how to do this sort of thing."

"It's easy, just hang on and put one foot in front of the other, follow me. We're gonna walk around in a big circle."

She did and it was fun, they laughed and spun around the floor while the band played and sang directions telling them what to do with their feet and arms. It was easy and Chase a good teacher.

She hadn't laughed or enjoyed a night out like this with Tom—well, ever. They never went out dancing and having fun with each other, even in their college days. They either were studying, or out drinking with friends.

She wished she hadn't thought of Tom or compared him to Chase, but this time she suffered no pangs of guilt or sadness overwhelming her. She stayed in the moment with Chase, and realized this must be what happiness feels like.

However, it's not a real date. We are just friends.

After the last dance they sat down and waited to catch their breath before leaving. The evening was over too soon for her, and evidently for Chase too.

He said, "since tomorrow is Saturday, how about we do something together? Get to see the non-medical side of Oklahoma?"

"What did you have in mind?"

"How about we do a trail ride? I've heard about a ranch not far from here that offers the real deal, they go up in the mountains and picnic and then return. It's an all-day ride, starting around 8 a.m.," he said.

"Well, I've never sat on a horse before. You think I'm up to it?"

"Only one way to find out. I'll pick you up at 7:30 in the morning, and don't drink too much coffee…..there are no john's out there," he said.

She couldn't sleep that night; she was so keyed up from the dancing and thinking about what could possibly go wrong the next day. Finally, sleep came, and no visitors showed up in her dreams.

The next morning Leotie prepared a light breakfast for her, and Annie limited herself to only one cup of coffee. She had no idea what to expect, this was totally outside her comfort zone, and she almost backed out before Chase arrived. Promptly at 7:30 he knocked on her door.

He looks even better in the morning sun than he had in the restaurant last night. How's that possible?

Leotie handed her a small brown bag, with two bottles of water, a couple of energy bars and apples. Just in case, she even stuck a half-roll of toilet paper into the sack. She thought of everything, and that's good because Annie would have just walked out the door with her phone and purse.

When they arrived at the Lazy K Ranch Annie's palms were sweating. She had never been this close to a horse before; she was ready to back out. Chase reassured her these animals were very well broken and not to worry.

There was a large corral in the middle of a grassy field, inside was about 20 saddled horses roaming about chomping at a large round bale of hay. A young teen boy and two girls of similar age tended to them, tightening up saddles and adjusting bridles. Then lining up the riders and asking their height, weight, and experience to assign them to an appropriate horse. Annie got Ole Sam, a red roan gelding with gray beginning to pop on his nose, and not too tall. He was very docile and rubbed his face on her stomach and snorted as she stood beside him. She liked the way Ole Sam smelled; grass breath tinged with horse sweat. Chase rode a big young paint named Sonny, who seemed a little rowdy, but he could handle him because he had lots of experience with horses.

First on the agenda was to help each rider mount their horse. A set of stairs joined onto a platform which the horse stood beside. All Annie had to do was walk up the stairs, stretch a leg out and over, sliding her feet into the stirrups. The ranch hand adjusted the stirrup length if needed. Before she realized it, she was astride the horse and holding on for dear life.

So far so good.

Once everyone was on their horse—there were about ten riders including the two guides. At first they walked them around the corral teaching the riders how to start, steer right or left, stop and back up. When satisfied with the pairings and the abilities of the riders, they opened the gate and headed for the woods walking in a straight line. Annie was in front of Chase at about the center of the pack. She sat ramrod straight and tense, her legs gripping the sides of the animal, one hand holding the reins and the other holding the saddle-horn. Little did she realize this was the easy part, they were on a flat grassy path circling around the woods.

After about an hour at a slow pace to get everyone warmed up and comfortable, the lead guide turned onto a trail leading into the woods. It was beautiful and cool, but branches overhung the path and would slap at those following behind the rider in front. Annie had to let go of the horn to protect her face from the limbs. Ole Sam didn't seem to mind and walked on, she loosened her grip and started to admire the beauty surrounding her.

"You are doing ok up there?" Chase yelled.

"So far so good."

Just as she said that the path started a sharp downward descent, she slid forward in the seat of the saddle almost toppling over Ole Sam's mane.

"Annie, lean back, and hold on to the back of your saddle when the terrain slopes down, and lean forward and hold the horn when you go uphill," Chase shouted.

She did as he instructed and righted herself in the saddle. Ole Sam walked on, stepping over the exposed roots on the path's deep ruts. Every now and then, he would make small hops over one of them, but she hung on. Causing her to tense up and grip his sides with her legs, which she soon rubbed raw, and her bottom started to hurt.

Then she saw something in front of them, she stopped her horse and said, "Uuun oh, no way, no way can I do that."

At the bottom of the hill was a bubbling stream about a foot deep. The creek bed was covered with large stones and rocks, with slippery green algae growing on them. There was a muddy path in and a rocky hill out on the other side. She created a traffic jam, as all the riders stopped when she did.

The guide shouted instructions to keep moving and coax their horses into the stream and maneuver up the rocky slope. The guide went first and waited by the bank, urging the next rider and then the next across and up the steep slippery hill. It was finally Annie's turn, and she sat still, Ole Sam wasn't up for this either.

"You can do this Annie, I'm right here behind you, you're doing great," Chase said.

I can do this.

She clicked her tongue and nudged Ole Sam in the sides with her legs. He stepped gingerly into the water; his front hoof slid off the rock. She held tight to the saddle horn, not breathing. Half-way across he slipped again, spooking him, causing a lunge sideways. Annie let out a little yelp and held on tighter. Ole Sam stopped and stood still in the middle of the stream, refusing to go any further.

"Annie, take your reins and swat him a little bit on the hindquarters as you prod him with your feet," the guide said.

As she did so, he lurched forward and in two steps was on the solid ground and bounding up the steep slope. Annie held on tightly and made it to the top. Chase was right behind her stopping beside her on the hilltop.

"That was great Annie, so proud of you, I was worried there for a minute," he said.

"Me too."

At about noon the group stopped on a flat spot of grass where the guides tied the horses to a rope strung between two trees to graze. They spread a blanket on the ground in the shade, handing out sandwiches and drinks to the hungry riders.

After lunch, the guide approached Annie and Chase, "I'm afraid Ole Sam has thrown a shoe and come up lame. We're gonna have to double up a ride, can she ride double with you?"

"If Sonny doesn't care, I don't care," Chase answered.

"The good news is the hard part of the ride is over, it's all downhill from here," the guide said.

What have I gotten myself into?

Annie was worried.

Lunch was over too fast for Annie, and it was time to get upon Sonny sitting behind Chase. He led his horse to a nearby tree stump, hoisted himself into the saddle, taking his left foot out of the stirrup, and then held out his arm. It looked like he had done this before. She climbed upon the stump with her knees first and then stood—not very gracefully. She grabbed his arm and stuck her left foot into his stirrup, struggling to throw her right leg over the saddle. Almost unseating Chase from his horse, but finally doing it. Sonny didn't mind the double load as much as she did. Terrified, she wrapped her arms tightly around Chase's waist and leaned into him with her whole body. He felt hard and muscular, and smelled like soap with a hint of the outdoors, she liked the feelings this evoked. All she could concentrate on was her breast rubbing up against Chase's back as the horse swayed. They were able to talk to one another since they were so close. All the way back Chase called out the types of trees and pointed out squirrels and other wildlife. Things she had not noticed on the way in because she was too frightened to take her eyes off the mane of her horse. The ride was over too soon, she liked his closeness, holding him tight and laughing together.

As they walked to the car, she realized how tired she was, her bad leg ached, and she had saddle sores from bouncing in the saddle. She was envisioning a hot soak in a tub of bubbles and a nap.

"I have never done anything like this before, and I had a wonderful time. I hope I wasn't too much trouble for you," Annie said.

"Not at all, I especially enjoyed the ride home," he said as he winked at her.

TWENTY-FIVE

Current Day

The following Monday morning at the hospital Chase brought Annie a venti caramel macchiato, her favorite coffee. They shared some small talk before the day began and laughed a bit about the trail ride. Chase was easy to be around, and she always had a smile after talking to him. It was a good way to begin her day.

Mondays were always busy, people put off going to the hospital on the weekends, but come Monday they rush into the ER, so in addition to all the ones already admitted, there were new patients flooding the floors. The day passed quickly, and at 5 p.m. she headed out the doors to her car. She heard someone shouting her name and turned toward the sound. She was shocked to see it was Tom.

What on earth is he doing in Oklahoma?

"Annie, hey Annie," Tom yelled sprinting toward her.

"Tom, what are you doing here?"

The expression on her face was not warm and inviting, she had frown lines and crossed her arms. He reached toward her to give her a hug and she stood firm, unmoving. She glared at him and shook her head.

"You're unbelievable. How did you find me? Are you stalking me?"

"No, no, it's not like that. Annie, can we go someplace and talk? I need to tell you about some things in person, the way we ended it was not good," he said.

His appearance puzzled Annie, but she agreed to go listen to what he had to say, they drove separately to a restaurant near the hospital. She wasn't about to tell him where she lived, and she wasn't sure how he tracked her down at her job, or why. She was a little miffed at him.

Once they settled in a booth away from the noise of the crowd at dinner, the wait staff took drink orders. Tom ordered two gins and tonics. She ordered water with lemon.

Maybe he's drinking more these days?

"Ok, what gives Tom? I'm curious, why did you hunt me down, all the way out here in Oklahoma? Our divorce was final a month ago, and I don't think we have anything left to discuss."

Tom placed his hands, palms up on the table reaching out to take hers, she didn't budge. Sheepishly pulling them back and down into his lap, while turning red at her obvious rejection.

"Yes, I know our divorce is final. I also know divorcing you was the biggest mistake of my life. I am here to tell you how sorry I am for cheating on you and leaving you when you needed me. I am a jerk, and I don't deserve you. But, Annie, I love you, I've always loved you and I need you. I want to try again for us. What we had once was good, wasn't it? Will you give me a second chance? Please, I'll do anything you want to make it up to you."

"Why now, Tom? Did Green kick you to the curb? What was it, the gambling, the manipulation, the drinking?" She paused.

He dropped his head, lowering his eyes obviously ashamed and guilty.

"I thought as much," she said. "You know I did love you, or thought I did at one time. Now I wonder what that really was, maybe co-dependence? I'm happy Tom, really happy. I'm sober and love my job and have made new friends here. I finally feel like I belong somewhere."

"Annie, we can stay here, together. I'll move, I'll do anything you say, just please. I'm begging you; I need you."

The drinks arrived and Tom took one and pushed the other gin toward Annie.

"Here, have just one with me for old time's sake," he said.

Annie picked up the glass and swirled it around as if she was contemplating taking a drink, then she threw it in Tom's face, as she stood up and grabbed her purse.

"I'm not the old Annie who would drink herself into a stupor and let you manipulate with lies."

Slamming the empty glass down on the table, "I don't need this anymore, and I certainly don't need you. Please do not contact me again, we're done. Fair warning, if you come around me again, I'll call the police and file a restraining order. They don't take stalking lightly around here, especially one of their own by a white man."

She walked with her head held high out of the restaurant pushing the door open with such force that it banged into the wall on the backside. Never glancing behind her, she got into the car, and sped out of the lot so Tom could not follow. When she pulled into Leotie's driveway, she blocked Tom's phone number and disabled the tracking feature. She didn't feel sad, bad, or sorry, if anything she was angry that Tom threatened her sobriety, trying to entice her back into co-dependence with him.

She needed to be amongst people that understood what she was feeling. She appeared strong on the outside standing up to Tom, but on the inside, she was jelly. Her hands shook as she called Ray to fill him in and then she headed to the AA meeting in town.

Later that night at the meeting she shared what happened with Tom, and everyone agreed to ending the co-dependent relationship to protect her newfound sobriety. They clapped for her and expressed pride in her strength. She finally found a place with people, who held her accountable and knew her day-to-day struggle because they shared it too. It was a place where she belonged, on the land and in the AA meetings. She was with her kind, the people that accepted her and a bunch of drunks trying to stay sober, just like her.

After the meeting adjourned, she called Ray and headed to the deli across the street, which had become their weekly routine. She loved having coffee, while talking with him about her week. He walked this path before her, was a mentor, and counted him as a good friend.

"I'm contemplating moving out here permanently, trying to get a position at the hospital and live here. What do you think of that? I'd really like your input," she said.

"Sis, I think that would be a wonderful thing for the hospital. However, you need to ask yourself, is that what you want? Look inside, ask for guidance from your 'Higher Power,' that's what I do when I have a big decision to make. Ultimately, you must choose your own path in life, don't ever let anyone take that power from you. Just remember, you don't want to do anything that would jeopardize your sobriety. That is the number one rule in life for people like us."

"You know I realize now you never give me a straight answer or tell me what to do, you always have me think about it and make my own decision. That's one of the reasons I love you so much. You're like the big brother I never had," she said.

"Hey, here in this world we're all brothers and sisters," he said.

The next day while at work and taking a break, she told Chase about Tom's stunt.

"I'm proud of you Annie, for not giving in to his pressure, and I hate to say it, but I'm glad you didn't take him back. I don't want to lose you."

"Chase, that doesn't mean I want a relationship. You're a great guy and I enjoy being with you, but I am not ready for anything more than friendship."

"I'm good with that for now, but I'm gonna wear you down," Chase said flashing his smile, as he seductively sipped his coffee.

Man, he's sexy, but I must stay strong. I don't want another man in my life right now.

She chuckled at his comment so he wouldn't notice her nervousness.

"I have news to share, I'm going to apply for one of the physician positions here at the hospital. What do you think about that? Can we work together as colleagues without killing one another or butting heads?" she asked.

"I think that's wonderful; it gives me more time to work on you with my southern charm and natural good looks."

"Hah, that's hilarious, just keep dreaming the dream," she said.

She started the application process that day, uploading her resume and licensing information to the hospital job posting portal. She also stopped by the HR department and talked to the director about her application. She came clean about her past, filling her in on her adoption story, her struggle with alcohol, the accident, divorce, and her newfound sobriety.

"It's standard procedure to do a background check. Part of that process is talking with references provided from previous employers about your capabilities as a physician and verifying licensing credentials. But I promise you a fair shot. The fact that you are Cherokee gives you preference over other non-Native applicants. Honestly, we usually don't get alot of applicants. If we do, once they visit us, they will turn us down quickly," she said.

She continued with a pensive look on her face and soft inviting voice, "you know Dr. Hayes."

Annie had to listen hard to hear her.

"Everyone has a past with things they are not proud of, and with the high percentage of alcohol abuse on The Nation, maybe your experiences would be helpful to get more patients into treatment programs, or even establishing a sobriety program at the hospital. I believe we should see how to use this as an advantage in hiring you. Would you be open to extra involvement in establishing community programs like that?" she asked.

"Of course, that would be awesome. In fact, my 12th-Step requires me to carry the message to other alcoholics while practicing the principles in my own life.' So, I'm definitely in agreement to do that."

She left the discussion with high hopes, feeling positive. Only time would tell, she didn't even care about the employment package, if she got the job, it was meant to be, and she'd take whatever the offer.

She shared her news with Leotie when she got home.

"I am so excited to hear this and you can stay here as long as you need to until you get your own place. I also have a great idea, go with me on Saturday to the ceremony at the community center. It's a celebration of the elders, the Cherokee Elder's Summit. Our medicine man healer and spiritual advisor will be there. You must meet him if you are to become a healer of the People. You need his blessing," Leotie said.

"Well, ok, tell me when and where. I'll drive. Do I need to wear anything special? I have no idea what to do; this Cherokee stuff is all new to me?"

"Just go as yourself, you can sit with me, and I'll explain everything to you. The Principal Chief will be giving a speech, and a good opportunity for you to learn more about your people, especially the elders. Their acceptance will mean a great deal if you are to be here permanently."

Saturday came fast, and when they walked into the building, she was surprised to see Chase there as well. He came straight over to her and Leotie, hugging them both.

"Where are you sitting, may I join you?" he asked.

Before she could reply, Leotie said, "Of course, we'd love that, wouldn't we Annie?"

Annie blushed and shook her head yes.

A dozen or so elders sat in the room that morning, as Principal Chief made his way to each table welcoming them. It was a time to hear from them, to learn from them. It was apparent they valued the elders here.

After the speech, and the food, Leotie said, "We must find John Walkingstick, he's an elder and spiritual healer. Come let us go."

Leotie spotted him and pointed him out.

"When you meet him, be reverent and just shake his hand. Let me do the talking,"Leotie said.

Leotie began, "Osiyo."

That was all Annie could understand. Finally, after a few minutes Leotie reverted to English so Annie could be part of the conversation.

"John Walkingstick, I want you to meet some friends. This is Dr. Annie Hayes, she and her people are born here, they are the Healer and Bearpaw clans. She was taken from The Nation, but she has returned and applied for citizenship. This is Dr. Chase Hunter, he is from the Eastern Band. They are both working at the clinic this summer. Dr. Chase has already accepted a position and plans to stay on at the new hospital. Dr. Annie has applied and is hoping for a job offer. They both wanted to meet you."

"Osiyo," elder John said.

"Osiyo," Annie and Chase repeated back to him.

"I'm afraid, 'Osiyo' and 'Wado' are the only Cherokee words I have learned so far, but I intend to take lessons," Annie said.

"Oh, do not worry, there are many of our young that do not know our tongue. These days there are very few fluent speakers left among the old ones, and it makes me sad. But, enough of that. What can I do for you?" elder said.

Leotie answered, "These two healers want your blessing upon them and their medicine. They want to honor our 'old ways' and the spirits of our ancestors. Will you pray a blessing over them?"

"Let me ask a couple of questions first. You, Dr. Annie, do you believe in the Creator?"

"As a matter of fact, I have a 'Higher Power' that I have been relying on for a while now. This belief helped me overcome many adversities and is guiding me to my true path. So, yes, I do."

He then turned to Chase.

"What about you, are you a believer?"

"Elder Walkingstick, I have been a believer in the Creator since my youth. I hold onto the teachings of balance, harmony, cooperation, and respect within the community, between people, and nature to guide me in my walk," Chase said.

"Osda," elder replied.

"Good," Leotie translated for Annie, shaking her head yes.

The elder instructed them to kneel, each one facing him and bowing their heads. He placed a palm on their heads and began to chant. Annie had no idea what he was saying, but felt it was a sacred moment. She closed her eyes and silently asked her Higher Power to come down and fill her with the words and actions she would need to treat her people, and to bless her medicine. She peeked over at Chase with one eye; he seemed to understand the language and nodded his head at certain times. Annie copied him.

When the elder finished his prayer, Annie noticed the HR Director standing in the corner of the room watching them. She hoped she had not offended anyone or made a cultural faux pas. She didn't know how to be Cherokee, but she knew she was one, and now she felt acceptance.

Elder Walkingstick wasn't yet done evaluating the young doctors.

"Pull up a chair, I want to talk more with you two."

Chase and Annie did as instructed giving him their full attention.

"It is important for you to see the full man when you treat our People, not just the sickness you see with your eyes. As a Cherokee healer, you should always seek the Creator's guidance first to allow you the skill and ask permission to perform healing. There may be times that the Creator does not allow healing, and you must be respectful of that too. There is a cycle of life and death is a part of that cycle. As healers we must be mindful of the role we play, we are not God— 'The Creator.' Annie, I encourage you to learn the tongue of your ancestors and understand the 'old ways.' It is important as you heal, many still use old remedies and hold to the beliefs from their forefathers and mothers. We should not replace those beliefs but enhance them. And to you Chase, you must adapt to the ways of the Cherokee Nation, and the Keetoowah Band, there may be some differences between them and the Ani'-yun'wiya Eastern Band of your tribe."

Chase shook his head, he understood.

"Yes sir, I intend to learn as much as I can about my ancestry and the culture. I'm hoping to get the job so I can stay here permanently, which would make this much easier to accomplish. My ancestors are on the Dawes roll, and I've already submitted my citizenship papers," Annie said.

"I have a good feeling about your chances," elder said.

He looked towards the HR Director, winked, and nodded at her.

"Well, this old man needs to go home. It's been a long day already."

Elder Walkingstick picked up a long stick from under the table, using it to pull himself out of the chair to a standing position. He then held it out for Chase and Annie to inspect.

"You know the story of this healing stick?" he asked.

"Many years ago, a healer of our people, a Beloved Woman, and War Woman—she sat on the governing council deciding over wars and fates of prisoners, this belongs to her. Our elders say that she pulled captives from their bonds as they stood in the fire pits ready to be burned at the stake, and she even freed slaves. The legends tell us of her skills to travel between the three worlds, from here into the spiritual realm. She performed rituals calling upon sacred spirits to help our people. Some believe even today she walks among us from time to time. This was her healing stick, she used in gathering medicinal plants and rituals. After healing, she would tie a piece of the person's hair onto it. See, the remnants are still there."

He held it up for Annie and Chase to inspect the dangling braids of hair.

"The People called her White Hawk, and she was buried in Ross Cemetery. You should learn from her ways. To become a Beloved Woman is a highly regarded honor of our People. Her picture hangs in the visitor's center beside other famous Cherokee like the actor Will Rogers, the first woman Principal Chief Wilma Mankiller, and Nation's Principal Chief Leader John Ross. Ross led our people for over 40 years, walked the trail of tears with the People, and helped set up our government."

After the chat, they both shook hands and expressed appreciation for his blessing and words. Annie knew she had a lot to learn about her Cherokee ancestry, but she was excited to feel like she finally belonged somewhere.

The following week the HR Director called Annie into her office and offered her a position at the new hospital. Her medical references were positive and there was no fault in her work history. The salary was about the same as she made at St. Vincent's and as a Native, she would qualify for free housing on The Nation. She had to wait for a house to open, or construction of a new home whichever came first. Until then she would stay with Leotie. Her life was coming together at last. She couldn't wait to share the news with Chase, Leotie, and Ray, in that order.

Chase was becoming increasingly important to her, and he brought her a coffee every morning.

She looked forward to seeing him first thing and they usually had lunch together, but she was keeping him in the friend zone, nothing more. She was not ready to get involved with anyone yet, but that was getting harder for her each day. Chase was right, he was wearing her down bit by bit.

She still mourned her old life with Tom occasionally, for it hadn't been all bad, especially in the beginning of their relationship, they practically grew up together. However, she tried her best not to go there in her mind, as it made her depressed and brought with it a craving to drink. Tom was her trigger, and as she learned more about herself, she learned to avoid triggers and turn her focus to working the 12-Steps.

To plan for her new role at the hospital, she started AA meetings held on The Nation in the community center each week. A few of the regulars from town who lived there agreed to attend and seed the new program. They were excited to have something closer to home and it wasn't long before fresh faces started showing up. She began inviting patients from the hospital, who clearly had health issues related to alcohol abuse. It didn't take too long until they were at capacity and moved into a larger room, then the meetings started happening two nights a week.

Annie took language classes, practiced with Leotie—Cherokee only immersion, and soon could understand simple phrases. She learned enough to make elders and patients comfortable with her. Before long her citizenship papers arrived, and she secured her id card. It was now official, she belonged.

Annie's life was good, and she was happy, but she still missed having a family she could call her own.

TWENTY-SIX

Annie had been working at the hospital for a couple of months and it was better than she could have imagined. Living with Leotie while waiting for housing, she was content and neither of them were in a hurry for her to move out. She took on a mentor role to young woman in the AA group fulfilling the last step in her 12-Step program, 'to carry the message to other alcoholics while practicing the principles in her own life'.

She finally felt at peace, at home and fulfilled with the urge to drink long dissipated, and still always carrying her first 30-day chip in her pocket.

Today she began her morning routine, scanning the ER admissions report which listed the patient's name, age, and diagnosis from the night before. She read half-way down and a name jumped off the page when she saw it: Polly Bearpaw. Her grandmother admitted to the hospital last night and was now her patient. The preliminary diagnosis of congestive heart failure and uncontrolled diabetes. Annie wasn't sure how to process this info. It was a dilemma. Her first thought was to exchange a patient with Chase; because Polly had made it clear, she did not want to meet her.

As she thought about it, she realized Polly didn't know anything about her. She would never realize Annie was her blood granddaughter unless she told her, and she certainly didn't plan to tell her today—not this way.

She made rounds as usual, working her way down the list and drew closer to entering Polly's room. Annie's nerves got the best of her, and it showed in her work. She misplaced paperwork, and messed up lab orders, everyone noticed the change from her usual proficient work. She was afraid Chase might think she was drinking again.

So, she decided to share with him at lunch about the upcoming afternoon rounds with Polly.

She shared her background and Polly's relationship quandary with him. She was glad she did because he noticed and worried about her. He was agreeable to swap patients if she wanted. She decided to go ahead and treat Polly. She was curious to see what this woman looked like. She thought she could help her without revealing her identity.

After lunch, Annie and the students gathered outside of Polly's door to discuss her diagnosis, and test results. Annie entered the room first, and the team filed in behind her gathering in a semi-circle around the foot of Polly's bed.

Polly appeared startled at all the people in her room, and then she noticed Annie. She locked eyes and would not look away. Annie felt the change in Polly's demeanor and her stomach lurched. She hadn't contemplated that she might resemble her dead mother and what the reaction would be from Polly. It was noticeable.

"Good afternoon, Mrs. Bearpaw. How are you feeling today?" Annie asked.

"Howa," she said with downcast eyes, and Annie understood OK.

"We have a group of medical students here today making rounds with us. Is it ok for them to stay and be involved with your care?"

"Howa," she gave one-word answers to everything, not looking at her when she spoke.

This is not going too good so far.

Annie launched into her overview of the patient's symptoms, what brought her to the emergency room, and then questioned the students on next steps with possible treatment options. She talked fast; she wanted to get out of the room as quickly as possible.

As they were turning to leave Polly timidly asked, "Excuse me, doctor. You look familiar to me, what is your name? Do I know you?"

"Um, I'm sorry I didn't introduce myself. I don't believe we have met; I am Dr. Hayes. I'm from Chicago."

She told a partial truth, shook Polly's hand as hers tremored a little. She hoped Polly didn't feel that, and then she turned and made a beeline out of the room. This was not how she envisioned meeting her grandmother for the first time.

Before she left the hospital for the day, she reviewed Polly's latest tests results. The findings weren't good, her sugar was out of control even with all the newer drugs they were using to bring it down along with a strict diet. She had fluid around her heart and in her lungs. She was an extremely sick woman.

Annie wanted to check on her before she left for the day. She poked her head in the door before entering to see if Polly was alone. She was listening to the TV with her eyes closed.

Tapping on the door lightly, she asked "May I come in?"

Polly roused from half-sleep.

"Howa."

Annie sat down in the chair beside her bed and said, "I wasn't honest with you today. There's something I must tell you. I'm….."

Polly interrupted, "You don't have to tell me anything. I know who you are. I can tell by looking at you, you are the spitting image of her when she was young."

She started to cry and put her hands over her face, crying into them as her shoulders shook with the depths of her emotions coming up and finally out. She was mourning for Byrdie once again, and Annie was sorry she had brought so much sadness onto this sick old woman.

"I'm so sorry for upsetting you. I didn't plan to tell you, but I knew you recognized me this afternoon. I don't want or need anything from you, you'll never have to look at me again. I will arrange for another doctor to take over your case. I'm so sorry to cause you such anguish." Annie stood to leave.

"No, wait, please don't go. Let me see your face and touch you. I wanted to see you, I am just so sick I didn't know if I could or if you would even want to see me like this. This just brings back so many bad memories of that time, of Byrdie, of what happened to her. It was so long ago, and I gave up ever finding you. I thought my prayers were not heard."

Polly took Annie's hand between hers and looked deep into her eyes. She then brushed Annie'shair away from her forehead, stroking her head, finally her hands cradling her face.

"I'd like to know what happened, why……if it's not too much for you? Can you tell me why she didn't keep me, didn't want me?" Annie asked as she leaned over the bed rail while Polly stroked her face.

Polly pulled her down kissing her on the forehead.

"These are tears of happiness, that you have returned to us. Sit down and I'll tell you the story I have never uttered to another living soul."

Annie sat on the edge of her chair, afraid to move.

"Before I begin, you must understand that you were born in a time when unwed mothers were looked down on in society, especially a 15-year-old Native girl. People assumed Byrdie had been wild and messed around with some young buck, getting herself in trouble. That's not true." She paused, clearly having difficulty breathing and talking.

"Byrdie was a straight A student with hopes and plans of going to college and making something of her life. She was a good girl and a responsible loving daughter. Working part-time at the bowling alley on the territory, as a waitress— trying to save money for college. She usually worked from after school until around 7 p.m., always getting home before dark. However, one night she worked late covering for another person until 10 p.m. She always walked home because we didn't have a car. Three men drinking in the bar had been watching her all night and were waiting for her in the alley off the main street. As she walked by, they grabbed her, dragging her into the darkness, taking turns with her. When the men were done violating her, my Byrdie was left there like trash, unconscious, bruised and bleeding.

When she came to, she walked and crawled home to get to me and her daddy. She didn't know who these men were, but knew they were from the reservation. We called the sheriff to report it, he was useless…didn't even come to the house to get a statement or file a report. She was just another poor Native girl, but if it had been a white girl, it would have made the front page of the papers."

"I am so sorry…. I had no idea," Annie said.

Polly kept talking incredibly low and staring off into space as if she were reliving the events as they unfolded.

"Well about six weeks later the sickness came on her and we knew she was pregnant. She hid the pregnancy from everyone, but the assault changed her. She didn't go out with her friends anymore and her grades plummeted. It was like she gave up on life, gave up on her dreams. Those men ruined her life that night, not you.

When you were born, she wanted to keep you, and I offered to adopt you too, but the caseworker from Catholic Adoptions showed up at the hospital and told us we weren't fit to have a baby. We didn't have any money, and Byrdie, who just turned 16 was still a minor. She had no job and no way to support a child the woman said. The caseworker went before a white judge and he took you away, placing you with a white family they had waiting for a baby. The people had money, offering you an education and life we could never give you. But we never forgot you. The saddest part of this was what the doctors did to my Byrdie."

"You mean there's more?" Annie said.

"Oh yes, since she birthed an illegitimate child, they sterilized her when you were born, it was the law back then. She would never be a mother. The guilt and shame from all this eventually took my Byrdie away too," Polly said as she wiped her nose on the corner of the bedsheet.

"It looks like something good came from it, for here you are a big-time doctor."

"No wonder my presence causes you so much pain. I'm so sorry," Annie said.

"From then on, Byrdie just gave up on life. She began to drink and run wild. She didn't care anymore. We watched her drink herself to an early grave, and she never forgave herself for letting you go. She used to say when drinking, that she should have fought for you, taken the 'warrior path' for you," Polly said with the tears starting again when she spoke about Byrdie.

"Don't cry Mrs. Bearpaw, tomorrow I will have another doctor take over your care, you will not have to see me again. I'm so sorry to have troubled you by bringing all these bad memories up again."

"No, Granddaughter, I have found you, the one stolen from me. I believe the Creator brought you back to me and our people for a reason. I want you to stay and be my granddaughter. I want to tell you about your mother and your ancestors that have come before. You have a long history, and we haven't much time for you to learn our stories from my tongue because I am old and sick. Start now by calling me 'Elishi', which is grandmother in Cherokee. I have longed to hear you call me that. My precious granddaughter I have found you."

Polly wept.

Annie stood and wrapped her arms around Polly, touched by her words and tears.

"There, there, it's ok 'Elishi.' I'm here now and not going away again. I'm here."

They remained like that for several minutes until Polly calmed herself. But Annie did not take her hands away from her, she wanted to touch her and feel the person connected to her soul. It was a surreal moment for her.

When Polly could talk again without crying, she asked, "am I dying? That would be so unfair to find you, just to have to leave you again so soon."

"I'm going to do everything in my power, and with the help of the Creator to keep you here for a good long-time. However, I am not going to lie to you, you are seriously ill. We must get that fluid off your heart and lungs and get your sugar under control. It's important for you to have regular care from a primary care physician. When was the last time you visited your doctor?"

"It's been a while. Can you be my doctor and take care of me?" Polly asked.

"Of course, I can do that, I'll even make house calls for you. However, you must follow instructions and eat right, limit the sugar, and take your medicines. Promise me you'll do that."

"I promise. When I get out of here, I want you to come to the house and meet your grandpa Charlie. I have a lot of pictures of our family I want to show you. We come from a lengthy line of healers. We have a lot of catching up to do," Polly said.

"I look forward to it," Annie hugged her again.

When she left Polly's room, Chase was waiting at the nurse's station to see how things went.

"It went better than I could have expected. She answered many questions, and she wants me for a granddaughter after all. Byrdie didn't throw me away, the courts took me from them. All my life I have struggled with my self-esteem, thinking I was unlovable that my own mother trashed me, I was wrong.

After discharge, she's going to tell me all about my heritage and the family I didn't know existed a few months ago. Wow, I have a grandma. How awesome is that."

Chase put his arms around her and hugged her tight, not caring that they had an audience watching. When she realized, she backed away, said thank you for your support, and stuck out her hand to shake his.

Chase just laughed at her and said, "Am I wearing you down yet?"

She just smiled, turned, and while pressing the elevator button, yelled back, "Not even a little bit."

She continued to treat Polly, making weekly house calls. Polly's health improved, as she became medically compliant, testing her sugar and taking the insulin as instructed. Polly also adhered to a sugar-free diet, and Annie brought her meals and new recipes to try. Annie fell in love with Polly and Charlie, and they reciprocated, welcoming her to the family, including her at holidays and other gatherings. She met cousins, aunts, and uncles; it was a new experience to have an extended family welcoming her to the clan.

One day, a few months into her house call visits, Annie walked in the door, and sitting on the kitchen table was a large cardboard box. Strewn around the table were several stacks of photographs. Some dog-eared and worn, and others were so old they were in black and white. Polly was pulling photos from the box and adding them to the stacks.

"What we got going on here Elishi?"

"I think it's time I told you about your clan, the ones that came before. I don't have a lot of pictures but some I think you'll want to see, especially of your mother when she was young."

"Oh yes," Annie said.

"Let's start with Byrdie, and I'll do my best to try not to cry."

Polly started with the stack near her, handing them one-by-one to Annie.

"Here's Byrdie's hospital birth picture, she looks like any other Cherokee baby, look at all that dark hair. She was special, and she never cried, she was the best baby. This whole stack is her childhood, school pictures, holidays, and special occasions. I want you to take these."

"She's very pretty," Annie said.

Annie noticed that the pictures of Byrdie lessened as she got older, they also became more revealing of the toll drinking was having on her. Annie pretended not to notice.

Polly picked up the next stack, "these are of me and Grandpa Charlie, when we got married, a lot of our early life. We had a happy home, until you know...." Her voice trailed off.

Then Polly picked up the smallest stack of old black and white photos of the Healer clan.

"Now, I remember my grandmother Fannie, she was born in 1926 in the Nation, right after Susan came back home from college. Fannie died in '96, at about 70 or so, I have a good memory of her."

Polly handed her another photograph of a woman dressed in a white blouse with billowy sleeves and a long black skirt.

"This one is my great-grandmother Susan, my 'Elishi,' Fannie's momma. I barely remember her, but she was special in the Nation. She was the first to attend college earning a medical degree, and returning to practice medicine in the early 1920's. That was unheard of in those times for a woman, especially a Native to go to medical school."

The picture of Susan showed a solemn faced young woman holding her medical school diploma.

"Granny, Susan appears a bit darker skinned than the rest of us, why is that?"

"Her mother was Agali—I don't have any pictures farther back than Susan, but she was mixed blood. Her grandmother was married to a Black man. Supposedly, a clan adopted him into the tribe as a child, so he counted as full Cherokee."

She put the pictures down on the table but kept talking.

"Now the most famous ancestor you have is White Hawk, she was your 6X great grandmother. She was a 'Beloved Woman' and 'War Woman' of the tribe, born in 1830 and lived to be over 100 years old.

She walked *nu na da ul tsun yi,* 'the place where they cried' , or the Trail of Tears, as a child, and is still highly revered for her healing and spiritual teachings as medicine woman. She also sat on the war council—that's why she was a 'War Woman.' It was a great honor, in those days, the women carried significant roles in governing of our People.

The only picture I ever saw of her hangs in the visitor's center among the honored ones. You should go there and see her; there is a resemblance."

"I will, I will do that soon," Annie said.

She could hardly wait to get to the visitor's center to look upon her ancestor's face, as more pieces of the puzzle of her life fell into place.

TWENTY-SEVEN

Chase had been talking for weeks about the Cherokee Nation's National celebration held each year in Talequah on Labor Day to commemorate the signing of the 1839 Cherokee Constitution. The weekend includes four days of events including games, sports tournaments, a parade, arts and crafts and the highlight is the pow-wow and fireworks show. The whole town closes on Thursday evening and events start early Friday. This year Annie and Chase would be joining in with the festivities and Annie would experience her first pow-wow. She had no idea what to expect, so she turned to Leotie for advice.

"What does one wear to a pow-wow, Leotie?"

"Dress respectfully and remember that dancing is a sacred form of worship of our people, the different dances tell a story. The festival is a fun time to reconnect with family and friends and to make new ones, but the pow-wow is a time to reconnect to our culture. There are also dance competitions. It's a lot of fun."

"I'm way outside of my comfort zone, Chase has been doing this his whole life, but this is all new for me," Annie said.

"A few things to know, don't take pictures of the memorial dances. When a new drum dance starts, do not enter the arena, wait for the drum to end, and then ask if you can take photos. Call the clothing Regalia—not costumes, many are handed down for generations. Have you ever heard the story of the sacred eagle feather?"

"No clue," Annie said.

"We believe the Creator gave the eagle as the highest and best medicine, the eagle flies higher than any other creature. We are to honor and respect the feathers as sacred. Each eagle feather has its own spirit, and to wear and be a guardian of that feather is a great honor. If a feather falls from one of the dancers, do not touch it or take a picture of it. It is important to also stand when the ceremony begins and at other times, just do as those around you. Oh, and you can join in the dance on social songs without Regalia, make sure you stay down the line, and your feet hit the ground on the hard beats of the drum."

"I really don't think I'll be doing any dancing, but with Chase you never know," Annie said.

She was excited and nervous, as Saturday night finally arrived, to go to the Inter-Tribal pow-wow held at the cultural grounds. She wore her best blue jeans, the ones without the holes, a button-up white cotton blouse and her cowboy boots. Leotie approved.

Chase brought a couple of lawn chairs for them, rather than bleacher seats. The opening drumbeats started with the Head Man and Woman leading the dancers into the circle. Annie watched enamored with the ceremony unfolding before her. The Regalia was beautiful, the colors were mesmerizing. The women shawl dancers held each end of their shawl in their hand and worn over their shoulders spreading out like a bird's wings with long fringes hanging down. In one of their hands, they also held an eagle feather fan. They danced with fast footwork, spins, and leaps.

The jingle dress dancers were younger women with footwork in a zig-zag pattern causing the metal cones sewn onto their dresses in rows from top to bottom to make tingling sounds as they moved around the circle. The metal cones made from rolled up tin can tops. They jingled in time with the drum as they danced. Each woman carried an eagle feather fan in one hand and the other resting on her hip.

The men's Regalia was equally striking, especially the porcupine roach headdresses. Chase explained the making of the roach from porcupine guard hair, deer's tail hair, or moose hair attached to a base making it stand up on the head like a tuft or crest. They were bright colors usually matching the dancer's Regalia, further adorning them with feathers, shells, and other décor.

Finally, after all the ceremonial dancers had competed, the MC announced the start of the social dance. Chase stood up and reached for her hand.

"What, oh no. You want me to go out there, with you?" she asked.

"C'mon it'll be fun, I'll teach you. After all you are Cherokee, and you should learn to do this."

She wanted to resist with everything within her, but she stood up and took his hand.

She said, "Whatever you do, don't let go of me."

"I won't, I'm stuck like glue. Haven't you realized that yet? I'm not going anywhere without you."

As she moved around the circle Chase showed her how to come down on each beat with her foot. The movement became second nature to the rhythm. She felt a calming hum inside, closing her eyes imagining a world centuries ago as they danced in the night around the fire.

Chase didn't let go of her hand all night. They stayed until all the dancers finished and the closing ceremony ended, making plans to meet early the next morning to visit the vendor booths.

He picked her up at 10 a.m. and they headed back to the grounds. Once they had made the rounds, bought some artwork, and eaten lunch from the food vendors, she told Chase there were two more places she wanted to see. First, she wanted to visit the Ross Cemetery to find her mother and great grandmother's grave and those of her maternal line. Then go to the Cherokee Heritage Center and see the plaque of her 6X great-grandmother, the Beloved Woman, White Hawk.

Ross cemetery was peaceful and quiet. She quickly found the previous Chief John Ross's resting place. A black iron fence surrounded the burial plot, and the actual grave was covered over with concrete. At the foot of his grave sat a polished black granite flat stone with his name, birth date and death carved into it along with the seal of the Cherokee Nation. At the head stood a very tall obelisk with his name and dates carved into the base, along with a piece of granite denoting he served as their Principal Chief for 38 years, with the inscription: "He led us through times of great achievement and great sorrow".

After a few minutes of showing respect, Annie started searching for the other graves, walking up and down, row by row looking for Byrdie's headstone. She finally found it, a small flat piece of pink granite engraved with the words 'Byrdie' beloved daughter of Polly and Charlie Bearpaw, 1962 - 2002. Her search for her birth mother ended here, she would never know her, never hug, or touch her, but at least she now had answers. A few markers away she also found a large stone for White Hawk, The Beloved Woman, her 6X great grandmother.

Annie ran her fingers over the engraving of White Hawk's marker, trying to connect to her past and to feel something linking her to this woman. Craving to find out more about these people—this bloodline that she didn't even know existed until a few months ago, she had a thirst to learn more about them, the more she discovered the more she yearned to know.

Chase did not interrupt her as she walked through the cemetery looking for connections, and names that may be distant relations. He was reverent and patient, traits that she admired. He was right about something else too; he was wearing her resolve down. She thought of him whenever they were apart, wondering what he was doing, did he miss her too? She pushed her feelings for him down and it grew a little harder each day.

They walked back to the car, and he instinctively reached for her hand, she didn't pull away, she reached back for his. They rode in silence to the heritage center, still holding hands. When they arrived, he opened her car door and as she stepped from the car, he pulled her into himself and kissed her hard on the lips. At first, she was shocked and started to pull away, then she felt his body and leaned into his kiss. She felt the flick of his tongue parting her lips. Her heart beat faster, and she felt a quiver in the pit of her stomach. She had never felt this way before, even with Tom. She didn't want to be the first to stop, but suddenly realized they were in a very public parking lot.

She extricated herself from his arms and said, "I'd like to continue this discussion later if we might?"

"Of course," Chase said as he flashed that smile.

Annie was not sure what to expect inside, she thought this would be a quick in and out visit.

Entering the rotunda, she felt a buzz starting inside her head, the anticipation of a revelation coming to her that had been a long time manifesting.

In the front lobby they stopped before the large paintings of notable Cherokee, where hung the large portraits of humorist-philosopher Will Rogers, and Principal Chief Ross. Then they meandered through the hallways rich with history. There was hand-made pottery, jewelry, baskets, artwork, weapons, and Regalia from the past. A large display for the history of the Trail of Tears, which caused both pain in the sight and reading of the account.

Finally, she found what she hoped for, a display for Beloved Women of the past. The framed piece held a message of peace and purpose of these women and their contribution to The Cherokee People. Beside the plaque, was a framed black and white photo of a woman with a blanket around her shoulders, holding a long stick in her right hand and eagle feather fan in her left.

Annie drew closer to inspect the picture and gasped at who she saw. She pulled back and pointing at the photo.

"Chase, I know this woman, I have seen her before."

"That's impossible Annie, you probably saw someone that looked like her. She died in the early 1900's."

"No, no, I know what I saw, and I saw her. I talked to her, she talked to me."

"What are you saying, how is that possible?" Chase said.

"Well, the first time I saw her was when I died in the car accident. I awoke standing on a windy, purple desert, crying. She was there, she came to me, she sent me back from there. She said it wasn't my time."

"Go on," he said.

"Then I saw her again in a dream. This was just a few weeks ago, she comforted me and told me that I had been lost and now I was found. She spoke Cherokee and I understood her," Annie's voice trailed off as tears started to well up in her eyes.

She drew closer to the picture again and ran her fingers over the glass covering the woman's face, she knew her. Annie felt a cold chill starting at the nape of her neck and permeating her body, she shivered.

"What's the matter, you cold?" Chase asked.

"No, it's just I feel something, something tangible, it feels real, like she's here beside me."

"You know some Cherokees believe that there are special souls whose spirits can move between the realms of the physical world and the spiritual world. Maybe that's what you feel. I've never had that experience, but I have heard of those who have special powers of healing that can do it, interpret visions, and have insight to discern those spirits that visit us. Maybe you're one of those, especially since you are of direct lineage from the Beloved Woman White Hawk." Chase said.

"I'm sorry, but could I just be here alone with her for a while? I've waited so long to find my place, where I belong, and I want to just be with her. Do you understand?"

"I get it, I get you. Someday you are going to realize that, and you can't live without me. Maybe Great-Great-Great-Great-Great-Great Grandma can put in a good word for me."

Chase looked up at the photo of White Hawk and said, "you hear that Woman? Tell her, will you? Tell her that the best thing to ever happen in her life is standing right beside her, and with that I'm gonna go outside and answer a couple of texts and phone calls. Take your time. I'll be waiting for you, always." Chase kissed the top of her head before walking away.

She hated to see him go but wanted to meditate and try to get a message to White Hawk without an audience and feeling self-conscious. She sat on the bench in front of the display, closing her eyes. The only thing she had with her was the chip in her pocket; she felt for it and began to rub it between her fingers. Then she started to talk to White Hawk as if she were sitting beside her on the bench. In her mind she was there, she could see her, she could feel her, and she could hear her. Grandmother reached out and touched her face, wiping the tears from Annie's cheeks.

Annie whispered, "You know God says the angels catch and bottle your tears as they are precious....."

Annie heard a voice. "My dear one, I have longed for this day. The day of reuniting you with your people, you who once we lost and now found. My clan is complete. You, my special child who possesses the spirit to see and travel into the land of no time. You can walk in this realm when you have prepared yourself and are clean and pure. Join me there, you will see your mother Byrdie, who will finally find peace. She walks to and fro on the plains crying for her lost child, searching, and searching, she cannot rest. I will keep you safe and help you to return to the land of the living. Go to Polly and retrieve the pipe for smoke, go to water to cleanse your body, then use the smoke to bless the four corners, North, South, East, and West. Bathe in the smoke to protect yourself from unclean evil spirits that may cling to you. Once you have done these things, drink the black tea. I will be waiting for you."

Then she was gone as a vapor. Annie opened her eyes and stared at the photo. "I know you….," she whispered.

She returned to the car sobbing. She poured out her heart to Chase at the profound loss she had experienced in life by not knowing her people and the power they possessed.

"The years of abuse and ethnic genocide at the hand of men chanting for progress, our people suffered for hundreds of years as they professed to 'kill the Indian but save the man.' Their land, culture and children stolen from them. Yet they….no, WE persevered. We saved ourselves; our identity survives and lives on in people like us.

"Chase, how can you not be angry about this? At what has happened to us and still happens to this day. I see the 'Missing Murdered Indigenous Women' movement, the billboards display the red handprint over the mouths of women, and this is 2023. No one looks for our missing daughters and mothers, when will it stop?"

"It will stop when it will. When those like you who are called answer. I knew the minute I met you that you were different, you have a purpose here Annie Hayes. We just need to help you figure out what that looks like. Are you game?" he said.

"You won't believe what she said to me in there."

Annie relayed the time spent with White Hawk, but Chase did not laugh.

"Well, alright we need to make that happen, sooner rather than later," he said solemnly.

They went straight to Polly's house to get the pipe, and the eagle feathers that White Hawk used for the Beloved Woman ceremony. She found them wrapped and stored in the deer hide pouch containing White Hawks medicine powders, crystals, and other talismans. These precious artifacts preserved for all these years, passing down the matriarchal line, and finally finding their place with Annie. She cherished this connection but was frightened at what lay ahead.

Polly said, "Go to John Walkingstick, the elder that blessed you, he will make the black drink. Take this pipe for it belonged to White Hawk, use it in your ceremony. You must *'go to water'* at dawn on the day you take your walk. My child be sure to follow all the 'old ways,' listen to the wisdom of the elder. What you are about to do is dangerous, and only special ones can walk between the two worlds."

The elder agreed to help her with the ceremony and the day finally came. She started with the cleansing process for 'going to water.' Chase drove her to the river, and as the sun rose, she waded into the water up to her chest. It was cold and she shivered. She raised her arms praying to the Creator, asking for blessings to fulfill her purpose and guidance for what was to come. She submerged herself seven times, then disrobing down to her undergarments. Releasing her clothing for the current to carry them away with her sins. At the shoreline, Chase waited with a towel and a new deerskin dress made for this day. This was the easy part, but she was emotional and apprehensive at what was to come. She shook from fear, not the cold.

As they drove back to the elder's house they found him outside under an arbor, a fire keeper was already there to start the holy fire. He lay the kindling first in the pit, and then the logs in the sacred pattern igniting the fibers with flint hanging from a necklace he wore. The fire jumped to life and began to dance before them. Chase and the fire keeper stood well back from the two beside the flames, they could not hear their whispers to each other. Annie took White Hawk's sacred bundle and removed her crystals, laying them around her while seated on the ground. Then she took the pipe from the pouch, handing it to the elder. He filled the bowl with a mixture of herbs and special tobacco and took a twig from the sacred fire to light the pipe puffing seven times. The bowl glowed a bright fire red. He handed the pipe to Annie and she did likewise, returning the pipe to the elder. He held the pipe aloft and in Cherokee prayed to the Great Spirit with words she did not comprehend. He then offered sacred smoke in the four directions, passing it to her to do likewise. The elder took the healing stick, which once had belonged to White Hawk, and lay it across her lap instructing her to hold firmly to it.

"Do not let go of the healing stick, this is your connection to the physical world."

He gave her the cup of black tea to drink. It was warm and sweet, tasting minty, and she drank all of it. From her open medicinal pouch, he handed the fan of eagle feathers to hold in her other hand. Soon her head tilted forward, and she lost consciousness. Chase was worried about her and bent down to check her pulse but the elder shewed him away.

"Do not touch her, her spirit is gone, she will return when her purpose is revealed, and her walk is complete."

Annie felt her spirit floating upward and then blacked out. When she awoke, she was on the same plain she visited when she had the car wreck. It was eerily familiar, and she wasn't sure what to do. Before she could complete her thought, she saw White Hawk on the horse and then she was beside her.

"My child, you are here finally. Look below on the canyon floor and there you will see all those that have gone before you."

When Annie looked down on the flat land below, she saw hundreds of people gathered and looking up toward her and White Hawk. In front of the gathering stood Byrdie. She knew her mother at first glance, it was like looking into a mirror. When she thought of her next, they were standing beside each other.

"My daughter, I have mourned for you since your birth. I hope you forgive me for not fighting harder for you?" Byrdie said.

Annie took Byrdie in her arms and hugged her tight to her chest, and said, "there is nothing to forgive. You did what you thought was best at the time, my adoptive family was good to me, and I am here with you now and that is all that matters. I am found by my people, and we will someday be together for eternity."

White Hawk introduced her to many that walked before her and her heart was overjoyed at the love that emanated from the crowd.

"You have a special gift of healing, passed down from generations before you. This gift is to be used with the new medicine, and not forgotten 'old ways.' The People need your insight to separate what's important or true from what is not, you have this ability. Now you must return to the land of the living, for a moment here is a great time in the earthly realm. If you linger too long, you will not be able to return," White Hawk said.

Annie awoke and the fire had burned down to nothing but glowing embers, the logs consumed but the fire keeper kept the embers alive. He and the elder chanting while waiting for her. She had been gone for hours but Chase remained, he rushed to her side, and she fell into his arms, exhausted.

"Chase, I remember it all, it was magical and spiritual and all that I could have ever imagined. I know what my true calling is for our people. I have a purpose, and now I must get to work. I have much to learn. Elder, will you help me?" Annie said, her legs wobbling as she stood. Chase steadied her by holding her elbow.

"Of course, my child, you have capabilities to do things that I have heard of but could never do. You are a special spirit, I am honored to teach you," he said.

He handed her the stick and said, "this belongs with you."

"Annie, what about us?" Chase asked as he turned her toward him.

"I am here, I will stay here, and I hope you decide this is where you belong too," she said.

"Oh Annie, like I told you before, I'm not going anywhere. You know in Cherokee language there is no word for goodbye, you will never hear me say that either. But I will say—I love you, and 'sv-se-yu-l' that means I will give up eating so that you may have food, at the deepest level I will give up my life for you."

He paused, "So, have I worn you down yet?"

He smiled as he bent in to kiss her.

The elder cleared his throat to remind them he was still standing there.

"Yes, Chase, yes I am ready to say I love you back."

She took the wooden chip from her pocket, throwing it into the embers. Together they watched it burst into flames. She didn't need it anymore; she was finally free from her past and ready to face the future with her love. She knew who she was and was no longer afraid. She was Cherokee, the Healer.

The End

BIBLIOGRAPHY

Allosso, Dan, *"Life with a Slave-Breaker (1833): Narrative of the Life of Frederick Douglass,"* written by himself (1845), 57-63 https://minnstate.pressbooks.pub/ushistory1/chapter/life-with-a-slave-breaker-1833/

Backus, Paige Gibbons, *"Common Diseases of the 18th and 19th Century."* American Battlefield Trust, February 2, 2022. https://www.battlefields.org/learn/articles/common-diseases-18th-and-19th-century#:~:text=Unfortunately%2C%20physicians%20of%20the%2019,well%20as%20bleeding%20and%20blistering.

Bell, Danna. *"The Cherokee Nation and the Civil War."* Library of Congress Blogs, November 10, 2022. https://blogs.loc.gov/teachers/2022/11/the-cherokee-nation-and-the-civil-war/

Bradford, Sarah Hopkins. *Harriet, the Moses of Her People.* The University of North Carolina Press, 2012. *Project MUSE*, https://muse.jhu.edu/book/19228.

Bryant, Marie Claire, "Underground Railroad Quilt Codes: What We Know, What We Believe, and What Inspires Us." *Smithsonian Magazine,* May 3, 2019. https://folklife.si.edu/magazine/underground-railroad-quilt-codes

Carter, Kent, "Dawes Commission," *The Encyclopedia of Oklahoma History and Culture,* Published January 15, 2010. https://www.okhistory.org/publications/enc/entry?entry=DA018

Dawson, Shay. *"Harriet Tubman-Davis"* National Women's History Museum. 2024 www.womenshistory.org/education-resources/biograpies/harriet-tubman.

Everett, Dianna, "Indian Territory," *The Encyclopedia of Oklahoma History and Culture,* Published January 15, 2010. https://www.okhistory.org/publications/enc/entry?entry=IN018.

Hart, Albert Bushnell, Curtis, John Gould, "American History told by contemporaries," NY The Macmillan Co; London, Macmillan & Co. ltd, 1897-1929, P579-583 https://archive.org/details/toldcontemporari03hartrich/page/578/mode/2up

History.com Editors, *"Trail of Tears.,"* A&E
Television Networks, November 9, 2009,
Updated September 26, 2023.
https://www.history.com/topics/native-
american-history/trail-of-tears

History.com Editors, *"Wounded Knee.,"* A&E
Television Networks, November 6, 2009,
Updated July 7, 2023.
https://www.history.com/topics/native-
american-history/wounded-knee

Horton, Jennie. Guest Post Library of Congress
Blogs, the 2020 Librarian-in-Residence with the
Reference Team in the Serial & Government
Publications Division. *"How Newspapers Helped
Crowdsource a Scientific Discovery: The 1833 Leonid
Meteor Storm."* Public Domain, September 2,
2020
https://blogs.loc.gov/headlinesadheroes/2020/
09/How-newspapers-helped-crowdsource-a-
scientific-discovery-the-1833-leonid-meteor-
storm/.

King, Gilbert. *"Where the Buffalo No Longer
Roam," Smithsonian Magazine,* July 17, 2012
https://www.smithsonianmag.com/history/wh
ere-the-buffalo-no-longer-roamed-3067904/

Library of Congress. Research guides: *Harriet Tubman: Topics in Chronicling America:* Search Strategies & Selected Articled. N.d. https://guides.loc.gov/chronicling-america-harriet-tubman/selected-articles

Lindsley, Harvey B., photographer. *Harriet Tubman, full-length portrait, standing with hands on back of a chair.*, ca. 1871. [Between and 1876\ Photograph. https://www.loc.gov.item/2003674596/.

The Far West, Shooting buffalo on the line of the Kansas-Pacific Railroad/Bghs. Great Plains, 1871. Photograph. https://www.loc.gov/item/2004669992

"Military Orders Relating to the Forced Removal of the Cherokee from Georgia to the Indian Territory." Orders (military records). Benjamin T. Watkins Family Papers, 1838. Box 1, Folder 7. Stuart A. Rose Manuscript, Archives, and Rare Book Library. (https://digitallibrary.emory.edu/purl/962f7m0f8n-cor

Moerman, Daniel E. *"Native American Medicinal Plants: an ethnobotany/Daniel E. Moerman."* Abridged Version C1998 Timber Press, 2009. P58,124,242,243,260,320,365,410,430,441,445, 504,516. (See table at end: Ethnobotanical Plants)

Old Aunt Julia Ann Jackson, age 102 and the corn crib where she lives. United States Arkansas, ca. 1938. [Between 1937 and] Photograph. https://www.loc.gov/item/99615221/.

Perdue, Theda. "Clan and Court: Another Look at the Early Cherokee Republic." *The American Indian Quarterly 24*, no. 4 (2000): 562-569. https://dx.doi.org/10.1353/aiq.2000.0024

Reese, Elizabeth Hidalgo, Yunpoví (Tewa: Willow Flower), *"The Long History of Native American Adoptions,"* Harper's Bazaar*, November 30, 2022. https://www.harpersbazaar.com/culture/features/a42097413/native-americans-scotus-adoption/

Reese, Linda. "Freedmen," *The Encyclopedia of Oklahoma History and Culture*, Published January 15, 2010. Last updated July 29, 2024. https://www.okhistory.org/publications/enc/entry?entry=FR016.

Smith, Crosslin Fields, *"A Lifetime of Healing."* Dog Soldier Press, 2023.

Smith, Crosslin Fields, *"Original Teachings, Designed to Stand as One, Early Keetoowah Teachings and Traditions."* Dog Soldier Press, 2021.

Speck, Frank G. and Broom, Leonard,
Contributions By Will West Long. *"Cherokee
Dance and Drama. The Civilization of the American
Indian series."* University of Oklahoma Press,
Publishing Division of the University. New
edition copyright ©1983 by the University of
Oklahoma Press. 1993 PP 45-51
https://www.oupress.com/9780806125800/che
rokee-dance-and-drama/

The Cherokee Nation, *"The History of the
Cherokee Nation,"*
https://www.cherokee.org/about-the-
nation/history/

The Last Cherokee Midwife," Cherokee Images
Blog https://cherokeeimages.com/wp/the-last-
cherokee-midwife-

The Native American Boarding School Healing
Coalition, *US Indian Boarding School History*,
https://boardingschoolhealing.org/education/u
s-indian-boarding-school-
history/#:~:text=There%20were%20more%20t
han%20523,they%20spoke%20their%20Native
%20languages

Timberlake, Lieut. Henry, The Memoirs of Lieut. Henry Timberlake, LONDON: Printed for the Author, MDCCLXV (1765), Collection University of Pittsburgh Library System, Americana:P32,39-44,47-51,64,77-80. https://www.archive.org/details/.memoiroflieu the00intimb/.page/62/mode/1up?q=dragging+ canoe

U.S. Congress. *U.S. Statutes at Large, Volume 4 – 1835, 19th through 23rd Congress*. United States, - 1835, 1826. Periodical. Https://www.loc.gov/item/llsl-v4/.

Virginia Museum of History & Culture. *"Civil Rights Movement in Virginia: Hampton Institute & Booker T. Washington."* https://virginiahistory.org/learn/civil-rights-movement-virginia/hampton-institute-and-booker-t-washington#

Wikimedia Commons contributors, "File:Original Cherokee Syllabary.jpg," *Wikimedia Commons,* PUBLIC DOMAIN https://commons.wikimedia.org/w/index.p hp?title=File:Original_Cherokee_Syllabary.j pg&oldid=850879505

Wikipedia contributors. *"Cherokee funeral rites." Wikipedia, The Free Encyclopedia.* Wikipedia, The Free Encyclopedia, 3 Mar. 2024. Web. 22 Aug. 2024. https://en.wikipedia.org/w/index.php?title=Cherokee_funeral_rites&oldid=1211553739

ETHNOBOTANICAL PLANTS REFERENCED IN THIS BOOK

Plant Name	Scientific Name	Page
Aztec, Cultivated Tobacco	Nicotiana capensis, nicotiana rustica	242, 320
Black Drink	Ilex vomitoria	242
Bloodroot (Dye)	Sanguinaria canadensis	441
Blue Cohosh	Caulophyllum thalictroides	124
Dahoon Holly Berry	Ilex cassine	242
Hazel Alder	Alnus serrulate	58
Jewelweed	Impatiens capensis	242
Laurel, Mountain	Kalmia polifolia	445
Mullein leaves	Verbascum Thapsus	504
Pale Touchmenot	Impatiens pallida	243
Pine, Virginia	Pinus virginiana	365
Sage, Sweet	Salix candida	N/A
Sassafras	Sassafras albidum	260
Smooth Sumac	Rhus glabra	410
Sweet Grass	Hierochloe odorata	236
Wild Cherry Bark	Prunus serotina	389
Willow Tree Bark	Salix alba	430
Yellow Root Tea	Xanthorhiza simplicissima	516

Source: *"Native American Medicinal Plants: an ethnobotany/Daniel E. Moerman."* Abridged Version C1998 Timber Press, 2009.

DK WILLIAMS

resides on a farm in Southern Indiana where she lives with her husband Jim. When she is not writing, she is usually in her studio creating watercolor art. This is her fourth novel.